June Carter Powell

THE SECOND ENDING
Revised edition

JUNE CARTER POWELL

Hi Gayle

This is my first novel.
I hope you enjoy reading it.

June

June 2021

The Second Ending

June Carter Powell

© 2018
Revised edition ©2020

Typesetting: R. Wainwright
Revision: Co-Editor, Dana Ramstedt
Cover Art (Kamloops Brandenburg Orchestra) © Murphy Shewchuk.

ISBN 978-1-989092-35-4

Photo of the Brandenburg Orchestra, Kamloops

Revised Edition published by Celticfrog Publishing.

CELTICFROG PUBLISHING

To the memory of my brother
Brian Richard Carter Sr.
August 4, 1936 – August 14, 1982

And

To the memory of my nephew
Charles Thomas (Tommy) Whetstone Jr.

September 15, 1965 – May 2, 2016

ACKNOWLEDGMENTS

Ted Joslin, past president of the Kamloops Author's Group for his encouragement.

Dana Ramstedt and Glenn Hall, editors who prevented me from committing too many indignities to the English Language.

Murphy Shewchuk—Cover photography

All photos printed with permission.

Michael Powell, long-suffering husband and musical partner.

Family and Friends for support during this writing project:

My sister, Carole Whetstone.

Daughters: Allison Perran (SCAAD), Gillian Wainwright, Heather Chernecki and Valerie Jensen-Hall; Sons: Richard Travers and Glen Alan Powell and grandson, Matt Chernecki, my stand partner in the Thompson Valley Community Orchestra, Twin Rivers Orchestra, Ordinary People Ensemble and The Kamloops Brandenburg Orchestra.

Jolyon Joslin for offering technical advice on such mechanical issues as how a ratchet works, the construction of a scaffold and other things every writer needs to know.

And last but not least, Francie and Presto who chewed my pencils regularly, sat on my manuscript and who poked my printer with a curious paw, thereby teaching me how to clear paper jams.

ONE

Stillborn rosebuds were nestled beneath leaves, frozen stiff in their dark green splendor courtesy of the cold snap.

"Enough of this morbid scene," Tony said as he and his wife stood on their back deck overlooking her garden. They turned away and he held the French door open for his lovely wife. "If you stare at your garden any longer your tears are going to freeze on your cheeks."

"My beautiful roses are frozen under all that snow," Elise said sniffling as she entered the glassed-in the sun porch. "It's not even Thanksgiving yet. Do you ever remember it snowing this early in October?"

"No, I do not, and I have lived here six years," Tony said.

He hung up their coats and then stepped in close behind her where she stood at the stove. He looked over her shoulder at the steaming brown liquid she was stirring. "Hot chocolate?"

"Of course, best remedy for chilly weather," she said, humming along with the song on the stereo.

He watched her as she flitted around the farm-style kitchen. When he had renovated the old house, his first wife, Yvette had accepted his choices without question. Thankfully, Elise loved the big kitchen, too. She said she found it quaint to cook on the cast iron top of the fancy antique stove.

She moved the pot to the far right, away from the hottest part of the stove top. It would simmer there until they were ready for a second cup.

After entering the nook off the kitchen, he wanted to draw the blinds so she would not see the garden. Instead of darkening the room, he chose to sit facing the windows.

Elise set a steaming mug of hot chocolate in front of him "Whipped cream?" she asked. A large spoon of the white fluffy stuff hovered over his mug.

"Certainly," he said, smiling like a child as he watched the dollop drop, sink out of sight and bob back to the top.

"Have you read the poster I showed you?" she asked, sliding the poster in front of him.

Why had she brought that up again? Why couldn't she forget about it? He did not want her cozying up to a lot of musicians. He wanted that scene out of his life.

"You have enough to do at home. Why would you want to join some silly orchestra?" He pushed the poster away, but she snatched at it before it fell off the table.

"Don't be like that. You know how long I've been hoping to join an adult musical group." She took the poster to the secretary desk she had restored over the summer and settled onto the delicate chair.

"I wonder how many people are coming on Friday." She picked up the receiver and spun the dial as she traced the phone number with her slender finger.

"I wonder what made that cop organize an orchestra?" he said taking a big swig of the lovely hot liquid. "Maybe he does not have enough to do upholding the law here."

His wife frowned at him, waving her hand for him to

be quiet. This was not going as he wanted. He had tried to talk her out of calling the number. Somehow, he had just pushed her over the edge. She had made up her mind about this.

You are losing control of your wife.

"Who said that?" Tony spun around and hot chocolate sloshed onto the linoleum floor.

Did you know she had already called him?

"Tony?" Elise said, scorn in her tone as she held the receiver to her ear, obviously waiting for someone to answer the phone. "Hush, besides, I didn't say anything." Still tethered to the phone by the coiled line, she reached toward the island and she grabbed the roll of paper towel and tossed it to him.

"Never mind," Tony said, catching the paper roll. Still grumbling, he bent to wipe up the sticky mess. That stupid poster! Ever since Elise brought it home, it was as if someone was whispering in his ear. He did not like it!

"Sourpuss," she said after she hung up the phone. "No answer. I'll try again after supper."

"I love it when you play your bass. Why—"

"I know you don't understand what it is like for me. I miss the experience of being with other musicians. I love hearing an orchestra getting ready to rehearse together," Elise said.

"It sounds more like dueling chainsaws to me," he said. He walked around the island to get to the sink to put some distance between them. *That* would show her he was upset.

"How would you even know?" she said, tipping her head as she studied him. He turned away from the sink.

"We don't live in a vacuum," he said. "I have heard musicians practice before." How did she always know exactly how to un-nerve him? This evening had started out so well. If he stayed on this track, he'd likely end up sleeping on the couch in his office. Cold and alone was

3

not how he had predicted this night ending.

"So, you have already spoken to the cop?" She answered by leaning against the counter and crossing her arms.

"I did, we are meeting in three days."

"Without an audition?" This was moving too fast! "Why did he tell you to bring your bass without holding an audition?" Tony said, trying to change her focus.

"I don't need one. He knows I've played in an orchestra before," she said loftily. "Besides, right now I am probably the only bass player in the area. We'll have a short meeting first and then try some easy pieces." Her face glowed with enthusiasm.

"And just how do you know all this?" he said, angry with her for not waiting for his approval.

"I'm sorry, dear; I thought I told you about it. Are you alright with this?"

"No, you did not tell me. You seem really excited about this. I still think the very idea of the Chief of Police trying to organize an orchestra is ridiculous. I doubt if he has any experience but, I guess I can live with you going out once in a while."

She hurried over to him, wrapped her arms around his neck and kissed him. He sighed in relief.

"He plays the piano and he directed a jazz group once." She ran her fingers through his hair. His body was being swayed.

"You dislike jazz." He stepped back and out of her reach.

"It's not my favourite music, but Brad said we wouldn't focus on jazz. There are many genres of music to choose. I want to know what kind of group he is organizing, so back off."

Tony bristled before asking in a somewhat civil voice, "Will he direct the orchestra in his basement all the time?"

"I think he may have something else in mind for a

permanent rehearsal room," Elise answered. She crowded him against the island and kissed the tip of his nose.

"You should quit while you are ahead," he said acidly.

"No."

"Nothing will come of it anyway," he said.

"I want to be part of this," she informed him. "If it is a flop, then so be it."

"Brad's just a cop," Tony said. "What does he know about music? Maybe he rode in the Musical Ride last summer in Kamloops." He gave a humorless laugh, his voice becoming harsh.

Thin ice, Tony.

"Frank! What the hell are you doing here?" Tony said, recognizing something in the voice. No-one was there. He glanced inquiringly at Elise. She chattered on as if she had heard nothing. Tony shuddered. He must have imagined it.

"Why are you putting Brad down without even hearing what he can do?" Elise asked. "Being a police officer doesn't make him a musical dunce."

"I hope you won't be disappointed," Tony said. A tiny nerve in his cheek began to send shooting pains up and over his eyes, nearly blinding him.

TWO

"Be careful," Tony cautioned when they arrived at Brad's house the next evening for the meeting and preliminary rehearsal. "Brad didn't salt the path after he cleared the snow away, might be safer to walk in the snow along the edge." To demonstrate, he slid his foot over the shoveled area and promptly lost his balance. With flailing arms, he fumbled to maintain his grip on the soft case that protected her cumbersome string bass.

"My bass!" Elise exclaimed. She dropped the stool she was carrying, lunged and barely saved her bass before it hit the frozen sidewalk.

"But what about me? I could have broken a leg," he said. When he'd recovered his balance, he took the instrument out of her gloved hands.

"The bass would cost money to replace," she said. "Musicians always save their instrument before they save themselves."

"I can believe that. I suppose it would be easier to replace me rather than your bass," he complained.

"Oh, no, "she said, "I don't want to replace you or my bass. I love you both."

"That is good to know," he said with a sarcastic edge to his voice. "Have you ever thought of playing the flute? This thing weighs a ton."

"Not really," she said. "I played the flute in my High

School band but that was years ago. I probably wouldn't even remember how to play it now."

"I am just thinking of you," he said, smirking.

"I don't notice its weight," she teased, "so quit complaining. I can manage it myself if it's too heavy for you, dear." She squeezed his bicep and giggled.

"I doubt that. You are too petite to carry this instrument when it is icy. Now *you* quit complaining and get out of my way." When she stepped aside, he continued along the illuminated walk toward the downstairs entrance.

"Tony, you're spoiling me." She laughed sweetly.

He smiled, even if she often behaved like a teenager, it was pleasant to hear her laughter tinkling on the frozen air.

"I know," he said, with the air of a martyr and concentrated on his footwork.

The beautiful summer garden, in bloom only weeks ago, was now also wilted and brown. As he plodded along, is footsteps crackled in the freeze-dried grass.

Chrysanthemums, blackened by freezing winds, stood on sentry duty by the basement entrance to the recreation room.

Tony grimaced as he opened the door a crack and peeked in. Musicians were already there tuning up their instruments. He pointed with a discreet finger at two flute players practicing trills and finger exercises in conflicting keys and time counts. "You could do a lot better than those two even if you have not played the flute for years," he whispered.

"They're just warming up their instruments," she said, giggling. "That's not how they play."

"I hope not," he said. Tony glared at her, which made her giggle all the more.

He hoisted the bass so it would fit straight through the door, wide end first. Once inside, he set it down on its side and covered his ears with both hands, a scowl on his face, but he allowed himself a weak smile when she dragged his hands off his ears and whispered, "Sourpuss."

Tony bristled for a split second before asking in a somewhat civil voice, "Will he direct the orchestra here all the time?"

"I think he may have something else in mind for a permanent rehearsal room," Elise answered.

"I would hope so, because the acoustics in here will likely be crap," he said looking around at the dark wood paneled walls. He gave a humourless laugh.

"Oh, Tony, relax. Leave if you must. I'm sure someone can drive me home," she said.

"I am relaxed," his voice becoming harsh. "From the racket I hear this evening, it is not very promising. However, I would rather drive you home myself, so I will wait for you." He pressed the nerve with his finger until his whole face ached.

A voice broke into Tony's thoughts.

He's watching you. Tony.

"Where are you?" he said, looking around the room. He had certainly heard someone give him a warning. Was it someone in this crowd of strangers?

Elise had turned away. The pain in his head was increased by the overall din from the clash of tortured instruments.

Then, he saw the policeman across the room. Even out of uniform, the man's six-foot six frame and wide shoulders cut an imposing figure.

Brad was indeed watching him. Tony shuddered.

The violinists were playing passages and phrases at breakneck speed, up and down the scales, as if their lives depended upon it. The flute players were still tootling disjointed melodies with trill and runs. The clarinetist was sucking on his reed to soften it and occasionally, a loud squawk would pierce the air as he attempted a sound test. The trumpet player appeared to be trying to drown them all out by blasting *You're in The Army Now!*

Tony flinched. The squawking and squeaking made him cringe.

"Whatever is the matter," Elise said reaching out to take the bass from his hands.

"Ugh." blurted Tony. "It is all this noise." He held onto the instrument. "I will leave your bass over there, out of the way of stumbling musicians." He pointed to the back of the room where an oversized desk stood, one drawer partly open to display a stack of sheet music.

"Where will you sit?" he asked.

"Thank you for caring, Tony," she said, "but I'm sure musicians know they must take care not to knock one another's instruments down. As for where I will sit, it will probably be between the viola and the cello sections."

Tony placed Elise's high, bass player's stool to the left end of the four violinists. "Here?" he asked as he moved the patented invention a few inches to the right.

"He'll tell me to move if this is the wrong place. Here is good." She indicated with a wave of her hand

Tony walked away, his brow wrinkled in response to the pain of listening to some very amateur playing. Some of the notes *were* sour, due to the instruments being cold. Not much in this musical setting was to his liking but Tony was not ready to acknowledge the real reason he found fault with everything musical.

He positioned himself in a secluded spot behind the desk so he could watch Brad conducting. He pulled a book from his backpack and settled to wait out the musical torture.

He watched with interest as Elise defrocked the huge bass of its soft leather case. Tony enjoyed hearing her play at home and from the way she spoke about music, he knew she was a good musician. However, he had never seen or heard her play in an orchestral setting, and he wondered how she would rate with other players. Practicing alone is not the same as being part of a group. That took co-operation and careful attention to tempo as the player listened to the music and watched the director simultaneously as he played each note. Orchestral playing is not for the faint of heart, or for someone as carefree as Elise.

When she pulled out the stand-peg on the instrument's bottom piece and expertly tuned it to the first violin player's instrument, Tony had to admit that she obviously knew what she was doing. He had avoided talking music with her in case he would reveal too much of himself. Tony wasn't ready to do that yet.

Brad stood by the piano observing the musicians coming in, each carrying an instrument. In addition to those with instruments, there were six people with empty hands. Tony checked the clock above a picture window which overlooked the street.

At seven o'clock Brad stepped up onto the makeshift podium, a small platform in front of the musicians, and tapped on his music stand with his baton.

"My name is Brad Thomas, organizer of this meeting," he said, assuming a businesslike air. "Welcome aboard! Perhaps you can each introduce yourselves to me and to the group." He pointed to Elise and said, "Would you like to start off, Mrs. Lorenzo."

"I am Elise and the gentleman who carried my bass in for me, "she said, nodding her head in Tony's direction, "is my husband, Tony. I'm looking forward to playing with this group,"

"Does Tony play an instrument?" Brad asked, turning to observe the partially hidden man leafing through his book.

"No, but he will help me bring the bass to rehearsals while the roads are slippery."

"We always need listeners," Brad said. Elise nodded.

Cynthia Bell assumed the position of Concert Master and Fred Hetherington, a well-known Rocky Creek fiddler, sat beside her. Cynthia's two teenaged music students, Brian and Liz Eriksson, beamed bright smiles in her direction.

"For now," Cynthia said quietly to the two teens, "how about Fred sitting with Liz as the second violin section leader and Brian can sit with me in first? Would that be okay with you? Some of the music we will probably play will need an experienced player to lead."

"Perfect!" Liz said.

"Sure," agreed Fred.

"You want *me* to play first violin with you?" queried Brian, looking surprised. Cynthia nodded.

"You are a very accomplished musician," she assured him

When that issue was settled there were the usual questions as to where each person should sit and a considerable amount of chair shuffling. Music stands were unfolded and shoulder pads clicked onto violins.

The trumpet player, who had earlier almost overcome everyone with an Army bugle call, suddenly became shy and hid behind his music stand. He introduced himself as Clancy Aldrich, his voice muffled with embarrassment. Red hair curled onto his forehead and one unruly strand stood straight up at the crown, resembling a beacon.

Tony allowed an amused smile to linger over his face as secret memories flashed into his mind. He quickly withdrew into his book again. Tony wasn't quite ready to admit he was interested in the orchestral plans.

Brad grinned at the motley crew.

"Are we all here?" he asked.

"I doubt it," Tony said into his hand. He saw Brad look up as the door was flung open with purpose.

A very tall young man in work clothes stomped in

11

carrying a cello. He had paint splotches on his pants; his wavy brown hair stuck out in all directions under a work cap perched jauntily on his head. The words INTERIOR PAINTS emblazoned on the brim seemed superfluous considering his pants were already advertising his employment.

Out of breath, the late-comer whipped the cello from its case with a flair and set himself up opposite Cynthia and Fred. When he removed his jacket and hung it over his chair, the crest on his T-shirt revealed his name was Matt Jacob. Confidence radiated from his demeanor as he rosined his bow and drew it across the strings while he turned his instrument to the note Cynthia played for him.

Tony had looked up from his book in dismay when he saw the fellow enter the room, but when he heard the full bodied, yet silky tone the boy produced while tuning, he was impressed. Even so, it was difficult to picture this wild looking individual as being a serious musician.

Tony thought that Brad appeared interested when he heard the velvet sound the young man produced. Would Brad recognize talent and training in the young painter or completely overlook him? An inexperienced director might not look beyond appearances.

In spite of having some misgivings about the player's wardrobe choices, Tony was somewhat comforted to remember that many artists had eccentric qualities. He glanced in Brad's direction. For a split second, their eyes met and an unwanted bond established.

"Everyone's here now so we should get the show on the road," Brad said. He tapped on his music stand again for attention.

Several people were standing by the door. Brad said. "I take it you are either musicians without instruments or people interested in making this endeavor work. If you play, grab a chair in the section you think you will be in and sit down. If you are chauffeuring a musician, please sit at the back of the room where there are extra chairs. I was able to rent some from the library."

He paused while prospective players jockeyed for space. "Perhaps it would be a good idea for those seated with the players to introduce themselves, too. After they had done so, he said, "Tell me if you are musicians?"

There were a couple of "nays," a "yay," and one "yep."

"Nice adaptation of Caribbean patois to Canadian slang," Brad joked. "For those needing instruments, come to me after the rehearsal. The High School has instruments for rent." This was greeted with applause.

"I really like the power this stick gives me," Brad continued. He looked at the baton and grinned, "And I hope that you will all bear with me when I explain that I was unable to find a director to work with us right away." Brad paused to soften the unexpected bad news. "Until we find that person, you will have to put up with me for a few weeks."

"Fine with me," said Tom, a big fellow with thick dark hair and a prominent nose, "as long as you just use the baton for beating time and not faulty players." From his hiding place behind the TV, Tony noticed Tom was one of the flute players who had been *warming up* when he and Elise had entered the room.

"No," Brad said, "but you'd be surprised what I can do with this stick." He waved the baton in mock aggression. More laughter. "I can play a whole orchestra with just the flick of my wrist, but I'd much rather play an instrument than direct. My aim is to bring music to Rocky Creek. There are school bands, but when kids grow up there's no outlet for them to continue making music with others. Playing together is what it's all about so I brought a couple of marches by Philippe Sousa to warm up with, and I have some simple quartet stuff. Let's play a few pieces before we decide what we want to do. I am heartened by the response to the flyer I sent out last week and grateful to Paul Eriksson and his friends for delivering them."

Brad joined in the applause that followed before picking up several music books from a stack piled up on a chair by his stand. He looked around before passing them out to the group. "There will be no auditions so you can all relax. The group here tonight will form the nucleus of the orchestra. At a later date, if other players want to come, I will consider auditions. I will give out some music and you can choose which parts are appropriate for you. We will take it from there. One more thing—there is a sheet of paper on the desk," he indicated with a sweep of his hand, "If you will each write down your name and instrument, address and phone number before you leave, I will have a record of prospective players."

Brad looked around at the assembly. "I recognize some of you from the High School Band concerts. Many of you help the music teachers to fill out the different sections.

"I see four members of the Eriksson family. I hope other families will join us. When everyone in a family plays an instrument, it indicates a good measure of dedication.

"Anyway, let's play a couple of pieces tonight just for fun. I have some easy music to try out. Most of us have played a Sousa march or two in school bands so turn to number five, *Our Director March*. I'm sure we all know it.

"We have a timpani. Cynthia, please play a G so he can tune." Cynthia played a low G on her violin. The timpanist tapped lightly with one of his sticks and turned a key on the drum's side until the note was satisfactory.

"Now if you will give us a two-bar drum roll when I give the downbeat, it will help everyone to come in at the right time." There was a flurry of pages being turned, a pencil dropped on the floor and the faint click of a violin shoulder pad being attached to the rounded part of the instrument.

Brad gave a downbeat with his baton and the music began, but ended almost as quickly when he tapped again for them to stop playing. It was a plea of sorts as he laid the baton on his music stand and put his hands over his ears.

"Stop!" he implored. "There's something rotten in the State of Confusion!" Nervous giggles rippled throughout the room. "Let's try again. This time at least get the first note right and the rest will follow — we hope. Relax, take a deep breath, and look over the first few bars of the music before we even try again. This is supposed to be fun."

Elise looked down at the floor. Tony tried to make eye contact with her but she didn't even look in his direction.

On the large desktop, were four new typewriter ribbons, a box of paper and a bottle of *Witeout* lined up along the right side of a large square of green blotting paper covered with ink smudges. He made a mental note to get some of the new correction product for himself. Not that he made any typing mistakes, of course, but it would be useful to have some on hand. Tony wondered if this was Brad's office. His place where he wrote down his memos.

From his vantage point, partly hidden behind the cumbersome black and white TV and a well-used Underwood typewriter sitting side by side on the desk, he could observe the self-styled director.

I told you he was watching you.

Startled by the strident voice, Tony involuntarily brought his hand up to his mouth.

"Get away from me. Whoever you are. I wish you'd leave me alone." He shivered and looked around to see if anyone had heard him speak.

15

Tony had started seeing Dr. Brown, a psychiatrist in Vancouver a couple of months after Yvette, his first wife died. It was before his sixth visit that he met the somewhat familiar gruff old man in reception. When he asked Dr. Brown about the man, he denied seeing him. It was then the voice had begun to plague Tony. He had hoped the voice was gone for good.

When he met and married Elise, the voice had indeed gone away, but ever since Elise brought home that stupid notice about the orchestra the old man was back and more aggressive than ever.

Julie Thomas stopped in front of the desk. She'd brought him a cup of coffee and a cinnamon bun on a side plate.

"Thanks," Tony said, staring up at her.

"Isn't this wonderful?" she whispered. "Brad has wanted to start a music group for years." She pulled up a chair beside him. "Do you mind if I join you? I love playing my violin but I'm not good enough to be in the group yet, so I'll just listen while I read. Do you play an instrument?"

Caught off guard, he stammered, "Oh, no, I'm the – ah, Elise's chauffeur."

She studied him for a moment. When he didn't say anything more, she shrugged and moved away making no more friendly overtures.

He watched Brad's every move as he guided the group in a slow- motion rendition of the well-known *Our Director's March*. He tried to shut out the good notes, the sour notes and the *not-quite-either good or bad notes*, wondering why he found it so difficult to block them out. His book began to slip from his hand. He grabbed for it and turned over a page.

"Let's try it again." Brad waited until it was quiet before he raised his arms and counted them in once more

"One, two!"

The drum roll was perfect, but the opening notes were discordant, causing some nervous giggles. Brad tapped on his stand for silence.

"Um — let's take another look at the music and we will try it again. Check the key signature first, and then the time signature. Third time lucky. Look up so you can see me. Believe it or not, a musician has the ability to watch the conductor and read the music at the same time." There was nervous laughter from the musicians.

"Now I'll count you in. One bar for nothing. Drum roll on the next bar. Play it for two bars before the music starts. One Two. *And here we go!*" The last four words were chanted in the rhythm in which he wanted the music to be played, mimicking the local high school band teacher's lingo. It worked, and Brad beamed with the pleasure of success.

Tony caught himself grinning when the group succeeded in getting it right. He told himself that it didn't matter how they did it; the important thing was that they did get it right in the end.

When the cellist began to play, he saw Brad look up. A perfect velvet sound flowed from his movements over the strings.

Tony's musical mind, the one he was trying to forget, leaped suddenly into high gear. He could not stop it as it imagined a cello concerto at a future concert, with Matt Jacob as the featured soloist. Who was his teacher?

He saw Cynthia and Fred exchange glances. Did either of them have the experience to draw out such marvelous talent?

Eccentricity was not always a bad thing.

Tony hoped that the lad owned a decent pair of black shoes. His sneakers, covered with blotches of green paint to match his pants, were not at all acceptable should he be required to wear a formal black suit for concerts.

When the music finally stopped, Tony craned his neck to see over the TV on the table. For a brief moment, his eyes met Brad's again, and their gaze connected. Tony quickly focused on his book.

He's watching you, Tony.

Shivers crept along Tony's rigid spine.

"Who said that?" The big man was indeed watching him. But why?

Your secret. Maybe Brad Thomas already knows it.

Tony read the same paragraph three times without comprehension. He tried to ignore the warning.

Surely even that ugly Frank had known Yvette was ill. After all, he was right there during the weeks I took care of her.

When he shifted his weight, his chair squeaked. He thought everyone in the room must be staring at him but when he looked up, he was surprised that no one was even looking at him at all. They appeared unaware of his torment

Brad seemed uncomfortable after he and Tony made eye contact, but he recovered quickly and continued directing the group of aspiring musicians.

Tony tried to focus on his book once more. He read two pages without knowing what it was about, so he closed the book and concentrated on Brad's baton.

"Obviously," Tony murmured. "Brad Thomas is not experienced. He is awkward and uncomfortable. He cannot do this."

THREE

Tony breathed a sigh of relief when at last the meeting
and play session was over and he and Elise were on their
way home. Elise's laughter bubbled over several times
while she talked about the evening. Tony gripped the
steering wheel of his Buick, tuned in to the throb of the
motor, and tried to cancel out her chatter. The car was so
large and luxurious it was like bringing a Jumbo Jet in for
a landing.

"For heaven's sake, stop talking for five minutes," he
growled as he guided it along the open highway. "You
will cause me to have an accident." Tony felt a sharp pain
as the tiny muscle in his left cheek fluttered. He squinted
to see the road.

"My tic dolorous is bothering me tonight," he said,
making a weak apology for his behaviour. "Loud noises
always give me a headache. That crazy trumpet player!
The noise he was making probably had something to do
with it."

"You didn't say it was bothering you before we left
home."

"No," Tony said, "because it started while he was
playing."

"He was too loud, but he was just excited. Now we
know why trumpet players go deaf. . . but they aren't all

like that. I am truly sorry it bothered you but perhaps next week I can go to rehearsal with Lorraine and Hank."

"Where is the snow plough?" he said, ignoring her remark. "This street is a mess and if I have an accident, I will blame them for not doing their duty. The lines are nearly covered completely with snow and ice. And your yakking is driving me crazy."

"Well, excuse me! If you'd relax and stop being so critical, it might be easier," Elise shot back. "You know they do the main roads first and our country roads are the last to be ploughed.

"I'll pull over if you want to drive," he said.

"Don't be silly. I am not criticizing you, but I'm also not responsible for your distracted driving, so quit blaming me, and the Public Works department because you are bad tempered, "she said.

"I'm not in a foul mood. I am in pain and the music was terrible and a waste of time. You are not seriously thinking of playing with that group, I hope. It was awful."

"I enjoyed it," Elise said. "It was a wonderful evening of great music. All those happy people. . . I am truly uplifted."

"Oh, come on, Elise," he said, frowning. "It was dreadful. Brad can't even keep time."

"He can so, and it was so much fun. Didn't you ever play anything when you were in school? Not even the recorder?" she asked, shaking her head.

"To please my mother. Gave it up as soon as I could. Why would anyone want to play that horrible instrument?"

"It was my very first instrument. I enjoyed making music so much that I wanted to go on to other instruments." Elise loosened her shoulder belt a little and turned to face Tony. He glanced at her. Her eyes sparkled with enthusiasm.

"It is cruelty to force a child to play that horrible

20

instrument, "he said, focusing on speaking every word correctly and with the right voice inflection, and never a contraction.

"I wasn't forced to play it," Elise said. "Giving the gift of music to a young person is the most wonderful thing we can do for them. Some children take piano lessons, but many kids play the recorder at school before they go on to other instruments."

"Nobody will learn anything about music with Brad directing, so who cares what instrument they played first," Tony said. "He has no clue how to conduct and he should be busy upholding the law anyway, instead of waving his arms around as if he is rowing a boat."

"He's doing the best he can, and he does deserve a day off once in a while. I appreciate his desire to bring group music to our community." Elise said, "Besides, who are you to judge?"

"I do not want to discuss this anymore," he said.

"Well, quit being unreasonable," she said, her voice rising. "Brad will be happy to hand over the baton when someone else can do the job."

"You should be satisfied with your home like other women. Why the hell do you think I choose to live in the country? I don't want to be involved in city stuff. I may as well live in Vancouver," Tony argued.

"You don't have to take part in it," she said. She shrugged her shoulders. "I love my home but I'm not going to stay in it twenty-four hours a day. You insisted I quit my job, but I want to do something besides dust the banisters. You are the most unreasonable man I have ever known," she said, with a huff.

"And you are the bossiest woman I have ever encountered. Why don't you watch TV? What about the Soaps?"

"Oh, for crying out loud! Just drive the car, will you. The Soaps are an insult to my intelligence." She crossed her arms and studied the road ahead.

Tony turned into their driveway, waited while the heavy gate swung open and then closed after his entry. He drove down the long drive, activated the garage door opener and parked the Buick inside the heated garage without speaking. He sighed loudly, got out and unlocked the door leading to a small hallway and three steps from the basement to the next floor where there was a mud room and laundry. With his back against it, he held it open, tapping his foot impatiently, while he waited for Elise to enter the house ahead of him.

"I give you everything a woman could ask for, and you want to go running off with the likes of Brad Thomas. It is all a pipe-dream, anyway. Stay home where you belong," he said when they reached the upstairs level. They hung up their coats and made their way to the kitchen.

"Forget it for tonight, please," she begged, putting her hands over her ears, "I enjoyed myself. I didn't marry you to be a prisoner in my own home."

"Why did you marry me if you do not want to make me happy?" Tony said curtly. "There must have been some reason. Try to remember what it was."

"I loved you at the time, but I won't put up with being trapped within these walls. I would like to make you happy, but not at the expense of my own happiness." She waved her hand in a wide circle. "In case you have forgotten, marriage is a two-way street."

Tony opened his mouth with a sarcastic retort, but a gravelly voice interrupted with a warning.

Shut up. You want to win this argument?

Tony flinched and looked over his shoulder. That was Frank's voice but how did he get in here?

"I will get the bass from the car for you," he said, happy to change the subject. "Why don't you put the kettle on so we can have a hot cuppa to warm us up before we go to bed?"

He hastily went back downstairs and into the garage again. He lifted the bass out of the car. Smugly, he studied his newest acquisition, his brand-new fully loaded Buick La Sabre. It was the only one like it in this part of the country. He locked the door, passing his hand over the sleek body of the car before he hauled the bass upstairs. He vowed to make another attempt at discussing things without losing his cool.

"Did you notice Hank's surprise when the drummer was tuning the timpani? I guess he has never seen anyone tune a drum before," Tony observed with an amused grin when he entered the kitchen.

"Oh, Hank played in the High School band, so he knew it had to be tuned, but how did you know the timpani is a pitched percussion instrument?" asked Elise.

"I worked in a music store once. I had no interest in it, but it was a job, "Tony lied.

"I just wondered," Elise answered, casting him a doubting look. "We had our backs to you, so how could you see his face?"

"What is this, a third degree? Some of you were turned to the side," Tony said, his voice becoming high pitched and reedy.

"I was just curious," Elise said, "I know you didn't really want to be there so the next time I could ride with someone else."

"It is my job to lift the bass for you. I do not trust anyone else touching it," Tony protested, with the air of a martyr.

"I appreciate your help, but at the same time I don't want you to do something you would prefer not to do."

"How do you know that?" Tony asked.

"You made your opinion very clear," Elise said, "I know you didn't really want to be there. Next time I could ride with someone else. I don't want you to be unhappy."

"I'm not unhappy, dammit," he snapped.

"Really?" Elise asked. She threw him a kiss, much to his surprise.

He clamped his mouth shut, but he murmured to himself, "If you cannot say anything nice, keep your mouth shut,' or something like that."

"Even if we get a director soon," Elise told him, "it won't sound very nice until we get used to playing together. Lorraine and Hank are going there anyway so it wouldn't be out of their way to pick me up."

"Right," Tony said with a sly smirk. "You may go deaf from the racket, but it won't get too much worse anyway. I thought you would care how I feel about you being away?"

"Of course, I do, but I won't be away more than a couple of hours a week. Is it such a long absence that it will seriously undermine our marriage?" she said.

"Oh, stop being so silly. You know that's not what I meant," Tony said.

Elise smiled behind her hand. "Somehow I don't think of you as being unable to handle me being away only for a couple of hours," she said, before Tony had a chance to formulate a retort.

"Let's just drink our tea and forget being so picky," Elise cajoled. "It's too late to argue and besides I hate going to bed feeling ruffled."

"Yes, that would be nice," Tony said. He softened his voice to a diplomatic smoothness and smiled patronizingly. "It's not that I am trying to make you give up your freedom to do some of the things that interest you. I just think you may get hurt if you put so much hope in Brad Thomas' mad schemes."

"I don't think it's a mad scheme," Elise said quickly. "I can hardly wait for the next meeting to take place. We are all excited about it."

Elise carried the two teacups and set them on the table Tony watched her every move as if he was afraid of losing sight of her. She filled them and set them on the table in the nook she and Tony used for intimate meals.

"Meeting?" he asked, after a moment's reflection. He pulled out a chair for her and seated himself opposite, "You have another meeting about this? I thought you already had a meeting? Why?"

"Of course, there has to be another meeting. We were just trying it out to see if we might have enough interest in the idea. I think Brad was pleased at such a good turnout, and I certainly enjoyed it," she said.

Using another tactic, Tony asked, "Did he say when it was going to take place and where? I'm curious. If he doesn't have it soon, nothing will be accomplished."

His mind was miles away, thinking of Yvette and comparing Elise to her. Yvette had been like a little girl the first time she had seen the house, running back and forth from room to room as if it was an enchanted castle and she was a princess. What's with Elise anyway? All she wants is the freedom to do what she wants.

Why did you let Yvette die if she meant so much to you?

"I had nothing to do with it," he said. "She died because she was ill."

"I beg your pardon?" Elise said, "Who is ill?"

"I was thinking of something else. What were you saying?"

"I was wondering why you care about this group. You've been running down Brad's plans for days now and suddenly you're offering us advice. What's got into you?" Elise leaned forward resting her elbows on the table.

"Nothing," Tony insisted, "but if you really want to find out if there are any interested people in this town, you have to do more than just talk about it. A dinner meeting or something. I am certain it is just talk anyway. Sooner or later the idea will be dead in the water." He nodded sagely.

"It will not be dead in the water," she retorted. After a long moment, her head snapped up. "I didn't even think of a dinner meeting, but what a wonderful idea. We could have it here," Elise said, her eyes lighting up. "This house is perfect. It would be so nice if we could do that."

Tony wiped the sweat from his brow with a white linen napkin, and sighed. He drank the last trickle of tea from his mug and stood up. "Uh-it was only a suggestion. I did not mean you should throw a party right away. Actually, I thought you might have it somewhere else. I just meant. . ."

Elise cleared the table and put the teacups in the dishwasher. "It would be absolutely wonderful," she gushed as she came closer to him. Standing on tiptoe, she put her arms around his neck, and kissed him lightly on the cheek. "You are so smart to come up with this idea. This will be just the right place to have it. Oh, I do love you."

"That is nice," Tony said dully, aware that he had just shot himself in the proverbial foot. He patted her shoulder awkwardly and stepped back. For some reason the distance between them gave him a false feeling of security. "When do you intend to do this thing? What if nobody comes? Or what if the whole town comes, looking for a free meal," he asked, in shocked resignation.

"I'm sure Brad will want to take your advice."

She chattered on excitedly, running thoughts together. "Oh, wait 'til I tell him the news! He'll be so excited. We could invite those who came to the rehearsal tonight. Maybe by then there will be others who have heard the news. We'll lay all our ideas on the table, and then after dinner together we could have a meeting. I've never chaired a meeting, but I do know how to entertain.

You could do that part of it, couldn't you? Oh, I just knew you would help."

"I am happy for you," Tony muttered. He stared into space and wondered how he'd managed to back himself into a corner.

Now you've done it. Why didn't you keep your big mouth shut?

"Who said that?" he said, glancing around the room.

You know who I am. Remember Camp London by the Fraser River?

"Go away. I don't even know you, and I wish you'd go away," Tony mumbled, envisioning the homeless camp.

You married her. She was the girl in the blue dress.

"Yvette?"

"Are you talking to me?" asked Elise, touching his arm. "I can't follow you. What mess? Yvette? Why are you talking about her?"

"Ah—forget it. Just make your phone call if you have to and we can talk about it later. I'm going up to my study. I have some work to do." Tony backed toward the door. "Have your bath and go to bed. I will be right behind you."

"I will call Brad first," she said. She checked the time. "I'm tired, but I probably won't sleep a wink tonight. You are a wonderful husband, but I wish you would quit talking in riddles."

"Could it wait until tomorrow?" Tony asked, ignoring her remarks.

"I'll think about it all night if I don't call him now." She reached for the phone book inside a drawer in the kitchen, ran her finger down the Ts, and quickly dialed his number.

Tony listened helplessly while she told Brad *the good news,* as she called it. He shook his head in disbelief as she rested her feet on the rungs of the chair.

27

He thought, *I don't know why I didn't just shut up! She's like a kid! Hopefully nothing will come of it anyway.*

Who's the boss?

As he passed by Elise's chair, he brushed his hand over her shoulder before he left the room. He stopped in the hallway and listened. She waved her arms and talked excitedly to Brad on the phone. He plodded up the stairs, dragging his feet.

"Tony suggested it, "he heard her say, "and he's willing to chair the meeting for us. Isn't he wonderful?"

"Wonderful?" Tony murmured when he was certain he was out of earshot, "I'm just bloody stupid."

***

Tony climbed the narrow stairway up to his gabled study above the third floor. He was glad that he had seen the possibilities for a hideaway room built into the attic when he remodeled the old house. It was the perfect place for an office, facing the tree line, away from traffic noises and streetlights.

Once in his sanctuary, he closed the door and immediately went to his desk. He dropped to his knees and pulled the drawer completely out and set it on the floor. He reached into the deep space. There was a secret compartment. He carefully pulled out a very old ebony baton and ran his fingers over the dark wood. His eyes lit up when he found the telltale groove in its handle.

"That was the time. . ." For a few seconds he relived an old memory but just as quickly it was gone.

He looked furtively over his shoulder to see if the door was closed. Just to make sure it was locked, he checked it again. Leaving the drawer on the floor, he selected a cassette tape from a shelf of the bookcase by the door and inserted it into the stereo. He dimmed the lights and pulled the blinds to shut out the silver moonbeams invading his personal space through the large gabled window.

With wide sweeps of the baton, he began directing the familiar music as if it were a live performance. When the tape was finished, he flicked the lights on again and turned off the stereo. After he put the tape in its case, he filed it on the shelf and made sure the baton was safely hidden. He replaced the drawer once more.

Whadaya gonna tell wifie if she catches you conducting your make-believe orchestra, Tony?

"Leave me alone. I don't have to explain myself to Elise. She loves me anyway."

If I were you, I'd make sure of that before you spout off anymore. It could backfire, y'know.

"You are not me," Tony said, "I don't need your advice. I know what I am doing."

Don't say I didn't warn you.

FOUR

After Tony had replaced the baton in its secret hiding place, he selected a book from his library without bothering to look at the title. The first words on the page were so shocking he closed the book abruptly and checked the title. He was flabbergasted to see the words *The Sex Life of the African Bumblebee*, engraved in gold letters on the spine of a very handsome book.

"Where the hell did this book come from? It is not about bees," he murmured. He plunked it down on his desk. "Why is Elise reading this crap? Probably belongs to Hank's wife. It figures! "

How did this book get into his private space if Elise had never entered his office? It certainly did not belong to him. He would never have a novel like that on his book-shelf. Someone else had to have access to his office. Someone. . .

Intrigued, he opened the book again and read the author's name. "Lois Black? Oh, a Penny Dreadful book, guaranteed to bore you to death, or put you to sleep." He set it on the edge of his desk and turned away, as if waiting for it to self-destruct. When it didn't blow up, he settled down in his favourite rocking chair by the window and decided to give it a chance after all.

Even if the book is full of filth, I am old enough to read it if

I want to, he thought.

At the end of the first chapter, he pondered the contents of the book. Well, fairly true to life. Yeah! Maybe it was not so bad after all. It is important, to know what my wife is reading. She is s-o-o-o impressionable.

He heard footsteps on the stairs. Frank? How did he get in the house? Or was Elise coming to check on him? She had never done that before. Absently he let his mind wander. She would never check up on him.

The book! He had to get rid of it fast. It would never do for her to catch him reading such a dreadful book.

With a grunt he dashed across the room and shoved it back in the bookcase. "Drivel! I have no desire to be that bored."

The footsteps stopped before they reached his door. He listened for a knock, and when it didn't come, he sat down again and rocked back and forth like a four-year-old on a rocking horse. The rhythm calmed him now as it had as a child.

Had he really heard footsteps? He was too unnerved to open the door to see who was there, but he rationalized that footsteps wouldn't just disappear into thin air, would they? Unless…

"It is Elise's fault," he declared. "Life never treated me unfairly before I married her. I may as well be a dead man, she never listens to me, anyway."

That's right. Death is the only thing that will get you out of this mess. I can help you.

"Who said that?" he asked, the calm he had felt a minute earlier instantly transformed into anxiety.

Brad was watching you tonight. He knows something.

Instantly angry, Tony leaned forward and pushed himself awkwardly out of the rocking chair. His reading glasses slid off his nose onto the floor. In frustration he scooped them up, grabbed the rocking chair and flung it across the room. He unlocked the door and wrenched it open, and stubbed his toe on the door jamb.

He limped down the stairs favouring his painful toe, lost his balance on the polished hardwood floor at the bottom, and twisted his ankle making a perfect three-point landing on his butt and both hands. Tony struggled to his feet and yanked his pants down to examine his bruised rear. He was glad that Elise was enjoying her bath and wouldn't catch him with his pants down. He imagined her remarks and smiled at the thought, although he was still in a vile mood.

When he was certain the bruises were only superficial, he pulled his trousers up and fastened his belt. Even the scent of lavender irritated him as it wafted through the cracks around the bathroom door. He tried to recall why that scent, as refreshing as it was, always seemed to upset him.

"Trafalgar Square in London?" he whispered under his breath. "The gypsy girl selling lavender sachets. . . her smile, so inviting. Years ago, but why does it bother me now? She was pretty but she was a gypsy. I had to walk away. You can never trust a gypsy. They rob you blind. I could have had any woman I chose in those days-except the one I thought I wanted."

He dragged himself past the large master bedroom with the ensuite he shared with Elise on the main floor. He could hear her humming as she splashed in the tub. Tony recognized the tune, so he moved away quickly. He would never play that song again. He didn't even want to hear it. Why had she chosen to sing *Moon River*, the last waltz that he and Jane had danced together?

He wondered where Elise was when he needed her. She could have at least come to see if he had any broken bones. She must have heard the crash when he fell, but. she just kept humming that cursed song.

"I hate that song," he whispered.

You've had a lot of women in your life, Tony.

"Dry up, will you," he muttered, "What do you know about it?"

I was there.

Oh, shoot! I still have to lock the doors. He sighed heavily, plugged his ears and held his breath so he wouldn't hear the song or smell the lavender as he walked past the bedroom door again. Rocky Creek was probably the safest place on earth, but he felt better for having locked the house up. Slowly he made his way to a small bathroom in the hallway outside the bedroom, and stepped carefully into the shower to avoid hurting any of his bruised and battered parts. If it was any comfort, at least those injuries were all on the same side.

His head was beginning to ache. About all he could do for that was take an aspirin.

As the hot water washed down his back, tight muscles began to relax. It poured over his head, the heat almost taking his breath away. He leaned backwards, allowing it to splash over his face.

"Damn ankle starting to swell. Bloody toe hurting. Headache. Nice bruise on my ass," he observed. "At least I have something to show for it." He poured several pitchers of cool water over his leg hoping to stop it from swelling but all it did was make him shiver. He put on his pajamas and robe and limped back to the bedroom in a brooding frame of mind. Now he couldn't even put his full weight on his foot.

He was pleased to discover he had two '292's' in the medicine cabinet so he took one and saved the other for the next day. Golly, but those things worked well. Almost as good as weed, but not nearly as much fun.

One thing about weed that was better than the legal pill he took was that it inspired romance. It was all about love. You could depend on a good doobie or two to *make love, not war.*

He got into bed and pulled the covers up to his chin. Soon she would come to bed. If he was lucky the scent of lavender wouldn't keep him awake.

The last thought he had before he drifted off into a sweet reverie was when his fertile imagination took him on a romantic trip into a fantasy world in which he was a king, and a woman who looked a lot like Elise, dressed like the gypsy girl, knelt at his feet and looked up at him in adoration. A giant bumblebee hovered above them, fanning cool air into the room with its wings.

He whispered into the darkness, "There won't be a dinner party. There won't be a dinner party."

The next morning Tony reflected that Elise probably came to bed quietly so she wouldn't awaken him.

He was aware of the unmistakable sounds of her breathing beside him. He was aware of another sound too—the crash of tree branches falling on the roof and the wind screaming through the forest behind the house. He closed his eyes tightly and tried to ignore them.

Tony knew Elise would hear the wind angrily battering the house. The wind burst through the cracks and crannies, whining like a banshee.

He looked over at his sleeping wife. She had pulled the covers over her head. Elise was such a light sleeper that he imagined she was hiding under the blankets to make believe she was asleep but he knew the sound of trees being lashed by the wind would prevent either of them from relaxing.

Tony marveled at the closeness he and Elsie shared in spite of the fact he was keeping a lot of secrets from her. He turned over to face her.

She stirred and peeked out from her cocoon.

"Good morning," he said.

"Good morning" she replied. "Did the storm keep

you awake? I had a hard time sleeping. I kept wondering if the house was going to fall down."

"We never have hurricanes here but I did hear tree branches hitting the roof." He smiled into the darkness as memories of his tenting nights invaded his thoughts. Tony was glad he had left those days and nights behind him, but sometimes he allowed himself to remember. He pushed away the thoughts and came back to earth. Beside him was his beautiful flesh and blood wife. He had to pay attention to her NOW. It was urgent.

"What was that crash I heard last night, soon after you went up to your study? It wasn't the wind because it was still calm until early this morning," Elise asked, turning over.

"Oh, it was nothing," he replied. "I stumbled over a chair leg. Nothing to worry about."

"You didn't yell so I thought you must be okay. Did you get hurt?"

"Some superficial bruises," he said.

He sat up and put his hand out to touch her soft, fine hair. He tried to tell her he was sorry he had been so short with her the night before but the words wouldn't come out. Instead he kissed her on the forehead, lay down again and closed his eyes tightly as if to shut out the unpleasant memories and the terrible voice that taunted him so often now. He heard her quietly get out of bed and pull the robe over her beautiful body.

"Are you getting up?" he asked, although it was obvious. She didn't answer but he could still hear the rustle of her reaching into the dresser drawer for clean clothes. He shut his eyes and squinted in the semi darkness.

Bravely he tried again. "Do you really have to get up yet, Lise?" he asked, using his pet name for her, "It's not even six o'clock yet and it's still dark. Stay in bed for a while."

"I s'pose I don't really have to get up right this minute. Why do you ask?" she said. Tony knew by the sound of her voice that she was smiling. Besides there was no mistaking the lilt in her voice.

"You are not going anywhere right away, are you?" Tony reached out and grabbed her robe, pulling her off balance, ignoring his sore toe and swollen ankle. She fell onto the rumpled bed, laughing.

"Go back to sleep, you silly old man!" Elise teased. "You know my farm days made me an early riser. I want to see if there is any damage to the house and trees. You must have heard the branches snapping and the wind howling around the house?"

"I didn't hear a thing until just now. What can you do about it anyway?" Tony insisted.

"We have to be ready," she said, "in case we lose power."

"Old man? I beg your pardon," Tony said, passing over her reference to storm damage. He had a fleeting memory of the book he'd been reading the night before. An old man would not have enjoyed any of that book. Unless he happened to be a very active old man. His mood was changing with every passing moment.

"I meant mature, of course," Elise replied with a chuckle.

"Well, I hope your version of mature doesn't mean just a passing mark." It was his turn to laugh. "You can't do anything about it if there is any damage anyway, so there is no use getting up if you do not have to," he repeated the thought.

"I can call for someone to clear the branches away. "

"Do you have to get up yet?" he asked once more.

"I can't stay in bed all day. Why do you want me to stay in bed?"

"Let me show you," Tony said as he held up the sheet invitingly. He turned the light on. "Did you see my bruises?" Those 292's were still working.

"Hmmm! Not bad!" she said, covering her eyes with both hands. "Ooh, that light is strong. Well--okay. I'll stay for another half hour — but I do want to see if our beautiful trees made it through the night. I'll get you a strong, hot cup of coffee and bring it to you in bed. How would you like that? It would warm you up."

"Later, wife, later! I am already warm enough," he said with an exaggerated wink. "We will deal with the bruises and the trees later. The bruises are not life threatening."

"My mother always said that I must think I'm gonna miss something if I sleep in." Elise chattered on, until Tony pulled her back into bed. Her laughter tinkled like golden drops of sunlight. She made a half-hearted effort to get up again, a mysterious smile on her face.

"You *will* miss something if you get up. And leave your mother out of it, if you don't mind. It is just you and me."

"You'd better have a good reason for making me burn daylight," she threatened, snuggling down beside him.

"Oh, I do," he said, eagerly reaching for her.

And he did!

FIVE

Tony paced back and forth across the plush carpet in his study, his mind racing. Only one week had gone by since he'd reluctantly agreed to host the dinner meeting, and already plans were being finalized for the event.

You said there wouldn't be a dinner party.

"Well, that could still change," he said. "Nobody will come anyway. People hate dinner meetings."

You are in denial.

"I just want to keep the peace. There will be no dinner party," he said confidently.

Really?

"I will not host a dinner party."

She's in the kitchen right now making a fancy dessert. They won't like what she is making.

"Why? My wife is a good cook."

Those people are used to bread puddings and cherry pies with the pits still in the fruit. Take a stiff drink? Take two.

"If I turn up at the dinner table crocked, she'll really be mad," he answered. "Why do you want to mess up my marriage?"

It's been messed up since day one.

"Get lost," Tony snarled. A maniacal cackle followed him as he limped down the stairs to the kitchen.

Elise was there cooking up a storm, according to the voice. Now it was laughing at him as well as taunting him.

Then what's she doing in the kitchen right now?
***

Elise was so completely engrossed in producing a work of culinary art that she didn't see Tony. He stood under the archway that separated the kitchen from the dining room. The island was cluttered with baking supplies. A package of cream cheese, chocolate chips and other tantalizing ingredients were open on the counter. She was leaning over a large bowl with her beater whirring into what looked like an extremely delectable mixture. Tony watched for a moment, his nose twitching as he breathed in the aromas. He stepped forward to peer into the bowl and sniffed deeply, his taste buds activated.

"Is that for dinner tonight? I smell cream cheese and chocolate."

"Uh!" Elise uttered in surprise. She dropped the mixer, the beaters rotating wildly, splattering food all over the counter and up the wall. "Oh, you startled me! Look what you made me do. Don't sneak up on me like that."

"I did not sneak up on you. You were concentrating on making fancy food for those people. How come you never cook like that for me? Do we even get some of it for our dinner tonight?"

"Of course," she said. "I do cook for you, but this is for the dinner party Sunday night. My sister calls it *Better than Robert Redford* but it has another name too-- *Sex in a pan.*"

Tony stuck his finger into the bowl and scraped out a sizeable sample of the filling. Dodging a disciplinary whack on his elbow, he grinned as he licked it off his finger. He smacked his lips with gusto and leered at her.

"A woman who can cook like that deserves. . .."

"Get out of my kitchen unless you intend to help me clean up this mess," Elise ordered. When he didn't leave, she handed him a soapy cloth and pointed at the splatters that had landed on the wall. "Wipe that mess off the wall, please."

"Just a small dessert for us tonight, Cupcake?" he wheedled, glancing idly at the cloth before he put it down on the counter.

"Cupcake? I'll cupcake you if you don't get out of my way," she threatened, looking fierce. "I knew you would want some for dinner tonight so I made an extra-large batch—but only if you get out of here pronto so I can finish."

"Why don't you answer me?"

"I told you twice I have already made some for dinner tonight. You aren't listening."

"I heard you. Of course, you want me to leave. I cannot even boil water."

"Oh, you can so," she teased. "You can prove it by making me a cup of tea right now. I didn't say I wanted you to leave. I said I have to finish what I'm doing."

"Do you have time to sit down with me and drink it?" he asked, putting his hand on her shoulder.

"We'll have to be quick about it. I love your company, but I can't get any work done with you poking things." She whacked his hand again when he reached for another sample. "And keep your fingers out of the food."

The voice broke into his thoughts with another snide remark. *Told you so!*

He suddenly blurted out, "I get the message. You want me gone, so you can make exotic food for other people. What about me?"

"Don't be silly. I love to cook for you— I just said I have enough for dessert tonight. There is nothing exotic about this dessert. It's just layered instant puddings, wafer crumbs, Cool Whip and cream cheese. I thought you were going to make tea."

"I'll do it now," he said, flustered.

When Tony had filled the kettle, plugged it in, and plunked himself in a chair by the table. He propped his chin on his hands. "We don't even know these people and they're already coming to dinner. Will they conduct themselves properly at a formal meal?"

"Of course, they will. It's not going to be really formal, though. I mean, we will all be dressed for dinner and we will have lots of good food, but quite casual."

"Is that Hank person coming?" Tony asked, pursing his lips.

"Hank? He's the guy who plays the flute, so I expect he will. Why do you ask?" Elise said.

"Does he even know enough to take off his shoes at the door? And that shabby old truck he drives is an insult. This is insane. It's a turnip truck. If he parks that thing on my lawn, I'll tell him where to put it, confound it." Tony pounded the table with his fists.

"Are you referring to his farm truck?" she said, with a scowl on her face.

"Yes, he drives that awful rattletrap we see going up and down our road. When I first saw that old crate, I didn't realize that the driver might be coming to dine with us. He slowed down yesterday when he drove past. Maybe staking out the place," Tony suggested.

"What do you mean by staking out the place?" Elise asked, looking up. "Staking it out implies he plans to rob us. He was probably checking out the address because of the dinner party."

"I wouldn't put it past him," snarled Tony, his temper beginning to flare up. "Any man who would drive a truck like that can't have very good morals."

"Oh, honey, that's silly. A man's truck has nothing to do with his morals. It only means he puts less value on appearances than some people."

"I still hate the thought of him coming here," he said, looking serious again. "What will the neighbours say?"

"They won't care. It's just a truck. When I was sixteen, I had a boyfriend with a truck just like Hank's," Elise said, with a twinkle in her eyes. "It was a status symbol of sorts because most boys our age just owned a bike. The more noise it made when he changed gears, the more prestige he had. It probably needed new shocks and sparkplugs, but he got a charge out of listening to it growl. It was just another feather in his cap — and mine," she said, blushing.

"Aren't you glad you didn't marry him?" Tony commented acidly.

"We never even thought about marriage." she said, laughing, "We were just kids. We didn't even think about serious things, like who is going to buy the groceries. Who thinks of marriage in Grade ten?"

"You are never serious about anything," Tony complained, shaking his head. "Lots of kids think of marriage when they are still in school. You just like guys who drive old crates. Maybe you like that kind of man better than me."

"Oh, for crying out loud, you give me a pain just listening to you bitch and complain. Don't you ever enjoy life? I love the joy of living and I'm not ready for the alternative." She turned to face him. "Unless you can stop being so miserable, I don't need you in my kitchen," she said, returning to the sink.

"Oh, I see. You want to have fun?" He playfully pinched her rear as she passed by his chair, and laughed out loud when she jumped. She smiled. He inclined his head as he observed that she didn't really mind being pinched. He leaned over and kissed her on the end of her nose.

When the kettle whistled, she reminded Tony it was time for him to make the tea as planned. She took two large teacups from their hooks and set them on the table in the nook.

"Shall I pour the tea now?" she asked playfully, when it had steeped for five minutes. That jogged Tony's British memories of his mother's tea parties. He looked up and grinned.

They drank their tea in silence, until Tony became serious again. "Don't you care if people see that rusty old bucket of bolts parked outside our gate?"

"It doesn't upset me a bit. It's none of our business what our guests drive. Hank is quite protective of his truck. He'll probably park on the road, so the mud and ice won't get his tires dirty." Elise laughed again. She glanced at Tony.

He couldn't help but smile.

"What's with you," she asked. "You act more as if you are about to reach puberty than adulthood. I can't figure out your mood swings."

"You should take this seriously," he insisted.

"Why? It is not important," Elise said, "and has nothing to do with us. A bit of rust isn't a crime."

"Well I still don't want it parked outside my gate."

"Oh, for heaven's sake, it's a public road. Don't be such a snob. You don't know a thing about the people in Rocky Creek, and you've lived here for four years."

"Quit lecturing me," he snapped.

"Just to jog your memory, you're the one who suggested they come here for the dinner meeting," she retorted. "They only live ten minutes away and will probably walk." Elise frowned. "It's a good way for everyone to get to know one another." She glared at him, placing her hands on her slim hips. "If you want nothing to do with it, then don't. We can probably get someone else to chair the meeting if you want to cop out."

"I resent the term *cop out*. They will be in my house." Tony said. "I am not a snob. Nothing good will come out of this orchestra stuff."

Elise drew herself up to her full five feet, two inches tall, and confronted him. "It's not just your house," she corrected him. "I want them to come so we can talk about our plans. If you don't want to attend the meeting, then don't. Leave as soon as dinner is over so we can discuss our options without upsetting you. Your behavior *is* snobbish; even childish, whether you think so or not. You judge people you haven't tried to know, and you think you're better than everyone."

"You *are* caustic today," he said. He agitatedly ran his fingers through his steel-gray curly hair, leaving it carelessly uncombed.

"Now you look like a golly-wog."

"What's a golly-wog?"

"Those boy dolls kids used to play with in the early forties were called gollywogs and had dark curly hair. Well, you look more like a gollywog with your *hayah* standing on end than you do a British gentleman, *dahling*," she said, imitating his Yorkshire accent. He tried to ignore her, but his lips quivered with amusement in spite of his resolve to remain aloof and dignified. Finally, he could hold it no longer, and he chuckled aloud.

"I don't know Hank," he said, when he finally stopped laughing. "What's he got that makes him so important to you? He certainly isn't handsome."

"He plays the flute and is married to my friend Lorraine," Elise said.

"You mean Lorraine Eriksson is married to that character?" Tony snorted. "She has terrible taste in men."

"He's a family man," Elise said. "They are a happy family."

"I'll wait until I see how he handles coming to dinner here. You may get a surprise," he promised.

"And you may also," she said.

He saw her look up in surprise when he suddenly

44

stood up and walked away from the table and out of the room. He ran down the stairs, through the laundry room, grabbing his winter coat on the way to the garage.

He slammed the car door and started the motor. As the garage door opened, he could feel that Elise was watching from the window as the back end of the Buick emerged into the driveway from the garage, barely waiting for the gate to open all the way.

He gunned the motor, sending the rear slithering sideways when he hit a patch of black ice. He swung his car around onto Maple Street, paying no attention to oncoming traffic. He drove erratically down the narrow country road until he went over the hill. She wouldn't be able to see the car now.

She was probably mad as hell that he forgot to clean up the mess he made when he surprised her. That was just too bad.

The snowflakes fell slowly, and settled on the windshield, rooftops and rose bushes. A steely calm settled over him. He stopped at a crossroad, pausing to watch a lone chickadee eating from a large bird feeder by a farmyard gate. The bird was soon joined by a flock of hungry juncos, their bright breasts contrasting with the stark white snow.

SIX

Tony was thankful he hadn't allowed that voice to coax him into downing more than one glass of wine before he left home. Even so, he felt light-headed when he pulled the car off the road and into the viewpoint's parking lot. He cut the motor and gazed out over the hood and the vista beyond the guard rail.

Far below, the mighty Fraser River shone silver in the wintery afternoon sun as it snaked its way through the canyon. Eventually it would be swallowed by the dark waters of the Pacific Ocean. He almost envied the river its fate.

The mood swings were happening more often now, usually without warning. "I hate the mess my life is in," he muttered to himself, becoming morose.

"One lie after another until I don't even know what the truth is anymore. Elise would be better off without me. She doesn't need me. Nobody cares what I do. I may as well not even exist."

You got that right.

Tony tried to ignore the voice pounding in his ears, but it was so loud and strident that he was unable to think clearly.

He got out of the car and walked over to the guard rail.

Go ahead and climb over, Tony? She won't even miss you.

He swung one leg over, straddling the rail and looked down at the tumbling river.

He read the warning sign with a sarcastic sneer. In large red letters on a white background, it warned: DANGER UNEVEN GROUND. Under it were the words OUT OF BOUNDS.

He sat on the rail with his feet resting on the loosely frozen gravel. He stared out at the sharply dropping bank and the great expanse of trees and water without seeing their beauty.

Tony shuddered and fought to hang onto his composure. Danger, eh? Who were they to tell him where he could go?

Hey, check it out. It might be fun. Have an adventure.

Numbed against the danger he was in, but with no thought of changing his pathway, he left the safety of the railing and walked quickly along a narrow descending path made by deer and moose walking single file through the scarce brush to a better spot for grazing. He stumbled when a rock shifted under his foot, and began to slide. He fell heavily and landed on his hip. His thoughts were scrambled He began to roll down the slope. With arms flailing, he struggled for control, and grabbed at shrubs and small trees on his way down. As an afterthought when he left the car, he'd put on a hat to protect his eyes from the glare of sun and water, but now it flew off his head when he fell. It twirled in slow motion to land out of his reach on a tree branch that jutted out over nothingness. One more thing he'd done wrong! One more reason even his wife didn't need him.

A voice he didn't recognize as his own, screamed "Nooooo!" His ear and the side of his head met the branches of a small prickly bush. The sharp needles, like dozens of tiny hands, angrily clutched at his hair.

Hand over hand he fought his way back up the hill. Only when he was safe from plunging further could he think clearly. He tried to ignore the pain in his hip and the blood dripping from his ear. He grasped the trunk of a miniature pine tree and buried his face in the rough green branches, unmindful of the discomfort. Breathing hard, he clung to the lifeline. The little pine tree had saved his life.

Why did you stop, you idiot! Let go. Life hurts more than death. You won't feel a thing.

"Go away!" he screamed. "I am not going to let go. I do not want to die. I just want to quit living like this. My wife. . ."

Only when he mouthed the words, did he realize how precious life was. Tony really did not want to die.

The voice screamed, *Liar! Nobody cares. You killed Yvette, now kill yourself. Coward.*

"I am not a coward!" he shouted into the wind, "and I did not kill Yvette."

A rustle in the frozen grass below startled him as a doe and two fawns almost as tall as their mother came into sight. Their noses twitched as they detected the scent of a human intruder. Tony watched them without emotion. The animals paused and looked back at him curiously before they wandered off, leaping easily from rock to rock until they were out of sight. Daring to look down the bank, he shuddered when he saw the jagged rocks below. The icy fingers of fear ran up and down his spine. He shivered.

When he finally willed himself to stop shaking, he plotted his precarious path back up the rock-strewn hillside. Cautiously he let go of the pine tree with one hand, slithered upward, grabbed another small bush and braced his fist against the pine for support. Tears mixed with sweat blurred his vision. Slowly and painfully from one handhold to the next, he dragged himself up the hill. Breathing heavily, he clutched the cold metal of the guard rail with his outstretched hand.

Tony wasted no time in scrambling over the rail where he sagged to his knees in the safety of the parking lot. He wiped his face on the tail of his sweater, and crawled on all fours across the gravel to the car. He slowly reached for the door handle and tried to pull himself up. He failed once, twice, three times, each time sliding down the slick body of the Buick.

With each miss he felt more of a failure and less of a man. Too weak to try again, he knelt beside the Buick's door with his head bowed. At last he laid his head against the waxed perfection of the Buick, feeling utterly exhausted.

He couldn't stay there blubbering. He had to get home. The eerie silence made it hard to think clearly, but he managed to push himself to try one more time.

The sharp gravel had cut into his flesh when he had fallen on the trail and the blood had soaked through his pants. He pulled up the leg of his trousers and examined the wound with distaste. Blood had oozed from a gash, run down his calf and soaked into his grey sock. He glared at his leg as if it had been its fault for bleeding all over his clothes.

Shaking with anger aimed at himself, he got up to one knee, then to a standing position. He took the keys from his pocket, relieved that he hadn't lost them. He unlocked the door, fumbled with the handle, forcing his frozen thumb to push the button to open the door. Fighting for breath, he settled into the driver's seat, slammed the door shut and locked it.

"Have to wait 'til I stop shaking," he whispered, as he stared at his scratched and bleeding hand. "I can't drive like this. I am a stupid ass."

He gasped, clutching at his throat as he fought for control. Finally, with trembling hands he got the key into the ignition. He combed his fingers through his hair, not bothering to look at his reflection in the rear- view mirror because he didn't care how he looked. Dirt and leaves fell to his lap.

Coward.

"Shut up. Leave me alone. I hate you. I want Elise."

What if she's not waiting for you to come home? What if. . .

"Elise is my wife. Of course. she waits for me." It was a comforting thought because he knew it was true.

He turned the key and panicked when he heard the roar of the motor. He turned it off again. Sweat soaked his body and beaded on his forehead. He wiped his brow with a blue rag he found in the glove compartment. It smelled of her perfume.

Elise probably stuck it in there. Just like a woman.

"I have to get home somehow," he said, scaring himself with the sound of his own voice. He looked through the bug splattered windshield and shuddered. His voice sounded hollow and far away when he said, "Bug blood. Bug suicide mission. Why can't I. . .? Have to wipe it off. Can't see. Never cleaned it off before the weather turned cold and now it's frozen on. I just can't get anything right."

He turned the key again, just part way so he could have power to clean the snow off the window, and sprayed it generously with window wash.

"At least I did something right today," he muttered as the ugly smear of bug blood and guts faded away in the melting snow.

The monotonous movement of the wiper blades lulled his senses into a near hypnotic state and then he suddenly couldn't bring himself to break the concentration. Finally, when he could stand the tension no longer, he turned the wipers off, and started the car. The rumble of the motor was a beautiful sound. His big, wonderful Buick. There was no other sound like it.

50

Tony slowly moved from the parking space to the highway, letting the car find its own way. He drove with eyes straight ahead, not daring to look at the trees, other cars or even people who walked along the highway, unaware that a maniac was behind the wheel. He didn't care that they admired his Buick. He didn't even care if they thought it was an ugly car, too big for the narrow road leading into Rocky Creek. A pretentious car. What did it matter what they thought?

When he arrived at his own driveway, he sat there with the motor idling until Elise came out to see why he hadn't pulled into the garage

"What's wrong, dear?" she said, opening the car door. "You look like you've seen a ghost."

"I am fine, "he said slowly, surprised that his words were slurred.

"No, you aren't fine. Do you want me to drive the car through the gate?" Elise asked.

"No, I can do it!" he snapped. He clutched the wheel and glared straight ahead as he drove through the gate.

"Did you have an accident?" Elise continued. "Your hair is filled with bits of gravel and twigs. And what's that red mark on your neck? It looks like dried blood."

"You're sure fond of giving me the third degree, aren't you? I cut myself shaving this morning. You don't need to know my every move, unless you're jealous," he said. He turned his tired body in the driver's seat, moving awkwardly until his feet touched the driveway.

"Whoa!" exclaimed Elise, ignoring his rudeness. She grabbed his arm to steady him as he almost pitched headlong into a cement pillar at the corner of the path in front of the house. "For heaven's sake, look at your pants. You can't blame blood that low on a wild razor, my dear," she said, looking into his eyes. "Now relax for a minute. Then I'll help you in. You are not okay."

"It doesn't matter," Tony said. "You don't care."

"I'm your wife," she said. "Why wouldn't I care what happened to you?"

"Sorry," Tony mumbled, too ashamed of his behaviour to look directly at her, "I didn't intend to be angry. I swerved to miss a deer, and drove off the road is all," he lied.

"Where? Did you hit something? I don't see any dents in the car but you look as though you've been pulled through a knot-hole backwards," she said, using one of her grandfather's picturesque comparisons. "Can you walk?" She pulled his arm across her shoulder to support him.

"Now I'll help you in and clean off the dirt. I smell perfume on your hair. How. . . ?" She leaned over and sniffed.

"I wiped my forehead with a blue rag I found in the glove box. You probably checked the oil the other day when you went for the mail, and stuck it in there. It smelled like your perfume."

"A rag? That was my silk scarf!" Elise said, raising her eyebrows.

In disbelief he thought, *I can't even get that right.* He mumbled an apology. She propped him against the car's rear door, and then reached inside to turn off the motor, took out the keys and closed the door. "Now I'll help you inside," she said.

Slowly, with Elise's help, he made his way through the garage and into the house, grabbing the door jamb for support.

He grimaced when he saw his reflection in the hall mirror. He raised his hand to wipe a streak of dirt off his cheek, the movement throwing him off balance again.

"I need to sit down," he said. He dropped into a chair outside the downstairs bathroom." He leaned forward and put his head down as a wave of nausea came over him. He tried to hide his torn pants.

"Thanks. I will be fine now."

"What happened to your knee? How did you cut yourself?" She spread the blood-soaked fabric apart to see the gash.

"I slipped on the ice getting into the car is all. It hardly hurts now," he lied again, "I just need to rest for a few minutes. Then I will be as good as new."

"Good idea," whispered Elise, "In a minute you'll be able to make it to the bathroom. I'll help you clean up and then we will have a cup of coffee together. I think you'll be fine. Maybe you can tell me what happened while we relax together." He felt, rather than saw her concerned gaze run over him, "No broken bones but a nasty gash on your knee. We'll wash it, apply some Ozonol and a bandage. If it is still bleeding in the morning, we may have to take you in to see the doctor."

"It looks worse than it is. I am not really hurt. I feel silly for being so shaken up over the whole incident," he confessed, surprised that it was true.

"It's nothing to feel ashamed about. We'd all feel the same,"

"Hank would be able to take it," Tony blurted.

"No, he wouldn't. Hank is not a superhero," Elise insisted. "He's normal just like you and me."

"Oh," Tony said. He looked down at his feet.

You sure botched that one.

He wanted to scream, "Shut up and go away," to the man behind the voice. Instead he said, "I'm just shaken up a little. Thank-you, Lise," he said. "I guess sometimes I do need help." He reached up to hold her hand and winced at the pain in his bloodied knee. "I guess I do love you," he whispered.

"I *know* I love you," she said as she gently tended to his knee, washed the dirt off his face and combed the twigs from his hair. He felt rather childish but he let himself go with the feeling.

SEVEN

Elise studied her frozen roses from the window and commented, "It's only October. Thanksgiving is just next week, so how can we have frost and snow so early? I wanted to cut some long-stemmed roses from my own garden for the table tomorrow night."

"Well, there is nothing we can do about it." He almost felt guilty when he saw her downcast face, and added, "If you order right away, they may be able to bring some in from Vancouver."

"I didn't think of that! They'll still look elegant on the linen tablecloth, even if they aren't freshly cut from our own garden, won't they?"

"Yes they will, "he said, "A rose is a rose."

What the heck do I know about a table setting? Beans straight out of the can still taste good to me. Possibly it's a primitive thing left over from living in a tent.

He said aloud, "Maybe the weather will be too nasty for your company to come, though. What about cancelling the dinner party?" he asked hopefully. "You could invite them another time. The weatherman said this morning we may even get a blizzard."

"It won't be that bad," Elise said.

Tony brightened considerably when he thought about it. A blizzard! Just what the doctor ordered. Hah!

55

He smiled at his wife, his eyes glinting with the sudden anticipation of an approaching storm as she gave the florist her order.

***

When Tony got out of bed the following morning, the first thing he did was to look furtively out the bedroom window. He moved away quickly when he heard her coming back into the room. It was okay to silently hope for a disaster but he certainly wanted to avoid her catching him as he gloated over it.

"Look at the blowing snow" he said. "I'd call this a blizzard." He felt considerably better as he fantasized about the situation should there really be a blizzard that night.

"It's too early for a blizzard. Quit worrying about the weather. Few people on the West Coast die of blizzards," Elise said with a positive twang to her voice. "They all have telephones," she added.

"Perhaps," he said, ignoring her, "they'll all be stuck in their driveways. Or on the side of the road. You wouldn't want that, would you?"

She moved to the window to survey her frozen flower garden once more. Tony joined her. He slipped his arm around her waist and she leaned her head against his shoulder. Without speaking they watched the snowflakes fall.

"Did you call the florist and tell them what you want? I will go and get them for you, dear," Tony said, moving away. "It might save time. I'm accustomed to driving in the snow, so I don't mind doing this for you."

"Would you do that? I'd be ever so grateful if you would," Elise said.

"I have an appointment in town anyway," he said. "After we've eaten, we can look after it.

Elise walked downstairs to the kitchen. Tony followed, carrying his briefcase in one hand and his wallet in the other.

She opened the fridge door and selected a fresh loaf of whole wheat bread, butter, and cream for the coffee.

"I like this coffee maker," she said. "Fresh coffee just the way I like it." She filled two mugs with the rich brown liquid. She handed one to Tony, who was lingering near the food. When the bread was toasted, he carried the plates to the table and pulled both chairs out.

Tony seated himself on the old wicker loveseat Elise had restored that summer, and thought about the ways he could have derailed this dinner party, but hadn't. He wondered about that.

She walked past him and bent down to kiss his forehead before she headed into the dining room. She ran her hand over the delicately embroidered arm rest of the old chair. Her mother had created the fabric with tiny petit point stitches long ago. Tears had come to her eyes when she inherited the precious antique after her mother's death.

He tried to relax, but his mind wouldn't allow his body to slow down. By the clatter of dishes coming from the dining room he knew Elise was adding the finishing touches to the table, all but the roses, which he had to pick up. He leaned forward to watch her through the French doors, crafted of stained glass by a Kamloops artist named Michael. The design accented the vintage architecture of the house perfectly.

As Elise moved a lamp an inch to the left, and placed the silver candelabra in the centre, her heard her say, "Nice."

Feeling more the man of the house again, he headed out to run his errand.

EIGHT

Tony sat bolt upright when he thought he heard a crash. When he looked around the room, he realized he had fallen asleep on the loveseat after getting home.

Elise was putting the finishing touches to the dining room table. Tony expected to see broken glass all over the carpet.

There was no broken glass. He felt bewildered. *What is happening to me?*

The Voice, bad dreams, and headaches. He rubbed his eyes and struggled to see through the fading daylight. Had someone spoken?

Elise was coming toward him.

"Did you just say something to me?" he asked. "I think I fell asleep."

"Yes, I was talking to you and wondered why you didn't answer me," she said. "I think you're still feeling some of the effects of that fall you had. I would appreciate some help to choose the wine, though." She beckoned with a wave of her hand.

Tony shivered. "I hate storms like this," he said. He stood up. "I haven't been sleeping very well. What do you want me to do?"

"What wine do you think would be best with the ham?" She was already at the door off the dining room.

"Let's get this show on the road," she said as she headed towards the stairs.

"Okay, okay!" Tony snapped. He flicked on the light and walked down to the wine cellar ahead of her.

He thought, *I hope I didn't drink her frickin' wine. I've had a few drinks lately. Not that many though. Never thought about saving any for the party.* He sighed as he resigned himself to the situation.

"Hank won't know the difference anyway," he said, with a slightly malicious edge to his voice.

"Perhaps that's to his credit," Elise said briskly. "White wine with chicken, red with beef and pork," she said when they reached the racks. She looked at the many empty slots, then turned quizzical eyes on him. Tony concentrated on his note-book, writing down the wines Elise would need. "A wine for the appetizer course," he said, "and then the main course, and the dessert course. What did you have in mind?"

After selecting several bottles and checking their vintage, Elise loaded up the wine cart and headed up the stairs, leaving Tony to lift the cart up.

"We need to think about a dumb waiter for this thing," he said. "I keep forgetting until the next time we have to go through this."

"I agree with you," Elise said. "We serve wine so seldom that I don't think of it, but you're right. We might have to purchase some dessert wines, Tony. Dry white brewed last year won't do for what I am serving. Anyway, take these upstairs. You can buy what we need tomorrow morning."

"I will look after it," he said. "The liquor store is not open tomorrow but don't worry. I will get some tonight."

"Listen to the wind whistling," she said, "This old house creaks and moans," Elise closed the heavy curtains in the living room."

"You should have heard it when I first bought this

home," he said. "I spent many hours working on it myself."

"You were so clever to be able to restore a vintage home to its former splendour."

"It was a labour of love," he said, modestly. "I hired carpenters and designers and enjoyed every minute I spent working on it myself. I would like to show it off, but maybe we would be wise to postpone the dinner party until another night."

"They will call us in plenty of time if they can't come. You're just an old worry wart. As they say in theatre circles, 'the show must go on.'"

"I wouldn't know," he said softly.

NINE

The following evening, as Elise had predicted, Hank and
Lorraine Eriksson and their two teenagers were the first
dinner guests to arrive. Hank's truck was parked a car's
length away from the ornate gate, its rusted side toward
the Lorenzo's front window. Tony stared at it in disbelief,
noting that the old crate had an extended cab, which he
hadn't noticed until the two kids pushed themselves out
onto the snowy road.

"Elise — they brought the children!" he blurted.

"Yes, of course," she said. "They are part of the
orchestra."

"I know, but we have alcohol. They won't try to drink
it, will they?"

"There are non-alcoholic drinks for those who want
them. You worry over the silliest things. Just relax and
answer the door. Their parents wouldn't allow them to
have liquor."

"Look where he parked that pile of junk," Tony said
in dismay. "Right in front of our gate where the whole
world can see it. It's even worse close up than when it's
on the road. Are you sure he can start it again after
dinner? I am not about to tow him home with my brand-
new Buick!" He glared at Elise when she giggled

helplessly.

"Stop that. You sound like a teenager!" he ordered.

"I'll always be a teenager at heart, and you will just have to get used to it," she warned.

"That does not change the fact he has never taken care of his truck."

"It's at least ten years older than your precious Buick. It may not look like much, but Lorraine says it's reliable, and he's worked it hard. Besides, he can always roll it down the hill and jump-start it."

He stared at her, incredulous. The stuff she came up with amazed him. He rolled his eyes and studied the ceiling, as if expecting a miracle to be imprinted there.

"Hank and Lorraine are wonderful people," she said, not waiting for him to answer. "You'll love them." She waggled her finger at him. "And you will be the perfect host, won't you, dear?"

"You mean to say that bucket of bolts is a nineteen sixty-one model?" Tony asked. "If I did not know cars, I would think he bought it in nineteen thirty. You would expect a guy to look after his vehicle better than that. That thing was at least fifteen hundred dollars new."

"He wasn't even born in nineteen thirty," Elise said.

"Do you have to question everything I say?" he asked, irritably.

Tony just had time to wipe the annoyed look off his face and assume his Company expression when Hank knocked on the door.

He wondered, "What would I do if they were important guests? Oh, yeah, take their jackets, and escort them into the parlour. While Elise pours the drinks, I'll hang their coats in the closet. Or should I pour the drinks?" It's been a long time since I did this sort of thing.

Brad and Julie Thomas were next, followed closely by Cynthia and her second husband.

"At least I know a few of the guests, and those children," he murmured into the shadows. "Brad and Julie, and the Bells. Everyone knows that hussy. I've lost count of her ex-husbands. I hope she knows how many guys have been in her life. Hate those facial piercings. Wonder where else she. . .? Black nail polish? Ugly. They have no idea how much work there is to get an orchestra started. One more couple to come. Hmmm? George Axelson and his girlfriend. Oh yeah, that cello player, Matt Somebody. A little far out. . ."

After he got over the initial shock of seeing Hank's truck parked right in front of his house, Tony was a gracious host. He didn't approve of it being there, but the contrast amused him just the same. He would have parked it in the garage, but Elise had told George to look for the Buick when she gave directions to the house.

"He has been here before," Tony had protested.

"Yes, but he said he had a difficult tune finding the address the last time he came here," Elise explained.

As each guest arrived, Tony personally escorted them to the parlour and presented them with a drink. Marcella passed a plate of hors d'euvres around

Brad does not look half bad in a suit, but he is too chunky in the belly. Tony couldn't help thinking the play by play as each guest arrived. *Who else is coming? Oh, yeah, the Knowltons from the wrong side of the track, or is that from the wrong church? No, the Blakes are from the wrong church. Yeah, I think its Fred Hetherington who's from the wrong side of the street. Does not matter, they are all dolts.*

The foyer was beginning to look like an elementary school cloakroom with boots and shoes lined up along the wall. Small puddles of muddy water covered the marble floor, in spite of plenty of boot trays and small rugs. Tony tried to combine being a good host along with the job of mopping up the water.

"Where are the girls?" he grumbled, getting up off his

knees. "We should have postponed the party. I shouldn't have to mop the floors." Elise appeared beside him and whispered, "Chloe and Marcella are working with food, dear, so can't do other duties." She hurried off to check on the wine and make certain there were some bottles of the non-alcoholic variety for the Knowltons and Brian and Liz.

"We have Orange Crush, Ginger Ale and some grape juice I bottled myself this summer for the kids and those who don't want wine," she chanted, as if taking orders in a tavern.

"Oh, good," Tony said, "I'll go downstairs and get the grape juice when I've finished the floor. It's already cool in the cellar so it won't need to be chilled."

"Let me do that," Brad said as he took the floor cloth from Tony and got down on all fours to clean up the mess he had made with his winter boots.

"Oh no!" protested Tony, without moving a muscle, "I should do it!"

"Nonsense!" said Brad, looking up at his host from a kneeling position, "It's my job at home when it's raining or snowing. No problem. We help each other with the duties."

Hank, not to be outdone, grabbed a cloth folded beside the black boot tray and did the mop shuffle across the slick marble floor. "Now," he said with a wink, "if I just had some music with a good beat…"

Tony cradled his bearded chin in one hand and huffed. Oh my! Unbelievable!

Brad stood up and grinned broadly. He brushed his pants with the back of his hand. "When we get our music going this winter," he said with a snicker, "I'll expect you to do that onstage, young man!"

"You mean in concert?" Hank asked, coming to an abrupt halt.

"Just you wait!" Brad threatened, "We'll make a star

out of you yet!"

"Well, it certainly won't be my flute playing that will get me there," Hank informed him with a chuckle.

"You got that right," Tony muttered under his breath, a smile on his lips.

When Matt arrived, he was wearing neat corduroy pants and a blue shirt. Tony furtively looked for some sign of paint splotches but finally came to the conclusion that he probably owned some clothes he hadn't worn for work. Without the paint cap on his head, his dark hair curled around his ears. Tony was pleased that there was something about the boy he could view with disapproval. However, he recalled, when he was singing for his supper on the corner of Broadway and Eighth Avenue, he had let his own hair hang down over his eyes, hoping it improved his image. He had been aware that nothing could really hide the nasal twang of his voice when he warbled some ballads, but perhaps the long hair had made him less noticeable.

He looked up at the young man and smiled in spite of himself. His youthful enthusiasm reminded Tony of his own excitement the first time he'd heard the amazing sounds of an orchestra surrounding him. He hastily brushed the memories away as he took the sopping towels to the laundry room and hurried to get the wine.

That done, he invited Brad, Hank and Matt to join the other guests in the candle-lit living room. Each man had damp spots on the knees of their crisply pleated trousers. Tony looked down at his own pant legs and noted there was a brown spot on one knee as well. He was pleased that the other knee had escaped the wrath of the muddy water caper.

The drapes were open and the heavily falling flakes made a strange contrast to the cozy, warm room filled with friendly chatter.

Tony's gaze fell on his wife, elegant in a pale green

pant dress. The delicate lace pants showed off her slim, well-shaped legs through the sheer fabric. The dark green crepe mini dress worn over them was the perfect style for a woman of her petite proportions.

He told himself, *my wife is better looking than Hank's wife. Lorraine's eyes are too close together. Being married to him it's no wonder she has that haunted look. Of course I...*

It occurred to him that Elise might think he was being childish, but on the other hand, it was true. *She is better looking than Lorraine. Some things are just the way they are and there's not much one can do about them.*

"I'll ring for Chloe to bring some more wafers," Elise said. She daintily sipped her glass of white wine, and pressed a button below an oak shelf in the parlour, where three tall candles flickered. "One more couple to arrive so we still have time to chat. The girls are almost ready for us to go into the dining room."

"How long have you lived here?" Hank asked her.

"Tony and Yvette lived here for several years," Elise told him. "I've only been here for four. I love this house, though."

Tony stared in her direction, surprised at her easy acceptance of his former marriage, although sharing Yvette's memory with total strangers was not something he wanted to do.

"Did you know Yvette well, Lorraine?" asked Elise.

"Yes. She was a real sweetheart," Lorraine said with sincerity. "She enjoyed singing in church every Sunday. We sure miss her there."

"Hmm," intoned Elise, "I thought she couldn't keep a tune at all."

"She wasn't really gifted with a musical ear," Lorraine said, "but God doesn't judge our musical ability as much as we do."

Tony listened in amazement. Not really gifted? Yvette was tone deaf. With a wry smile, he recalled having to escape to his study when she sang with the radio. Fortunately, she could sing with gusto in church on Sunday mornings, without upsetting anyone, and it did save his ears and sanity. She was a wonderful girl, but that tinny voice was a bit much.

"She looked after all the spring cleaning a lot better than I do," he heard Elise say. "Tony says he never had to even think about cleaning windows or pruning our big cherry tree because she handled everything."

She was a responsible wife, Tony thought. *Always got somebody in at the right time to do maintenance work. She would never run off to play with some dumb orchestra without my permission. I will always miss her dedication and uncomplicated love.*

"Do you prune the trees?" Brad asked. "The roses and hedges are easy, but I wouldn't attempt to prune your cherry tree. Your garden is like a park and this is a beautiful house." He glanced out the window. The back deck's trellised enclosure was lit up by two lanterns mounted on pillars.

"Oh, look," he remarked, "the shadow of your cherry tree is like the grotesque ghost of last summer sprawled out on the fresh snow. "

"Oh, my goodness, look at that!" Elise said. She beckoned Liz and Brian to come to the window to see it, too. Tony watched them carefully, expecting the two teens to begin talking loudly but they were very quiet as they observed the eerie shadows. He grudgingly had to admit they actually had very polished manners.

"We love this big house and the grounds," Elise said. "We hire professionals to keep the trees pruned, although the first year we were married we even sprayed the trees ourselves. I'm sure our neighbours were amused by our antics." She looked over at Tony and smiled. He hesitated before he took up the story.

"She's right," he said. "It probably did entertain

them. I hear that the trend nowadays is to not allow the fruit trees to get so large."

"Yes," Brad said, "keeping the trees small makes it easier to spray and pick the fruit. But do tell us what happened with the sprayer. I'm curious."

"I bought it at a garage sale. When we took it out of the box we realized that there were no directions with it," continued Tony. "We knew you had to pump the plunger to build up the pressure, so I climbed the ladder with it in my hand while Elise stood below and pumped with all her might."

Elise laughed as she enlarged on the tale. "There was only a thin little spurt of spray, too weak to travel far enough to get the fruit," she said. "I pumped until I was out of breath. After Tony realized he had to wait for me to stop pumping before he took his finger off the valve, the air pressure built up and the spray shot out of the nozzle with an enormous burst."

"The flow hit a mass of branches and the wind blew it back in my face," Tony said, "I began to cough. We noticed some people gathering across the road to watch. I was impatient to get in the house to clean the Diazanon off my skin."

"He was in such a hurry that he left me to carry all the equipment to the shed by myself. Tony had a red mark on his cheek and neck from the spray. He had to see his doctor. The branches that did get the spray had nice wormless fruit. The next year we got a man in to spray the trees."

"I would have helped you with the spraying," commented Hank quietly

"Me, too," said Matt.

"Even though we were strangers?" asked Tony, in surprise.

"Of course. It would be the neighbourly thing to do."

They were interrupted by a heavy knock on the door.

"There's George now, so everyone is here," Tony said. He welcomed the final guests into the parlour and offered them a drink.

Tell them to go home.

TEN

Tony had disapproved when Elise chose to set the table with white linen napkins, their corners embroidered with red roses. He insisted they were unsuitable with the white damask tablecloth. However, Elise did as she pleased, and by the murmurs of admiration from the guests, she appeared smugly aware that she made the right choice.

She had also pleased herself when she hired the two girls to serve the meal. Money was not an issue, but Tony felt it was going overboard to waste such niceties on the simple citizens of Rocky Creek.

Chloe and Marcella stood at opposite ends of the table until everyone was seated. Dressed simply, they blended in with the guests as they unobtrusively carried out their duties. Marcella poured drinks, and Chloe passed around the hors d'ouevres. Tony and Elise took over serving the meal, according to their own custom, the girls always nearby.

Tony and Elise were seated at either end of the oak table while Brad was on Elise's left and Julie on Tony's right side as guests of honour, while the other guests seated themselves according to the place cards. The heavy silverware spoke of wealth, and tall crystal candlesticks completed the formal air. Crystal bud vases, each with a single pink tea rose were at the left of each place setting filling the room with a delicate scent.

Elise served dainty crackers with an avocado dip and her special cheese ball while Tony deftly exchanged cocktail glasses with wine glasses of Pinot Gris.

Tony grimaced when he heard Hank whisper to his wife at the table, "What am I supposed to do with these?" He held up a set of chopsticks awkwardly jammed between the fingers of his right hand.

Lorraine laid her hand on his arm and said quietly, "It's sushi, dear. Just watch Tony." Tony couldn't help smiling when he observed Hank's concentration as he expertly utilized the chopsticks.

George remarked in a stage whisper to his host, "I prefer my sushi well done." Tony stared at the ceiling, ignoring George's effort to be humourous.

He signaled to Marcella, waiting by the kitchen door, to take care of the situation. She quietly and quickly whisked it away and substituted the sushi with a small piece of cooked Coho salmon, beautifully presented on a Royal Albert porcelain plate, the parsley garnish giving it a festive air. George was surprised and Tony snorted, barely concealing his disapproval at what he considered his guest's uncouth behaviour. Elise nodded at Marcella and smiled from her place at the opposite end of the table.

After the appetizer course, Marcella cleared the table and Chloe brought in the main course, placing the food on the sideboard. Tony switched wines to Blue Nun with non-alcoholic drinks for Tim, Maxine, Brian and Liz. Tony accepted their grateful thanks with a somewhat feigned grace, but grudgingly observed that the Eriksson children were quiet and possessed excellent table manners. It was all done with the finesse and split- second timing of a ballet. Lorraine, Maxine and Julie looked on with interest and obvious admiration.

The main course consisted of glazed ham, served with rounds of deep- fried plantain, and pineapple slices.

Fred Hetherington hesitated over the plantain, which resembled banana slices, but when Elise explained that plantain was a tropical fruit, related to the banana, and had to be cooked, he agreed to try it. Small potatoes roasted with their skins on, smothered in butter sauce, accompanied the ham, as well as a green salad, sprinkled liberally with dried cranberries, and a choice of dressings.

Between them, Tony and Elise had orchestrated a decadent meal with an ovation of Baked Alaska.

"Great meal!" Hank said, patting his stomach.

"Elise does all the cooking," Tony said proudly.

"Lucky man," Brad agreed. "Julie is queen of our kitchen. I can barely boil water without burning it."

Tony smiled wanly. "Then we have something in common," he said, with the air of a man making a painful disclosure.

The small talk around the table, fascinated Tony although he never would have admitted it. He listened in silence and even found himself smiling at some of the observations of his guests. *If one was a writer*, he thought, *a few of the casual remarks would have been juicy reading.*

"You looked familiar when we met two weeks ago at our house, but I didn't get a chance to talk to you," Brad's wife, Julie said to Elise.

"I recalled later that we were partners on a project at the garden club the year before last," Elise answered.

"Oh, yes, now I remember. I recognized your beautiful blonde hair," Julie said.

"I'm one of the blonde-haired Johansson's," Elise replied, "the famous ones."

"The fiddlers Sven and Lars Johannson?" Julie's eyes widened in surprise.

"My cousins, but none of their talent spilled over to me, although I try to borrow some of their fame as my own by being related to them." Elise giggled and Tony flinched.

"You could hardly play fiddle music on a bass, though you could play a fabulous accompaniment. Have you ever tried it?" asked Julie.

"Oh yes, when we were kids, they always came over at Christmastime to play carols and of course it usually ended up with a jam session."

"What?" Tony murmured. Elise had never mentioned her cousins. It was her fault they had secrets. He was always up front about everything.

"Did you always have music in your home?" Lorraine asked Maxine, who was quietly listening.

"We had an old pump organ when I was a kid," Maxine said. "Mom played in church when she was young."

Hank glanced anxiously out the window at the thickly falling snowflakes which were making it difficult to even see the street. "I hope my truck will start when it's time to go home," he said in a wee small voice.

"I hope so, too!" murmured Tony, his words lost in the chatter.

He dabbed his mouth with the corner of his napkin and noted that George was still clutching his fish fork when the main course was served. He rolled his eyes and looked at the ceiling. When Elise's giggles rose above the chuckles of everyone else, he tried to signal to her to be quiet. She was having too much fun to notice his discomfort.

After the first effort to control the conversation Tony watched with disapproval as Elise chatted happily with her new friends. Lorraine was a neighbour, but Maxine, Julie and Cynthia were new acquaintances and yet she talked to them with the easy familiarity usually reserved for special friends.

When Chloe served the dessert, it was accompanied by sweet rosé wine, its bouquet reminiscent of a summer day in the sun.

73

Brad is keeping an eye on you, Tony.

Tony glanced nervously at Brad, who was engaged in an animated conversation with Hank, not appearing to be watching him at all.

"I did advertise for a musical director," Brad was saying, "but of the three I interviewed, only one had enough experience and he was very expensive. I might have to conduct it myself until someone suitable is found."

"Have you directed an orchestra before, Brad?" asked Hank.

"No, but I directed a jazz group for a year or two," he said, "It's important to keep the group together until we can hire one that we can afford. I'll keep looking, of course."

"You're a cop. What do you know about music?" asked Tony, butting into the conversation.

"I had my first piano lesson when I was in kindergarten," Brad said.

"Oh, really?"

"He plays very well," Hank offered.

"We should move to the Family room downstairs now and attend to the meeting," Tony said, ignoring the comment.

Brad's annoyed by your rude dismissal, the voice announced. Tony flinched but kept his cool.

After everyone was seated downstairs, Elise served tea and coffee to the adults and hot cocoa topped with a marshmallow and whipped cream to Liz and Brian. They looked at one another and grinned as they drank it with obvious enjoyment, wiping off the white moustaches with a Kleenex. Even Tony had to smile.

While he efficiently gave out sheets of paper on which the agenda was typed, Tony made a point of avoiding eye contact. He looked up briefly when he called the meeting to order, but still maintained a manner of indifference.

"I agreed to chair this meeting as an impartial person," he said, in a monotone, "until someone is elected to accept that position. The agenda is before you. A show of hands will determine whether you accept it or not." He went over the main points as they read the agenda.

"Several items are on the agenda," he said. "Number one is to decide what your goals are. Do you want to just have fun, or do you plan to play well enough to put on a concert before Christmas? Number two is to select a leader to chair future meetings. Number three is to decide how you will finance your activities and to elect a treasurer and a name for this group." He gave them a brief five minutes to consider the agenda.

Elise moved that the agenda be accepted, seconded by Hank.

"All in favour?" he asked. Twenty-two hands shot up, too quickly for the question to have been accepted, Tony thought. He winced.

"Now," he continued, having regained his composure, "that the agenda has been accepted, we must decide what the goal of this group will be. Elise," he said, turning to her. "Would you please write up the minutes of this meeting, so the group has a record of what is being discussed?" She hastened to open a large, antique drop-leaf mahogany desk, with brass hinges, and a brass knob with a stylized L engraved on it. She retrieved a small writing pad and a pen from the drawer.

"How many of you just want to have fun playing light pieces together, meeting once a week, with that being the only goal?" Tony asked.

Tim and Maxine Knowlton raised their hands. Elise scribbled furiously.

"How many people want to have weekly rehearsals, with the intention of performing a concert at the

Community Centre twice a season, and doing smaller volunteer concerts at Senior Care Homes and Hospitals?" A short discussion followed, and the consensus was that, in spite of this being an energetic goal, it was the most popular opinion.

Tim voiced his concerns. "We aren't ready to make that decision," he declared.

"It will be just a jam session unless we have some idea of what we can easily play together," complained Maxine.

Tony said not a word, but he smiled and nodded his agreement.

"That's only partially true," offered Hank, "because we all have had some experience. Most of us have played in bands and small groups, trios and duets over the years, and in our younger years, we also played in small orchestras."

Tony opened his mouth to speak, but thought better of it, and closed it again.

George Axelson agreed. "Yes," he said, "Cynthia Bell is an excellent violinist, and could assume the position of Concert Master, and Matthew Jacob is an accomplished cellist. We have two very good leaders right now, and I know we can do this." Cynthia smiled and nodded while Matt's grin spread from ear to ear.

"Matt," Cynthia said, "is also a violinist and a fiddler. We can do anything we really want to do," she declared.

Tony stared at the blank wall behind the guests. *This is not the way the meeting was supposed to go*, he silently protested. *I wish I could turn it over to Brad right now!*

Yeah, they have you over a barrel, don't they? How are you going to escape this one?

I don't know. Maybe if I just follow through, he can take over.

"I know most of you are serious about the music," Tony said, "so let's go on to the next issue, the nomination of officers. The first one is a president. The sooner you put someone in charge, the easier it will be to make things happen the way you want. The nominations are open now." He looked over the heads of the assembled group, still avoiding eye contact.

Brad was voted in by acclamation. There was applause for the popular police officer.

"Good," Tony said, "now let's continue with the nominations." He hesitated for a moment, enjoying the attention, but at the same time, the anxiety caused him to perspire. He took a handkerchief from his pocket and wiped his brow.

Whew! Tony began to relax. *As soon as this is over, I'm out of here! I was scared they were planning to keep me. Now I'll be able to leave.*

Hey, you handled that well.

Tony looked over his shoulder and swallowed nervously, his frustration mounting.

Yeah, now I have to continue to the end of this meeting. Is there no escape?

Not yet. You'll call attention to yourself if you go too early. You didn't think you could do it, but you're doing fine.

After some deliberation, a large pot of coffee and two plates of Elise's chocolate chip cookies eaten, a name was chosen for the group.

They settled on The Rocky Creek Community Orchestra.

"Oh, isn't it grand?" Lorraine crowed.

"RCCO sounds pretty good, too," murmured Hank.

"I can just see the concert posters on every telephone-pole," muttered Tim, changing his tune considerably from the first vote. He had been adamant in declaring that RCCO wouldn't be ready to play concerts for a long time.

"Ooh. What will we play for our first concert?" asked Maxine, breathlessly.

Tony snickered to himself, thinking, *Mary Had a Little Lamb* maybe. They might even play that in tune without getting lost.

He smiled, pleased with his own furtive joke and for the first time that evening, looked directly at Brad. He turned to address Maxine, "I'm sure Brad will have some wonderful ideas," Tony said. "We must continue with the nominations so we can close the meeting." Tony skillfully guided the meeting back to business.

With the election of Brad as President and acting Musical Director, Elise as secretary, RCCO was off to a good start. Hank was given the position of stage manager, even though the group didn't yet have a stage to manage. Maxine was voted in as treasurer, with no money in the kitty, and Matt and George, Members at Large.

Tony was amused by this, but he was beginning to relax enough to plot his getaway.

When the first board of directors for RCCO stood to take their bows, he led the applause and brought the meeting to a close. As he slipped to the back of the room, he winked at Elise and disappeared down the hall and through the side door to...

"I need a cup of strong coffee," he said to himself and he quickly got one from the coffee maker in the kitchen. He then went up to his den, being careful to avoid the squeaky step at the top.

Tony was pleased that he was able to bring the meeting to a close and escape without being noticed. It took talent to do things like that. Living on the streets in Vancouver had taught him a lot. Tony grinned as he walked on cat feet upstairs and stood at the door to his den, his private office and sanctuary.

"No one will ever know what goes on up here," he said aloud, "and I certainly won't tell them."

He opened the door silently, slipped inside the room and disappeared.

ELEVEN

Throughout October they held a number of coffee meetings. The board finalized plans for a first concert to be performed by Rocky Creek Concert Orchestra. December the eighteenth was chosen as the ideal date, which would give the group six weeks to rehearse the music.

"That should give everyone a chance to really work on the pieces to get them as perfect as possible," Brad said, when they gathered in his basement music room for a first rehearsal, just after Thanksgiving. "However," he added, "we should reserve a venue right away. I know it seems early but if we do it soon it will be one less thing to worry about and should the concert not go ahead, we can easily cancel it."

Tony slipped into the comfortable spot partially hidden behind the TV set. He looked around the room, observing that this space did appear to be Brad's office. He planned to catch up with his reading and possibly take some notes while Elise rehearsed. Perhaps she would begin to see the light and give up on RCCO before too many weeks had gone by.

There were a few raised eyebrows when it was Brad who stood before them holding the baton.

"Is this where all the rehearsals will be held?" Hank asked.

"Yes," Brad said. "It should be large enough to hold as many players as we will probably have in Rocky Creek."

"I thought you advertised in the paper for a conductor," Hank said, with a frown.

"Of course, I did," answered Brad, defensively, "but only three people answered. Until we get someone to take over, I am willing to carry on with rehearsals just to keep the group from folding before we get started."

"That makes sense," Fred said.

Brad nodded. "A guy from Mission thought he could drive here weekly, but he wanted a lot of money," Brad continued. "A woman from Vernon was willing to relocate if she took the job. Not being a sure deal, it wasn't worth her time. I agreed with her. Then there was Iqbal from Turkey. I can't pronounce his last name." He paused to enjoy the joke at his own expense, "but he is a well-spoken musician with plenty of experience. He was looking for musicians who could play the saz cura, domra and the ballalaika. I said. . ."

"What?" asked Hank.

"What's a saz cura?" inquired Maxine. "It sounds like a pill for something infectious!"

"I know what a ballalaika is, but I've never heard of a domra. I think they are all World Instruments," George announced.

"You are correct, George. *Saz Cura* literally means *Russian Folk instrument,*" Brad said.

"Gee," said Hank, "I've heard of them all, but the only folk instrument I understand is the guitar, the most popular one of them all. Our own Fred Heatherington swaps his violin for a guitar on Saturday nights at the club." He nodded towards Fred, whose cheeks had turned a ruddy red at the unexpected recognition.

"And most of us have heard Ravi Shankar play the Sitar on recordings," piped up Matt, to everyone's surprise.

"Yes, he made the Sitar popular in our time. An interesting instrument. Anyway, as interesting as Iqbal was," Brad continued, "I had to turn him down, but I have his phone number so I can get in touch again. He lives in the Lower Mainland now."

"Good," offered Cynthia Bell. "Perhaps at a later date we could use Iqbal as a soloist with the group and play some Eastern or Russian music."

"Yes," suggested Elise, "It's a very good idea to keep in contact with these people with the possibility of a future concert showcasing a new and unusual soloist."

"In the meantime," said Brad, "let's look at some of the music I found in a box stored in my attic. I think you will enjoy learning these pieces. Tony, would you mind giving out the music for me? It's just written for strings, but the flutes can play a First violin part; we have no violas but one of the violinists can play the part as long as they know how to transpose. Sometimes a third violin part is included and that is actually the same as the viola music. Do what you can."

Tony had been watching with amusement while Hank was unfolding his wire music stand. He knew most experienced players gave up on that difficult piece of equipment as soon as possible. Maybe Hank was a novice musician after all? Tony wanted to laugh when he saw him struggling with the two pieces that held the music upright, were now sticking up at an impossible angle. There were wonderful black metal stands on the market that were easy to set up and less frustrating. Still, it was entertaining to watch. He smiled in spite of his resolve to stay in the background.

Tony had been so engrossed in the music stand process that he was startled when he heard his name called. However, as he looked around at the assembled group, he decided the best and probably the least of all the available evils was to just pass out the sheets of music before retiring to a quiet spot to read his book. He noted that it had been in the same place since September when the group had met for the first time in Brad's rec room, the only difference being that the TV was plugged in now.

Why me? Why does he think I know what he is talking about?

You know why. Your secret...

Then he noticed that Brad was looking directly at him.

Good luck.

Tony walked from chair to chair, pausing to suggest the appropriate part for each player. It wasn't easy. He had a vague idea that Elise could probably handle it, but when he saw Hank's confused expression when he examined a first violin part, Tony felt less hopeful.

He's still watching you.

Brad Thomas did this to me on purpose! He's trying to trap me. Tony was certain he heard a voice cackling in the background. He looked over his shoulder but no-one was there. If only he could run away! He felt the sweat trickling down the centre of his back in an unpleasant sensation. He was hot and yet shivering. As soon as possible he would be able to escape. For now, he was entrusted with giving out music. If he messed up, Brad would complain, but if he did the job perfectly, he left himself wide open to questions. He set his jaw into a stubborn square and carried on as if the job was big joke. That ought to confuse Mr. Thomas. For the first time that evening, Tony smiled.

"Some of these notes," explained Hank, "are too low for me to play on the flute."

"Oh, really?" said Tony, feigning surprise, "Well, do the best you can. I am afraid I can't help you. I am just doing as I am told." He gestured toward Brad and smirked as he walked away.

Lorraine stared at the music Tony had given her, and looked confused. She murmured, "I can't read this clef. Maybe the copier made a mistake." Tony came back and looked at her music.

"Oh, it's just *viola* music," he said, purposely pronouncing the instrument name as *vi-ola*, like the diminutive flower from the pansy family. He wrinkled his nose, and he pointed to the instrument name at the top of the page. "Brad said it was in the right range of notes for your French horn. Looks like a number thirteen." He scrawled the numbers on a piece of scrap paper, smiling when Lorraine compared the number thirteen with the clef on the sheet of music. "Maybe bad luck to play the *viola*, whatever that is. Just play it as if was French horn music. That should cancel out the bad luck."

Brad looked exasperated after all the negative discussion. "Give it back to me, you guys. I told you it was string music, but if you wind and brass players can't read it, we can't play it with everyone. Doesn't anyone know how to read this clef?" he asked. Fred's hand shot up.

"I can read the alto clef," he said. "Give it to me; I can play it."

"Never heard of it," claimed Tony, as he walked from chair to chair giving out music books. "What will they think of next?"

Brad looked at Tony with a quizzical look on his face. He squeezed his chin against the palm of his hand, squinted his eyes, and muttered, "Hmmmm!"

"Tell you what," he said, "tonight we can just play some school orchestra music I also found, and for next week I will try to get some music from Vancouver, so we have something to play. I just didn't think. Sorry about that. Tony, pass this music out instead." He patted another set of books beside his chair, "and before you all leave, put the other books in a pile by my stand."

"No problem," said Lorraine.

Tony didn't agree with her, but he kept quiet. No use bringing any more attention to himself. He already felt trapped. It wasn't really difficult to hide in a crowd, though. Tony had been doing it for years.

How else would he have survived on the streets of Vancouver?

TWELVE

"We got through the first real rehearsal with hardly any problems," Elise commented as she and Tony were having dinner at home the following night. A fire blazed merrily in the stone fireplace, the flames painting shadows on the walls of the small private dining area just off the kitchen.

"Whew! It's finally warming up in here," Tony said. "I have been cold all day. Would you like me to clear the table for you? We could sit by the fire and talk."

"Yes, please," she said. "A quiet evening with you is the perfect way to celebrate starting our very first orchestra in Rocky Creek."

Elise put the leftovers in the fridge while Tony put the dishes in the dishwasher. When they had completed the chores, Tony took her hand and led her to the couch by the window.

"It wasn't really good playing," he said, "but I suppose it could have been worse. Do you think Brad will really tackle the *New World Symphony*? "

"He might," Elise said, wrinkling her nose, "but of course he has to wait until he knows how advanced we are. He said we could import people from Vancouver. Orchestras borrow players from other groups all the time. I'm not sure we have the money to pay professional soloists for the concert, though. I haven't played *New World*, but I heard it's not an easy symphony."

"I hope he will not play it, but Brad is impractical," answered Tony. "There must be experienced community players in Vancouver and areas who would be able to play the solo parts," he said.

"Right, I expect there are, but I don't know any. Do you?" Elise said.

"Not personally," Tony said, "but I have heard that many of the more experienced amateur musicians and actors and even singers are quite happy to play the more prominent parts in an orchestra or a show for the experience. They don't ask to be paid for the performance but money for their transportation would be welcome." He took the poker from its hanger by the fireplace, opened the mesh guard over the grill, and moved the logs around until the coals were red again.

"Oh, what a good idea," Elise said. "I will mention that to Brad in case he hasn't thought of it."

"I wonder if he really knows what he's talking about. Perhaps you should quit now."

"Only time will tell," she answered. "I'm not quitting. If you need the car some weeks, you could just drop me off and do whatever you have in mind. I know it must be a bind for you to drive me there every week, but you could pick me up on the way home."

"I do not mind, but that is a good idea," Tony said, his fertile mind calculating how much time he would be stuck having to listen to them butchering a great composer's works.

"I'll carry the bass up the stairs for you. Do you think you should trust someone else to do that? I wouldn't want them to drop it and break it. You should call me when you're ready to come home."

Smart move, Tony. You've got her eating out of your hand.

"Okay, "she said, warmly, "but I'm sure musicians know how to handle instruments. I would appreciate us driving home together, though."

"Of course, I want to do that," he said, a satisfied smirk on his face.

"I'd feel so much better if you were the driver on these snowy evenings," she said.

"Me, too," Tony said. "Sometimes I even surprise myself with my brilliance," he murmured.

THIRTEEN

Brad was still ironing out the wrinkles at the last full rehearsal. Tony barely managed to hide his annoyance while he waited for Elise to put her instrument in the case for the ride home. He felt sure the group couldn't be ready for the concert in another three days, which was all the time they had left. Of course, the dress rehearsal on Friday night would be terrible, because dress rehearsals are always terrible.

Tony smiled a secret smile when he thought of the days before he met Elise. He'd tried to forget them, but every so often a memory would flash into his mind unbidden. Sometimes he thought of something amusing but often the memory was too painful and all he wanted to do was go up to his den and hide. Some little remark would remind him of someone he had known and his mind would be off and running.

Tony had listened to the RCCO as they not only disagreed with the conductor's directives regarding *The New World Symphony* but was shocked when they often defied the composer's wishes as well. However, he was impressed when Brad insisted every player should pencil in important instructions on his music so they would automatically play the way he requested. Brad did some things right.

"Pencil in the cues lightly so they can be erased if need be. Nothing," he added, "is ever written in stone so be ready for last minute changes."

"I don't want to deface my music," claimed Hank.

"That's why we use a pencil. You have to write things down, so you'll remember them," Brad explained. "You don't have to engrave them in with a heavy hand," he said, "or write a whole story. Just a few words, or a tiny diagram works."

"You mean a picture?" Hank asked.

"No, not a work of art," Brad said with an amused smile. "A mark that resembles a tiny pair of spectacles means to watch the conductor. Like this," he said. He drew a crude sketch on the small blackboard. It's easy to make and will alert you to pay special attention to your leader."

"Oh," said Hank. "What's it supposed to be?"

"Use your imagination," Brad said. "Pretend it's an alert code so you'll remember to pay attention.".

Tony grinned knowingly behind his hand. "Been there; Done that!" he murmured.

"Huh?" Elise asked.

"See you all at the dress rehearsal," shouted Fred, flinging open the back door of his car to put his violin case on the rear seat. "Bye!" He slammed the door and climbed into the driver's seat.

"Wait!" George called out, as he ran across the cramped parking spaces in front of Brad's home. He banged on the door of Fred's car to prevent him from leaving. Fred opened the car window.

"Yeah? What's up?" he said.

"The dress rehearsal Friday night is officially our last session before the concert, but a few of us could get together tomorrow night at my place if you would like to have an extra practice," George suggested. He beckoned Hank and Lorraine to come over to talk.

"Are you still in your little bachelor apartment?" Fred asked."

"I can fit quite a few people in there if I put everything away. When you came over last week Fred, I was just being a bachelor," George said.

"I'm game," Fred spoke up, "as long as I don't break a leg on the debris."

"I'll clean it up! It's not always like that," George promised.

"Count me in," Hank said. "I can just jump over it. What about you, Lorraine?"

"Sure," she said. "With kids in the house, we can handle anything." She called to Brian and Liz and got enthusiastic nods.

"Will there be room for my bass?" Elise asked. "Matt's already left so I'll give him a holler in the morning before he goes to work. It would be nice to have a cello, too."

"We'll have two second violins, two firsts and one of each flute, clarinet, French horn, bass and maybe a cello," George said. "That's nine people and instruments."

"Sure," Hank said. "Let's give it a try."

"I'll bring cookies!" Elise hollered out the car window.

"We can definitely fit your bass in," George said.

Tony didn't say a word. He drove home slowly, keeping his eyes on the road. Elise chattered enough for both of them anyway.

***

The next evening when they met in George's place, Fred observed that the bachelor suite seemed smaller than ever when filled with musicians and instruments. "I see you really have tidied up, though," he said.

"Well, I did promise," George declared. "I'm not always a slob. We can be more at ease without Brad here, I think. He's the least imposing person behind the podium, but sometimes he makes me nervous."

"He is one hellava nice guy and he just wants us to do our best, so let's make a supreme effort to play well. The symphony is a big job even for a professional," Fred agreed.

"Oh, you mean *New World?* I think we're all brave to play it," Elise said with a chuckle. "Not being a string player, Brad might not realize how we are challenged."

When Tony had first entered the one-room suite carrying Elise's bass, he looked guiltily around the tiny digs and thought of his own house with its spacious rooms, a perfect place to host a rehearsal., but he kept that to himself.

The hideaway table had been folded flat against the wall. Tony helped George heft the coffee table on top of his desk to make more floor space.

To escape the din of brass, woodwind and strings which he knew would surely assault his highly-tuned ears, Tony had planned to escape the torture by spending a quiet hour in the library.

After making certain there was enough room for Elise to comfortably play her bass, he clambered over the violin case blocking the door leading to the elevator. He paused and listened to the wind howling and changed his mind. As much as he wanted to escape, he knew his place was to be here to look after his wife. He sat down by the bath-room door and willed himself to relax.

He rolled her soft leather case into a compact package and put it on the bookshelf between *The Mastery of Music* and *Mozart in the Jungle*. He idly wondered what that book was about. Maybe juicy reading.

"We should clear a space for Matt to fit in," Elise said. She pushed her music stand closer to the wall, put a stack of music sheets on the bookshelf and stood someone's violin case up in a corner. "When I phoned him this morning, he said he would be late. She looked around the room and smiled. "We aren't as cramped as I expected," she said. "Let me see, I think there are about nine cases stored under chairs and in corners. "We are jammed in here like sardines but it's okay as long as we can breathe!"

"If any more people come," Brian said, "they might have to sit in the sink."

"Or the bathroom!" said Liz, giggling.

"I hope it won't come to that," Lorraine said, "but I wonder if anyone will complain. Did you ask your landlord if we could play here tonight, George?"

"Yes, he said everyone would co-operate for the sake of the concert. He even put our poster on the bulletin board this morning. He's a good guy," George said.

Fred, as the only true professional, volunteered to run the rehearsal. "Until Cynthia arrives anyway," he said.

Tony rolled his eyes when he thought of the odd situation that occurred when Cynthia had been appointed concert master. She was a music teacher with a lot of experience, but Fred had played professionally with major orchestras in Vancouver and the Lower Mainland as well as in Europe. However, there seemed to be no professional jealousy involved, so he kept his mouth shut. This would never have happened in any place other than Rocky Creek.

"I'm playing second violin but I can still lead," Fred said. "I won't use a baton to conduct," he said, "so you'll have to watch me when I give the downbeat. I will take a deep breath, move my violin upward and nod just before I draw the bow across the strings. Like this," he said. He demonstrated. "Got it?" he asked.

"Yep!" said Brian.

"What shall we play first?" asked Elise.

"I'm concerned about the Dvorak, so let's do that first," murmured Lorraine.

"What's a 'Dav-hor-shak?'" questioned Liz.

Hank laughed. "Oh, you will get used to calling

music by the composer's name. It's the *New World Symphony*. I like the way you pronounced Davorak."

"Shh," said Fred. Hank and Liz snapped to attention when the violinist hunched his shoulders, leaned into the room and took the promised deep breath. When he drew his bow across the strings, they all played the first note together as one. Fred literally beamed with satisfaction when the room filled with music.

Cynthia came in quietly, and simply sat in an empty chair. She smiled approval toward Fred who had assumed the leadership for tonight. When he saw her, he offered his seat but Cynthia shook her head. "You are doing fine," she said. "Maybe I can learn something, too."

Interesting, Tony mused. He vowed to be more understanding toward Elise because he knew she had missed playing with an orchestra since moving to Rocky Creek.

Next year, maybe but no need to hurry with the nice stuff. I do not have to be more understanding right away. Plenty of time for that. This will be a failure, anyhow.

Matt came in with cello case in hand, and was directed to sit next to Elise. He nodded an affirmative when Elise showed him the little spot she had cleared just for him.

Tony looked around the room and observed everyone paying full attention to their music; no gossiping or giggling.

"Could we go over the section where the famous *cor anglais* solo comes in? On my music the cue says *corno inglese*. What does that mean?" asked Hank.

"I know it's confusing but it just means *English horn* in another language," Fred explained. "They use Italian or German as a rule. I've played *New World* many times and always become tense when we get to this part. I hope Brad works on this at the dress rehearsal because it is an important solo."

"*New World* is challenging and *The Nutcracker* is hard, too," Hank said.

"Right, so we need to rehearse the Overture first," Fred said, "because the duet between violas and violins needs some work. We have no violas, so our second violins are playing that part on the violin."

"Is that why we have a third violin part for the Overture?" asked Brian.

"Yes, and it is very important. I'm glad I was able to persuade Brad to use a modified version of the viola part for you because it was way too difficult to play well," Cynthia said.

"Me, too," Fred said. "I've played for years and I was having to omit some notes."

"Dad, if I can't play all the notes fast enough does it matter if I have some left over at the end?" Liz asked Hank.

"Yes, it does matter," Hank explained. "It's better to leave some notes out in the middle so we can all end at the same time."

"After we've played the Overture, we'll rehearse the symphony. Your dad is right, Liz," Fred said, turning sideways so he could be seen by everyone. "Don't scramble for the notes. That applies to everyone. Play straight beats if you have difficulty playing every note in music that's written in a quick tempo. When you have a pattern of fast notes, play the first one, and aim for the last one in the group. Unless it's a solo part, another instrument in an orchestra nearly always shares your part, even if you don't realize it. If it's a trio or quartet that might not apply because each one is a solo instrument. In a big orchestra you can be sure all the parts are covered."

"I didn't know that," Hank said.

"Not everyone does, but it's true," Fred said. "You must not stop playing even if you aren't able to play every note."

"Why?" asked Hank. "Won't that look silly?"

"No, you continue playing because," explained Fred, "you mustn't draw attention to yourself. You can always watch the lead player in your section, too, even if he or she sits with their back to you. It is all about the music and the success of the concert, not about individuals. Stage personality is very important so you will have a good relationship with your audience. If a player does anything to draw attention to himself, the audience focuses on that person instead of the music."

"What if I really *am* lost?" inquired Lorraine. Nervous giggles greeted this query. Even Fred grinned.

"That happens," he agreed. "Don't share any of your problems with the audience. Tread water if you have to, but maintain your stage presence until you find your way, and you will recover. It is not the end of the world to make a mistake. However, the audience will enjoy the concert more if they don't have to worry about it."

At the end of the rehearsal Fred straightened in his chair and sat with his back to them while he busied himself with putting his music in his folder.

"Mr. Hetherington, you are just like a real teacher," Brian said. "I didn't understand what the conductor was trying to tell us when he waved his baton. Now I will always watch for the downbeat, so I know where I am."

"It makes a difference if we understand the gestures Brad uses when he directs us. It's a sign language but do you think Brad always give the right signals?" asked Lorraine. "He is not very experienced."

"He is improving," Elise said. "There are gestures that mean to play quietly, signs that mean pick up the speed, and body language that tell the players to play loud or soft and signals that indicate articulation. We will really have to pay attention.

"Tomorrow night when we each practice by ourselves at home, let's remember the things Brad told us," Elise said. She pulled the soft case around her bass and snapped it closed.

"Break a leg," advised Liz when she packed away her violin.

"How come you like that stage-door advice?" Brian asked. He cleaned the powdered rosin off his violin strings with a soft cloth before he slipped the gold satin bag over his instrument and laid it in the case.

"I think it's the same as being able to say, 'off with his head!'" Liz said.

"No, it's not a threat," Brian said. "Nobody is about to lose their head. It just means good luck. Mr. Hetherington helped us a lot. We're not so bad after all." He nodded toward Fred and grinned.

"Just call me Fred," said the violinist.

Tony said nothing. He got up from his cramped space in the kitchen and unwound his long legs. He had to admit to that their playing wasn't really all bad. Still, the parts that were bad made him cringe!

FOURTEEN

The snow-covered evergreens wore festive strings of red, green and gold Christmas lights which shone brightly in the dimness of an early December morning. An air of excitement quickened Elise's step when she walked into the breakfast nook that morning.

"The concert is tonight!" she announced needlessly to Tony, already seated at the breakfast nook.

"I know," Tony said morosely. He put his elbows on the table and pressed his hand against his bearded chin.

"How come you didn't sleep in this morning? This is a first! I am usually eating breakfast by the time you surface. You must be excited about the concert too."

"Oh, I am!" he said, his smile almost too large to be genuine. He stifled the groan that lurked in the back of his throat like a tiger looking for a weak link in the cage to make its escape.

"Did you make enough toast for me, too?" She looked at Tony expectantly, as if waiting for the gently browned slices to appear before her.

"I made four pieces," he said, "They are in the kitchen staying warm in the toaster. I will get a plate for you. Sit down, dear, and I will bring it to you." He hurried off to get a side plate.

98

As he carried the still steaming toast from the kitchen, he glared at the toaster.

Elise raised her eyebrows, and gave him a weak smile but she accepted the meal graciously. "Were you trying to make Indian smoke signals?" she asked. After all, it was good of Tony to think of her on this exciting morning.

"I think we need a new toaster," he said, "This one burns everything. Anyway, I'm hungry, so I will eat mine anyway. I will buy a new one this afternoon. I rather like burnt toast, don't you?" He piled his plate with two dark brown objects resembling floor tiles, and tried to cover up his mistake by spreading plenty of strawberry jam on them. He watched as Elise smirked across the table at him.

"Oh, yes, I do," she said, her dimples activated as she obviously struggled to contain a chuckle. "They say cinders contain more vitamin C than toast just browned to perfection. Extra brown toast has always been a favourite of mine. My mother loved it."

"Glad you like it," he said, a solemn look in his eyes. "Are you sure you want to eat the toast I made? It does not look as good as when you make it."

"I'm honoured that you cooked breakfast for me. Come, let's eat before it gets cold."

"I doubt it will get cold. The flames have barely been extinguished," he said.

Deep in thought, Tony helped himself to the second piece of toast already on his plate, and absent mindedly spread peanut butter and more jam on it. "I planned to get the flu," he muttered under his breath, "and miss this doggone concert, but I feel healthy. At least I thought I was before I ate this burnt toast. I don't want to disappoint Elise after all she's put into it?" He smoothed his lips into a half smile, beginning to see humour in the situation.

When he took a big bite of the overloaded toast,

strawberry jam dribbled down his chin. He grimaced and put it down on his plate with a snort, while he cleaned the sticky red juice off his beard with his napkin.

He knew Elise was trying not to laugh but her keen sense of humour was making it difficult to contain the giggles. He looked at her with a twisted grin and soon the two of them were laughing heartily together. He reached across the table and put his big hand over hers.

You idiot! Now you'll have to face the music.

"So what?" he said.

"I beg your pardon?" inquired Elise, her eyes wide.

"Nothing, I was thinking of something else. It will be a wonderful experience. I can't wait to see you onstage tonight," Tony said.

"Really?" murmured Elise, "I'm so happy you'll be there. I thought maybe you wouldn't come."

"Of course, I will. You will be the most beautiful woman on that stage," he told her.

He thought, that's true. The lovely Lorraine is no competition for my wife. Her jaw is too square. I don't understand how Brad could let this bunch of amateurs murder Dvorak's beautiful *New World*. It's sacrilege. And who is this Jackson person? If he messes up that *cor anglais* solo, I'll shoot him. What if he doesn't even show up? I suppose some Canadians will call it an English Horn, but I prefer to use its proper name, even if some local yokel plays it.

"Would you like to see my new dress?" Elise wiped the toast crumbs from her lips and took a step toward the hallway.

He looked up, surprise in his eyes. "Of course, honey. I'd love to see it," he said. "When did you have time to buy a new dress? Did you tell me? I forgot."

"You probably didn't hear me. You've been so distracted recently that sometimes I've felt as if I don't even have a husband." She dashed off quickly to put the

100

dress on. Tony was in deep thought while waiting for her return.

It's not too late to insist she return it to the store. You're weak.

Tony shuddered and looked over his shoulder. He mouthed the words, "Go away and leave me alone. I'm not weak. I'm a husband."

When Elise emerged from the bedroom, Tony was taken aback by how lovely she looked. The simple black dress was perfect. He could visualize her wearing the diamond necklace and earrings he'd given her for her birthday.

"You look fine," he said. "It is pretty. The beauty is from you, not really the dress." He laughed uncertainly, although the sentiment was genuine.

"I take it *fine* in this case means you do like it?" queried Elise, inclining her head slightly. "I have to look more than fine if I am to wear diamonds."

"Of course, I like it. Diamonds will be perfect. You know that is what I mean. I would never say you looked fine if it was not true," Tony said, his tone, bordering on irritation.

He began to mumble. "Such gorgeous music," he said, "and they intend on playing it for a first concert. It is sacrilege."

"Are you're talking to yourself, or to me?" Elise asked. "I can't hear you when you mumble." She looked intently into his face, but he lowered his eyes and looked away as if he hadn't heard her. It wasn't the first time Tony had done that.

FIFTEEN

"Wow," Brad said, "these players are so enthusiastic, they're arriving at the hall earlier than they even need to." He glanced at his watch. "They have forty-five minutes to spare. That sure makes me feel good."

Tony nodded, but said nothing. He wondered if Brad could actually pull off this concert, but as long as Brad thought he could do it, Tony decided not to say a word. He laughed to himself because Brad had even carried his scores in a briefcase to the hall himself, too nervous to leave that task to Lorraine, the music librarian, as he should do. Tony remembered doing the same thing years ago.

He could imagine Brad hiding in his dressing room so he could check the scores again and no doubt make last minute notes in the margins. He recalled doing that, too, in days gone by.

The Nutcracker Suite was the first item on the program and intended to get the audience in a good mood. He hoped it would. It wasn't easy music and Brad not being a violinist himself, Tony knew it was difficult for him to put himself in their shoes. If Brad had thought of that earlier, Tony was sure Cynthia, as concert master, would have been more than happy to advise him.

Before he sat down in the theatre to see the show,

Tony made a trip to the men's dressing room where he observed that Brad was combing his hair once more in an effort to tame the rebellious lock that never wanted to obey a parting.

"Perhaps you should go backstage to make sure Hank and his stage crew have done their work," Tony suggested.

"Oh, yes, of course," Brad muttered. His face was pale and Tony wondered if he was going to become sick instead.

"Would you like to come with me just to put everyone at ease?"

"Me?" queried Tony, "I would probably scare them, but sure, I'll come with you. I was just on my way to walk my wife to the dressing room. I like to make sure she's okay before I relax.

"Can't she find her way?" Brad asked.

"Of course she can, but it's just one of the niceties of the concert world," he answered. Brad looked at him strangely, but didn't say a word.

The ladies were helping one another to get ready. When he inadvertently opened the door in time to catch Maxine pulling a black taffeta blouse over her head, there was some excited giggling, but he was glad no one screamed. He hated women who screamed.

He casually looked around, noting that Cynthia had no hardware on her face tonight.

"Cynthia, my dear," he said, meaning every word of it. "There is something wonderful the way a long gown compliments a woman. You look very sophisticated."

"Why, thanks, Tony," Cynthia said. "Have you seen Hank in his black suit and white shirt? Now that is a sight for sore eyes!"

"I'm sure it's a real treat," muttered Tony. "I can hardly wait." He rolled his eyes as if the vision was too much for his mind to absorb. Cynthia chuckled.

"I had better go now," he said to Elise, as he walked toward the door, "so I can get a good seat. The auditorium is filling up fast."

He walked by the men's dressing room, and decided to go in to offer good luck to the guys.

George was standing by the door looking disheveled. It was obvious that he had struggled for a while trying to put on his tie, because it was beginning to look tatty.

Tony held out his hand and said, "Here, let me tie this thing for you, George." He took the tie from his hand, smoothed it out with his thumb and expertly tied it. He patted George on the shoulder like a caring father and held up his hand when George began to thank him profusely.

"Hold it," he said. "I'm not really a good Samaritan. I simply could not bear to watch you strangling yourself. Save your strength for the concert." They both laughed self-consciously. Tony walked quickly toward the door, glad to escape.

Go sit somewhere and be quiet, or you'll have to help the girls too. You know these theatre types. No modesty. Disgusting.

Tony walked down the stairs and into the hall, feeling George's curious stare as he walked away.

He chose a seat with a good view of the bass section so he could see Elise onstage. He picked up the program lying on his chair and checked to make sure her name was spelled correctly.

He could hear instruments being tuned behind the curtains, and he noted with amusement that some musicians peeked around the baffles backstage to watch the audience coming in. From his chosen vantage point he could just see the curtains moving apart. He imagined their excitement and, in some cases, probably the colleywobbles.

Old forgotten memories forced their way into his mind while he watched the patrons coming in. Unable to get rid of the lump in his throat, he studied the pattern on the tiled ceiling, the monogram on the chair backs. He cleared the mist from his eyes.

***

Backstage he knew the excitement must be reaching its peak. He imagined he saw Elise part the curtains with her fingers so she could look at the people coming. Wasn't that her blonde hair shining in the lights?

He imagined the excitement they were feeling, although he tried hard to squelch it.

Tony remembered the first time he waited in the wings before a concert and was amazed that there were actually people waiting for the concert to begin. He remembered a more experienced musician saying "I hope so. We sold tickets for that purpose. Relax and everything will be fine. Imagine the audience are all in their pyjamas." He had forgotten who it was, but it didn't matter.

What really mattered was the advice he had received when he was a young boy.

"Stay in the zone."

"What does that mean?" he had asked.

"Stay focused on the music, not the audience. You can do it."

His eyes misted again. He knew why he had thrown it all away, but it still hurt after all these years.

"Break a leg," someone would undoubtably say.

At exactly 8:00 p.m. Cynthia assumed her role as the Concert Master. When she walked onstage to tune the instruments, the audience applauded her entrance. She acknowledged them and nodded to the oboe player to sound an A, tuned her own instrument to the note, and listened as each section tuned their instruments. She moved from centre stage to sit quietly in the concert master's chair to wait for the director. Tony smiled his approval at her professionalism.

Brad came in with a flourish, and stepped onto the podium with confidence. Out of respect and tradition, the orchestra members stood while he bowed to the audience, the tails of his formal suit coat flapping importantly.

Tony craned his neck to see Elise. She was definitely the most beautiful woman on stage. Her small stature was accentuated by the enormous size of her string bass. With her head held high, she placed her left hand around the fingerboard to support its weight.

So far, so good, eh Tony? The Nutcracker Suite is an excellent choice to begin a Christmas Concert. Of course, Brad will mess things up when he tries to conduct.

Tony spun around. He could have sworn that Frank was in the seat behind him, but it was still empty.

He observed that Elise wouldn't look directly at him, but he knew her thoughts were probably drawn to him in the front row. The difficult opening notes of the Miniature Overture had successfully set the scene of *The Nutcracker Suite*. When she looked up, he nodded encouragement. The duet between the violins and violas, violins substituting for the darker-toned violas, was fantastic. Tony was impressed.

Even *The Dance of the Sugar Plum Fairy* was as fanciful as it should be. Hank's flute soared above the rest in *The Merlitons.* He saw Elise smile. Tony wondered if she was imagining the muscular Hank cavorting barefooted with one of the sugar-plum fairies; not that such a scene was even in the well-known suite but the vision amused him.

When he glanced around at the musicians, Tony noted that most of them were smiling. He stifled the possibility they were just happy because they had successfully arrived at the end of the movement at the same time. They hadn't always been so fortunate.

He noted that Liz and Brian appeared more relaxed than the older people but that was probably the gift of youth. When he was their age, he didn't suffer stage fright either.

Elise missed the first few notes of the *Waltz of the Flowers*, then stumbled over the next four bars before she was able to play the notes fluently. Tony suffered a few seconds of actual pain as he allowed his mind to wander into a realm he had denied himself for too long. Looking ruefully at the end of her bow, as though she half expected to see the missing notes sliding off the point onto the floor to settle in a heap beside her chair, he knew she struggled to look nonchalant. He was proud to see that she focused on the music, and the conductor, just as she had been trained to do.

Tony smiled as he shared in the feeling. It was not really something he wanted to do, but he was unable to help himself.

When the final notes faded away, Tony saw her glance up from the music and look in his direction. She smiled and Tony noted that Brad was smiling, too.

He wondered if Brad knew she had missed some notes. Tony could almost see them on the floor but he knew that feeling was left over from days gone by. Nobody can really do that unless... Tony didn't want to go there so he closed his mind and focused on the hardness of his chair.

He had truly enjoyed the first half of the concert, and he had actually relaxed while waiting for the last note.

He was jarred out of his reverie by a strident voice cackling in his ear.

They made a mess of that. Lots of sour notes and some left out entirely. Waltz of the Flowers too heavy. The cellos were droning like a fleet of bombers.

"Who said that?" Tony asked, looking around. The gentleman sitting next to him looked amused and turned away. Tony wiped his brow on a Kleenex and wondered how much more he could take.

Surely you aren't going to stay here.

He thought, *I care about my wife.* At the intermission he strode up to the stage to wait for Elise to meet him on the last stair. He escorted her to the foyer where the Women's Institute served some delectable refreshments. When he found himself hemmed in with so many people, he had a few moments of anxiety, but he forced himself to focus on Elise instead of himself. He put his arm around her shoulder and whispered, "Well done, sweetheart; you were awesome. How about a cup of coffee? I just saw Hank walk by with a fudge brownie. The sweets may not improve his flute playing, but you can have all the sweets you want. Would you like one?"

"I would," Elise said. "Was the music really okay? I'm so nervous tonight."

"That is normal—it is your first concert in a long time and I love you." Tony whispered the words into her ear, a slight smile playing about his lips.

"Are you really enjoying the concert?"

"Of course, I am," Tony said.

When the intermission was over someone flashed the lights on and off as a signal to go back onstage. Elise leaned into Tony's chest, and looked up into his eyes.

"Break a leg," she said. She shot him a big smile. "Are you sure it was okay? I'm still nervous."

"You are an excellent musician," he said. He gave her an affectionate squeeze. "I will walk with you to the stage, if I may."

After the intermission he walked back to his seat, and turned his head to see her again. Elise's blonde hair shone like a halo in the overhead stage lights, an effect he found quite appealing.

He listened with amusement to the clarinet players

making odd wheezing sounds as they tried to soften their reeds. Someone was blowing air into the end of his horn, and a trumpeter went through his *warming up* scales once more. He watched Hank swilling out his flute and wondered if it was plugged with unplayed notes. For some reason the fantasy tickled his sense of humour. It was like a Disney movie scene.

SIXTEEN

The intermission dragged on. Tony looked at his watch, noting that members of the orchestra appeared uneasy. Where was Brad?

Someone remarked loudly enough to be heard by most of the audience, "The intermission should have been over fifteen minutes ago. Where is the conductor?"

"Maybe he thought the concert was finished," answered someone in the next aisle. Amused snickers could be heard from a couple in the back row.

"He didn't do all the usual bowing and scraping, and nobody has thrown flowers at him yet," someone else said. Tony squirmed with embarrassment. Is that how conductor showmanship looked to the audience?

It broke his heart to see Elise looking so distraught. How could Brad treat his friends that way? It was fine to create a little suspense but there was a limit.

The thirty-two members of R.C.C.O. waited quietly for their conductor to take charge. Tony began to fidget until he could stand it no longer. He stood up and looked around. Something must have happened.

People are leaving. Isn't this what you wanted?

No. I can't stand by and watch this, he thought.

Tell Elise she made a mess of Waltz of the Flowers. *Why don't you walk out?*

110

Tony strode down the aisle to the backstage doorway, ignoring a sign on the door stating there was no admittance. He pushed the door open. In the confusion nobody seemed to notice him.

The dim lighting backstage made it difficult to see clearly but he could make out a heavy-set figure sitting in a chair. As his eyes became accustomed to the dusky interior, he saw the person was hunched over with his head in his hands. It was Brad.

"What's wrong?" he asked.

"Uh—nothing," the big man said.

"Get out there, man," Tony snapped, giving him a rough shaking. The conductor looked up, but stayed anchored to his chair.

"What the hell are you waiting for? Some fanfare?"

"Can't," mumbled Brad, his voice sounding nothing like Sgt. Brad Thomas, the burly, self-confident officer.

"What do you mean?" Tony said, as he tried to drag Brad out of his chair.

"I can't go onstage again," he whispered.

"Why not? Are you sick?"

"No-but. . ."

"This is no time for drama." Tony yanked Brad to his feet and glared up into his face. "Get out there NOW!"

"I can't do it," Brad whimpered, trying to squirm out of Tony's grasp. "I just can't go back on stage," he said.

"You are the conductor. You have to go onstage because they cannot play without you. The audience is restless. Are you willing to let your friends down?"

"I already did that." Brad looked as though he was getting ready to bolt so Tony grabbed him by both arms and held him firmly.

"They needed more time," Brad said. "It's all my fault. I don't know how to conduct the *New World Symphony*. I'm a failure!" He closed his eyes tightly as he continued to struggle. "I want to, but I can't." He bent

111

over and gagged. Tony backed away hastily.

"I get the message," Tony said, more gently when the dry heaves had subsided, "but if you just walk away it would not be fair to the orchestra members."

"I'm a failure," Brad repeated, choking on his words. Tony took a crumpled Kleenex from his pocket and handed it to him. Brad pressed it to his mouth. He studied his shoes intently.

"You did not fail," Tony said. "So they made some mistakes. Big deal! To your credit, they recovered nicely. You should make an effort to do the same. Nobody ever died because he played a bum note, and as far as I know, there have been no deaths from stage fright."

Brad uttered another expletive. "I am not going out on that stage. I don't give two hoots what happens. I don't care. I'm going home. Why do you care anyway?"

"My wife is on that stage," Tony said.

In a more subdued voice Brad said, "I understand but I can't. I don't *want* to let them down. I'm a miserable failure."

Tony frowned. He bit his lip and sighed deeply before speaking. "This is silly. Just give me the bloody baton. Where's the score? Never mind the frickin' thing. I'll conduct it from memory. Don't sit there staring at me. Just tell me if there are any cuts," Tony asked through clenched teeth. Brad shook his head and stared at Tony in shock and disbelief.

"You?" he blurted. "You are going to conduct? That is ridiculous! You've never conducted it before either. Or have you?" His tone turned to one of speculation.

"Maybe," Tony said, still staring. "If I delay, I will lose my nerve, too. In your case, it is just nerves. In my case, if I don't do this, I will have lost everything for good. Please do not leave the hall. Do you understand?"

"I think so," Brad said. He stared at the floor.

Tony set his jaw into a stubborn square. He peeked

around the curtains before he strode onstage. When he stepped onto the podium, he heard guarded comments from the players and struggled to keep them from eroding his nerve.

What am I doing? All my work to carve a new life for myself will be instantly smashed to smithereens. Ten long years I've worked to get out of this scene and in one foul swoop I will mess up my whole life again.

***

"What?" muttered Hank, as Tony took his place in front of the orchestra.

"Is he crazy?" whispered George to his stand partner. He fumbled with the music, which, in his nervous excitement, he had forgotten to open at the right page.

Fred looked at Cynthia, and frowned. She was the concert master, second in command to the conductor, and she had already lifted her violin to her chin, so he did the same thing. Brian, who sat beside her had followed suit.

"I'm scared!" Lorraine mouthed the words to John Hobart, a horn player from New Westminster, brought in specially to play the difficult First Horn part. "If he has no idea what he's doing, we'll be lost."

"Don't worry, he'll just follow us — he won't lead," whispered John, "Surprise guest conductors never lead. It's just too bad it's this piece. I've played *New World* many times so just follow me. Okay?"

Lorraine nodded, feeling the confidence that exuded from the professional musician.

"Where's Mr. Thomas? What happened?" whispered Liz to her stand partner. "Do you think he's mad at us because we made a mistake in the Nutcracker Squeak?" Fred shook his head and mouthed, "Shhhh! Stay in the zone."

Elise stayed focused with an effort. When the young cellist beside her looked confused, she whispered, "Tony would never do anything to show himself up, so don't panic. He knows what he's doing." She hoped that statement was true.

"Oh, a guest conductor!" said someone in the audience to the person sitting beside him, unaware that his stage whisper was loud enough to carry in a building built for good acoustics. "It's not on the program, so it must be a surprise." He removed his cowboy hat and hung it on the back of his chair, got to his feet and began to applaud loudly in recognition of the *guest conductor*. The applause spread throughout the hall, until everyone was standing to show their appreciation.

Tony gasped and half turned to acknowledge them, before giving his full attention to the orchestra. He noticed that the same people he had seen leaving a few minutes ago, had hurriedly returned to their seats. He smiled confidently and waited until the chair shuffling had subsided. He knew that even if he was nervous, this was something he could do right.

Don't turn around and look at the audience, you jerk. Someone will recognize you.

He did consider escaping into the safety and darkness of the wings beside Brad, but instead he said, just loud enough for the orchestra members to hear, "We are going to knock their socks off!"

He wiped the sweat from his brow with the back of his hand. Matt Jacob laid his cello on its side, stood up and offered him a handkerchief from his pocket. Tony smiled, accepted it, and carried on, the diversion giving him courage.

The audience applauded loudly when he used it to wipe the sweat from his forehead. Tony turned toward them and smiled. Someone said. "Bravo!" and the applause swelled to a crescendo again, and then faded away as Tony once more turned his attention to the orchestra.

He gave the downbeat and beamed as the orchestra

responded. He dared not look at Elise, but he knew she was watching.

Guest conductor, eh? What a brilliant idea, he thought. *Chosen at random.*

When he cued in the English Horn soloist, he recognized the beautiful tone before he realized he knew the player.

Oh no! I think he recognized you. You should have known that would happen.

Is that Robert Jackson Cates? Hmm--it has to be him. Nobody plays like my old friend Robert. I wonder what he is doing in Canada?

While the closing strains of the *New World Symphony* faded away, Tony signalled for Brad to come onstage to share in the glory. Brad shook his head and moved further into the shadows.

The applause was deafening. Tony basked in the moment, enjoying it thoroughly. He bowed low, and signalled for the orchestra members to stand. He shook hands with the leaders of each section. Just like the old days in England.

He thought to himself, *now what should I do? Will they know I've done this before or assume I am acting? Once a showman, always a showman. We thrive on an audience.*

Tony slipped behind the curtains for a brief moment, found Brad in the shadows again, and tapped him on the shoulder before leading him onstage. This time Brad didn't protest. He, too, was hyped up by the success.

Tony whispered to the younger man, "You deserve recognition for all the hard work you have done. Without you, this moment never would have happened." Brad gulped, and stifled a cough.

Together they walked onstage and took a final curtain call before going through all the pomp and ceremony a second time. Brad shook hands with each section leader and then, regaining some of his old confidence, he shook

Tony's hand before they both disappeared backstage.

As the applause came to a thunderous crescendo and slowly faded away, a stagehand turned on the lights backstage, and in the theatre. Tony looked up into Brad's eyes when the two men found themselves alone for a few moments. He marveled at how huge the cop was, standing tall, his wide shoulders erect.

Hard to imagine this great hulk of a man having a backstage meltdown. He certainly cut a fine figure right now.

"Shall we talk over a cup of coffee tomorrow, Brad?" he asked quietly. "I guess there are some things we need to discuss."

"Yes. How about nine o'clock at the Gateway coffee shop?"

"I'll be there."

"I won't have to arrest you or anything, will I? I know you have some secrets, but I didn't mean to get them out of you this way."

Tony laughed nervously and shook his head in answer.

"I hoped I would not have to talk to you at all, but I knew you were onto me."

"I guessed there was something, but I wasn't quite prepared for this," Brad said. "You have conducted *New World* before, haven't you, Tony?"

"A few times."

"You were too good, so I knew it wasn't an act, but I guess most people would think so."

"I know" Tony agreed. "I should have remembered that."

"I wonder how many people figured out what really happened back there tonight?" Brad mused.

"We'll soon find out. We aren't finished yet. There's the reception to live through. Almost forgot about that." Tony groaned.

116

"I suppose we can't get out of it, eh?" Brad reached for his jacket as if planning to run away.

"I'm afraid not. We're the stars tonight. Come on. We have to do our best. Remember, nothing that happens onstage is ever unrehearsed."

Brad shuddered. "This won't be easy."

"Look Brad, this is show business and it does not matter why you decided to bring in a guest conductor," Tony said. "We have no choice but to go along with that idea. Elise might ask me some questions tomorrow, but she will not do it tonight," Tony said with certainty.

"How do you know?"

"It's an unwritten law; you never discuss glitches the night of the concert. Did you forget that rule, Brad?"

"Yeah. I guess I'm not much of an actor," Brad told him, "In my job we only deal in facts."

"You will win an Academy award tonight, my friend! We want this evening to be one the musicians will always remember, so we have to carry on as if nothing happened. The person who began applauding the *guest conductor* gave us an out. No explanation is needed."

"No?" Brad asked.

"This really is your orchestra and I was just the guest conductor."

Brad took a deep breath. "I'm ready." The two men walked out to the foyer together'

The foyer was crowded with musicians and patrons. Brad hesitantly joined the crowd filing around a long table set with plates of cookies and cakes prepared by members of the Women's Institute.

"How did you manage to pull that off without making any mistakes, Mr. Lorenzo?" asked Bill Grant, Mayor of Rocky Creek.

"When did you rehearse?" inquired Jack Summers, the cowboy who had removed his hat for the occasion.

117

"You must have spent hours with Brad going through the motions of conducting," remarked the bassoon player.

"He is an excellent teacher," Tony offered, with a knowing smile.

"Tony's an exceptional student," Brad told Vladimir Bostock, editor of *The Rocky Creek Times*. He tried to balance a plate of cookies and a cup of coffee while he talked.

I'm not quite ready to talk to the editor yet, Brad thought, and turned his attention to Cynthia, who had just come into the room. *Where the heck is Tony when I need him? He is quite the escape artist.*

Brad looked up in time to see Tony trying, without success, to avoid the English Horn player. He strained his ears to hear the conversation and slowly edged closer, keeping the two men in his sights while chatting amiably with Cynthia. Snatches of the conversation reached his ears.

"You look a lot like Richard Lawrence," Robert Cates said to Tony, "even the same arm movements. Incredible!"

"Yeah, someone else just said that to me, too," Tony lied "Who is that guy anyway? If he really does anything like me, he's in trouble. I had no idea what I was doing," Tony was saying, skillfully avoiding direct eye contact.

"I heard that he died in a plane crash, so you don't have to worry about influencing him. Swell guy. It's uncanny how much you look like him. Who was your teacher?" Robert Cates said

"Brad Thomas, our director, worked hard with me," Tony continued lying fluently. "Great teacher. Wonderful man!"

"When you first came onstage, I was worried but when you actually started conducting, I really enjoyed playing. I hope you do it again. You're a natural. Have you ever considered a career in music direction?"

118

"I gave it a passing thought years ago. And your name?" asked Tony, pretending not to have recognized the speaker.

"Full name is Robert Jackson Cates. I return to England next month to do a concert with the Leeds Classic Orchestra. Very nice to work with you, Tony. I hope to see you again." He offered his free hand.

"Me too. Oh, I have to see the concert master. I have always wondered how come they call a lady in the First Chair position a Concert Master?" Tony asked, looking toward Cynthia.

"They would still call her a Concert Mistress in Britain," Robert Jackson Cates observed. "It probably has something to do with the women's movement toward equality in this country. It hasn't reached such a feverish pitch in England yet but I'm sure it will."

"Who can blame women for fighting for their rights? Only a strong woman like Cynthia would have that kind of drive. Tonight, she showed she is a true professional when she accepted me as a surprise guest conductor," Tony said. He moved away, grateful to put distance between him and Mr. Cates.

"Thanks for a wonderful performance," Brad said to Cynthia. "It sounded glorious from where I was standing. You are an expert leader, Cynthia."

"Thank-you, Brad," she said, "I must say you surprised me with the guest conductor thing, especially Tony Lorenzo. How come you decided on doing that? When he came out holding the baton by the *wrong* end, I wasn't sure what to expect."

"I missed that! I should have warned you, but it was a last-minute decision. I had no idea Tony was so talented," Brad explained, his voice cracking, as he expertly transferred the attention from himself to Tony.

"He is," answered Cynthia. "He handled it as if he wasn't really acting. What an interesting man. Oh, here he is now. I think he's trying to catch up to you, Brad. Did you notice that your friend from the newspaper is here? I wonder what his take on it is."

"I've dodged him twice tonight. Oh no! He just spied me again so I suppose I have to talk to him. I heard him say to someone that he enjoyed the concert so maybe it won't be so bad," remarked Brad, wiping his brow.

"Don't dodge him anymore," Cynthia said. She took Brad's arm. "You know he'll make something of it. That's his job."

They walked toward the newspaper editor.

"Come and join us, Tony." She smiled when she noticed him attempting to hide behind a pillar "You two guys are displaying a lot more humility than most directors," she said. "Time to come out and be proud. You were both fantastic."

Both men managed a weak smile in return, appreciative of Cynthia's upbeat manner.

Now you've done it. You'll be sorry, if you ask me."

"I didn't ask you," said Tony.

SEVENTEEN

Elise studied her husband at the breakfast table the following morning. "What happened to Brad last night?" she asked.

"Just stage-fright. He was brave to even rehearse *New World*, then to put it on the program for his first concert." Tony shrugged his shoulders. "It was a poor choice."

"Was he upset that you conducted it?" Elise asked as she buttered the nicely browned toast. "I knew it was probably stage fright, but still he must have had some pangs of disappointment when you directed it so well. You made it seem so easy."

Tony laughed ruefully. "No, he was not upset that I conducted it, but he was stressed when he realized that he was too nervous to do it himself. He had rehearsed the orchestra so well that it was easy for me to take over though. I have an appointment with him at nine this morning and I don't want to keep him waiting."

"What does he want to see you about?"

"Brad wants to talk to me about what happened last night. He made a couple of poor choices for a first performance—anyway I must run. I will be back as soon as I can," Tony said. "Could we talk later?"

"Okay, but I still want to know how or where you knew Robert Cates," Elise said. "He seemed to know you also. What are you hiding from me, Tony?"

"I am not hiding anything. I'd heard him play before," he told her. "His name seemed familiar when I saw it on the program. "

"You have been a different man since that poster came out, she said. "Like you knew him well before."

"I had forgotten that I met him at a reception once years ago." He looked at his watch. "I have to get out of here or Brad will have my head. He might even arrest me."

"Why?" inquired Elise, really worried now. "Have you done something wrong?"

"No, but he's the one with the badge. I am sure he'll find some reason," Tony said. "Bye now—I will see you at lunch-time."

After an obligatory hug he headed downstairs. Elise heard him open the coat closet and assumed he was getting his coat and hat.

A minute or two later she heard the basement door slam, and expected he would get into the car and drive off.

Elise watched him from the front room window, surprised that he walked past the car and continued walking. She waited until he became a tiny moving dot on the snow-covered road before she walked away. "Who is this man?" she wondered. "Do I really know him? Are there two Tonys? More important is which Tony is my husband?"

***

"Good morning!" Tony said cheerfully as he slipped into the booth across from Brad Thomas at the Gateway Coffee Shop. The aroma of freshly brewed coffee tantalized his taste buds as soon as he had opened the door.

Brad looked up from the newspaper he'd been perusing while he waited for Tony. Save for a couple of truckers taking their morning coffee break, the neat little coffee shop was empty.

"I suppose I made a fool of myself last night," Brad said before Tony had barely seated himself. He smiled self-consciously.

"No," Tony said. "Not at all. Everyone gets stage fright at one time or another."

"I'm curious to know how you did such a professional job of directing the *New World Symphony*?"

"I wish I could explain it, Brad," Tony said thoughtfully. He stared out the window at the snow-covered hills. "I just had to do it. I was unable to help myself."

"I understand," Brad said. "Will you have breakfast?" Brad asked. "I'm never lucid until I've had my first cup of coffee in the mornings so do you mind if we order it right away?"

"No, Elise and I had toast and her homemade strawberry jam for breakfast early this morning. I would like a cup of coffee though."

"You lucky dog. Home preserved jams are better than store bought jams. Look, my favorite girl is on today," Brad said. He smiled in her direction. "Lynette always has a happy smile on her face, no matter what the weather. One can't help being in a great mood when he's greeted by such a nice person."

"I feel better if the people around me are friendly," Tony said. "I do believe that."

"Hi Lynette. You look as fresh as a daisy this morning!" Brad greeted the waitress.

"I'd prefer daisies to snow drifts," she said. She gestured toward the window. "What will you guys have? Just coffee, or breakfast?"

"A couple of coffees to warm us up," Brad said. He nodded his head toward Tony and grinned.

"Sure," Lynette said. She flashed her lovely smile and

started to walk away, but after a couple of steps, she turned back and added, "I came to the concert last night. It's exciting to have our very own orchestra in Rocky Creek. Stroke of genius getting the guest conductor in, too." She stared at Tony and exclaimed, "Ooh! Aren't you him? Do you live around here?"

"Yeah," Tony said, somewhat embarrassed by the attention.

"Was it hard to come in and conduct? I'd be terrified," she said.

"I *was* nervous," Tony said truthfully, "but Brad is a good teacher, and he can be quite persuasive. Handcuffs and all."

Lynette raised her eyebrows in mock alarm and chuckled flirtatiously as she hurried off to put in their order.

When she was out of earshot, Tony said, "Elise guessed there was a problem last night."

"Did she ask why you got involved in such a big way at the last minute, even though you didn't want her to play in the orchestra at first."

"Well, yes, that too. We are having some domestic problems, actually," Tony replied. "Mostly since the RCCO started up."

"I thought she might be upset by your behaviour," Brad said. "I still can't believe I had a panic-attack. I guess the pressure brought everything to a head, eh?"

"It did but your reaction was just anxiety; nothing to get excited about," Tony explained.

"The music I chose was too difficult for a novice conductor to handle. I couldn't make myself go onstage."

"*The New World Symphony* is not as simple as one might think," Tony agreed.

"How could you take over like that? You must have had musical training, and experience to do it without even a rehearsal. It would take more than guts to pull that off.

You weren't just acting, were you?"

"No," Tony said, with a deep sigh. He stared out the window, nervously fiddling with the two top buttons of his shirt. "Please no guessing. I will eventually tell you my story, but give me some time."

"Okay, I can do that," Brad said. "I prefer to deal with facts, not guessing games."

Tony cleared his throat. "Me, too," he said. "Remember Richard Lawrence who directed the Leeds Classic Orchestra, in England? He was well known all over the world." Tony moved the cutlery from left to right, arranging it neatly and in line with the white paper place mat. "There was a rumour that he died in a plane crash ten years ago." Tony waited for Brad to react.

"I think I heard something about it," Brad recalled. "He conducted some major orchestras on the Continent. A tragedy to lose him."

"I knew him, but he wasn't a friend of mine," Tony announced.

"Really?"

"He was popular with audiences but not musicians."

"He was rather well known. What did you have against him?" asked Brad.

"Nothing, but I was not that upset to hear he was not coming back," Tony said, with a mysterious air.

"Where did you know him?" asked Brad, his forehead wrinkling as he focused on Tony's eyes.

"In Leeds," Tony said with downcast eyes. He leaned forward and put his elbows on the table.

"What were you doing in Leeds? I thought you were a Canadian. There were plenty of write-ups about him."

"It's my hometown," Tony said. "Richard Lawrence is not dead. I-uh- um-knew him," Tony stammered, not looking directly at Brad.

"You must be putting me on," Brad insisted. "You said he was reported to have died in a plane crash; now you say he's alive. Was there foul-play?" Brad frowned, wandering back into police officer mode. "How do you know he's alive?" he said.

"Because," Tony said hesitantly, "I –a-um-worked under him well after those reports came out."

"Doing what?"

Tony ignored Brad's question. "The rumour that he was killed in a plane crash over the Swiss Alps was false. I wanted to disappear, so I used it to cover my disappearance. I knew he was still alive." He pressed his index finger on a spot under his left eye and squeezed his eyes shut.

"I guess that makes sense," Brad said, studying Tony's face intently. "Why were you running away?"

"I was engaged to an opera singer. She waited until the wedding ceremony to leave me."

"No wonder you find it hard to talk about it."

"It has taken ten years to forget her. If I had minded my own business, I would not have to answer these questions now," Tony said.

Brad ignored the reference to his backstage meltdown. "I heard someone mention his name at the reception," he said, "but what you are saying is confusing unless he is listed as a missing person. His name has not come up in any of the listings."

"I have no idea if he is listed," Tony stammered. "I thought you might be mad that I conducted *New World*," he said, skillfully changing the subject.

"Not at all," Brad said, "I'm glad you were there. People have no idea how awful it is to be unable to face the crowd. In all my time as a member of the RCMP, I have never panicked like that."

"Panic attacks are usually a surprise," Tony said, aware that the secret smile playing about his lips was probably only partly hidden by his moustache.

"After we finish our coffee we can move to my office

where we can have some privacy," Brad suggested. "The cafe is beginning to fill up now. Leave your car here and I'll drive you back to pick it up."

"I walked over," Tony said. After a moment's reflection, he asked, "Won't people talk if I go in the police car?"

"I doubt it, "Brad assured him. "I'm off duty."

"Will you open a file on me?" asked Tony. "

"Not yet," Brad answered. He reached for his jacket hanging over the back of his chair.

Tony took his time retrieving his black leather coat from the open rack at the rear of the coffee shop. He carried the matching gloves in one hand and slung the coat over his arm. An icy blast of winter took his breath away when he stepped out into the cold. He hastily put it on and hugged it close to his body as he rushed to catch up with Brad.

The two men walked through the small parking lot, picking their way around piles of snow which had been shoveled in untidy clumps away from the parked cars. Brad casually remarked, "A woman, eh? Never underestimate the power of a woman. I've been married for ten years and I still don't understand my wife." They both chuckled knowingly.

Brad opened the passenger door of the black and white Dodge Polara and waited while Tony got in and put on his seat belt before he closed it. Once in the driver's seat he shuffled his paperwork around and turned on the radio, checked his mobile phone and opened the strong box between them on the bench seat. He read the list of mobile data on the display terminal, observing that Tony watched every move he made. He decided not to turn on the vehicle's recording device.

"Oh," Tony said, "I thought with all that fiddling around, you were looking for your revolver."

"I don't believe I'll need it today," Brad said, half

smiling, "We always put troublesome people in the back anyway. The doors in the back can only be opened from the outside," he added, with a humorous smile. He watched Tony's reaction.

"Good," Tony said, relaxing against the wide cushioned seat. He returned Brad's grin. "This baby is huge," he said. "Is it a seventy?"

"No, a seventy-one," Brad answered, "but they're talking about replacing it with next year's model. I hope they won't because I like the leg room in this one."

"Will you have any say in the decision?" asked Tony.

"Not likely they'll bother to ask me," Brad said with a crooked grin.

Don't get too comfortable. He's watching you.

Tony shivered and nervously looked over his shoulder.

EIGHTEEN

The police station was a short drive from the Gateway Coffee Shop, but Brad took the scenic route. At the bottom of Jordon's Hill, he turned left onto Martin Way, to a landscaped side street, where Dr. Herbert Davenport's office and Caruthers's General Store set the boundaries for the township.

The Police Station at the end of the street imposed its supremacy with its dark brown siding, local rock foundation and large paved parking lot. Four windows facing the street were protected by steel mesh and a prominent sign over the entrance proclaimed that the building had been constructed in 1857. Brad pulled into one of the three parking spots reserved for police vehicles only.

He smiled amiably when Tony stepped out of the cruiser, studied his surroundings and pulled his collar tighter around his neck. Brad would never grow tired of that reaction from his passengers as they stood outside the imposing building.

"Still cold?" he asked. Tony nodded sheepishly.

Once inside, Brad greeted the receptionist at the large oak desk which blocked the entrance to the back rooms and cells. He sidestepped the desk and held the swinging door open for Tony. At the first door to the right, he invited Tony to come into his private office.

Brad hung his coat on the rack and slid into a chair behind the desk. Tony followed and sat with his back to the window. Brad's office was a cramped room, with just enough space for a desk, two chairs and a couple of filing cabinets.

"Coffee?" he asked. "We can get some from the machine down the hall."

"No, thanks," Tony said.

Brad glanced at the clock on the wall. "I'd like to be home for lunch," he said. "Ninety minutes should give us enough time to have a good chat.'

"I hope so," Tony said. He leaned forward. "I have never been in a police station before. I had no idea what to expect."

"Maybe cells with barred gates? We have a couple of those in the back for holding prisoners until they can be taken to a facility. They're both empty today."

Tony shivered again. "I want to get this over with," he said.

Brad nodded, picked up a pen and held it poised over his yellow legal pad waiting for Tony to begin. Tony hesitated, nervously looking at the tape recorder.

"Not right now," Brad said. Tony sighed in relief. "It may be necessary eventually."

"Oh," Tony said, remaining deadpan. He took a deep breath. "I told you a woman caused some trouble for me and I wanted to escape because I was unable to handle the tabloid questions."

"Hmmm," murmured Brad. "Why?"

"It was all about why Jane and I never got married. Our wedding day was a fiasco. The worst day of my life. My best man and I waited for more than a half hour for her. Her father waited with us, so I thought everything was fine, but when Jane did not show up, her dad talked to the minister about the delay and discovered that she was crying in the Bride's Room. I was stuck telling three hundred guests Jane did not want to go through with the wedding. I was so distressed at that point, the guys took me out to a pub called *All the King's Horses,* where we got politely polluted." He lowered his eyes and concentrated on the black and gray tiled floor. He pressed his hand to his cheek again.

"What guys?"

"Doug was to sing while we signed the register and Ralph was my best man. I have carried this burden for too long. I have to talk to somebody."

"Sure. I get you. Who was your fiancé?"

"A well-known opera singer." Tony hesitated.

"What's her name again? Does she still sing?" Brad prompted.

"Jane Morrow."

"I see, "Brad commented. "How well known is she? I can't recall hearing her name."

"She sings regularly with the Inglewood Opera Company in London. I follow her career on the telly."

"Oh, in London."

"I created her, you know," he explained loftily. "If not for me, she would still be singing in cheap night clubs."

"Really? She should be independent by now."

"I gave her the breaks she needed. Without me…" Tony's voice faded away.

"I see," said Brad, "so she must have had a hard time. Have you talked to her about it?"

"No," Tony said, "That was years ago. She jilted me, so she got what she deserved," he said irritably. "There was no way I wanted to help her after that," Tony said, with a finality that closed the door on more discussion.

"You're married to Elise, so not really a good idea to have another woman in your life. She lives and works in

131

London, anyway and you are in Canada"

"You are talking in riddles," Tony complained.

" I'm just trying to understand where you are coming from, Tony," Brad said gently. "You just told me that you still follow her career, but in the same breath you won't help her."

"Leave me alone. I never wanted to talk to you about it," Tony snarled.

"Okay," Brad said, "You never got over her, did you?" he asked, unable to drop it. If he gave up the story that was unfolding now, it would be difficult to get Tony to open up again.

Tony was too upset to carry on, but he knew Brad was confused. Likely he wondered who the hell he was. *Maybe Brad's imagination was getting out of hand,* wondered Tony. *Perhaps he even thinks there was more to it than there really was.*

Tony knew Brad watched with interest as he fidgeted with his gloves, pulling them on and off. He massaged his cheek again and wondered if he was blushing. The nerve in his face twitched, the pain shooting almost to his eye.

"Let's call it a day," Brad said, making the difficult decision for both of them to stop the interview. "I'll drive you home so you can have lunch with that pretty little wife of yours."

"That would be great," Tony said, looking for all the world as if the last ninety minutes hadn't happened.

"She volunteered to join a work crew to clean the hall after our concert last night. She has to check things out after lunch today. I suppose I should go with her," Tony said, visibly relieved that the meeting with Brad was over.

"Good idea, "Brad said, "she could probably do with some help. We can make another date. I want to help you deal with this. Let me check my appointments." He turned the pages of a dog-eared appointment book and

132

asked, "How about Monday morning at ten? I have a day off. I can pick you up."

Are you gonna fall for that? the voice cracked in his ear.

Tony stood up and reached for his jacket again.

"I'll drive you home," Brad said, "but we must meet again because we need to get to the bottom of things. Unless I know the whole truth, I can't help you."

"Why do you think I need help?" Tony asked.

"Just a strong feeling I have," Brad told him. "You helped me, and now it's my turn to help you solve a problem."

"Oh," Tony replied weakly, only because he felt he had to say something.

NINETEEN

Elise had already assembled the cleaning supplies needed for the after-concert cleanup. With plenty of clean rags, spray cleaners, brooms and mops, she was well organized.

"I'm coming with you to help." Tony said when he came inside.

"Wonderful," she said, "I guess you won't want to clean the toilets, but I am grateful that you are coming. Lorraine and Brian were there this morning to put all the chairs back in the storage room, and they did some other cleaning, but my job is to clean the bathrooms. Nice to have you with me."

"Toilets?" he asked, turning up his nose with distaste. "Your job is the bathrooms? Why can't someone else do that? They saved the worst job for you."

"Oh, no, it's one of the easier jobs, "she answered, "and we have disinfectants and brushes. I've done a lot of worse jobs than that, I assure you."

"Well, "Tony said hesitantly, "I suppose so, but why can't Brad do it?"

"Brad has already done more than his share of labour," Elise said. "He worked with the stage crew before your meeting this morning. He also transported the four stage extensions that Hank built. Hank and Brad dismantled them to be stored in Brad's shed. Hank picked up the music stands we rented from Melodies-on-the Rocks and returned them, so both guys have been busy."

"Oh," said Tony, rather lamely. "Stage extensions? I had no idea Hank built those."

"After we eat our lunch we can be on our way," Elise said. "There's probably a couple of hours work left to do. Lorraine collected all the music from the orchestra members last night. She'll sort it all and erase some of the rehearsal marks players wrote for their own use and put the parts in folders. All that's left to do now is my final cleanup jobs, and then I have to lock the doors."

"You have the keys?" he asked.

"Yes, and the security code."

"You know how to set it?" Tony asked with a surprised look on his face.

"Of course, I do. It's part of my job as the last person here today," she said.

"No-one told me you had made all those arrangements."

"You weren't included in the plans because you made it clear you didn't want to be there. It was probably at one of the rehearsals I rode with Lorraine and Hank so you could have the car," Elise explained. "We asked for volunteers to do certain jobs after the concert to cut the cost of renting the space."

Tony sat down in the nook at the far end of the kitchen.

"What's for lunch?" he asked.

"Not sure yet. Maybe leftovers," Elise said.

"I honestly was unaware we had to do anything. The Community Centre must have maintenance people."

"They do, but we made a deal to do all the maintenance jobs ourselves for reduced rent."

Oh, yeah! You were the high mucky-muck, the great Richard Lawrence! Look at you now. Pitiful!

135

Tony nervously put his hand up to his mouth. Who said that? That slimy Frank? A vision of the man's unkempt, straggly hair, swarthy skin and bloodshot eyes popped into his mind. He tried to focus on Elise's words, but his head throbbed. He looked down at his lap and tried to be inconspicuous as he wiped the perspiration from his forehead. When he looked up, he was aware that she was studying his face.

"Is something wrong, Tony?" she asked. "You seem upset, and your face is flushed."

"No, not at all," he replied. I wish you would stop picking on every move I make."

"Let's drop it. I'm not into squabbling with you."

"Well, then leave me alone. I don't need a third degree every time I open my mouth. You aren't my mother," he snarled to an empty room. Elise had already walked away. Funny how that was happening more and more these days. He sat quietly and waited for her to come back, his mind in a turmoil.

A few minutes later, she returned with a plate of tuna sandwiches and a bowl of coleslaw. "The tea is brewing," she said. "I will get the plates and cutlery and we can eat. I'm hungry. What about you?"

"Me too," he said, looking keenly into her eyes. He had always been fascinated by her dark blue eyes. Navy blue. Unusual for a fair blonde to have such deep blue eyes.

"Did you have a good talk with Brad this morning?" Elise asked after they had eaten.

"We had to cut it short. The cafe was filling up with customers very early. Truckers and bus drivers and passengers, "Tony said. "We went to his office where it was fairly quiet. All he really wanted to know," he lied, "was how I was able to conduct *New World* last night".

She cleared the table and put the dishes in the dishwasher.

"I'm wondering how you did it, too."

"Just good acting. Anyone could have done it," he said. Tony smiled condescendingly. "Are you ready to go and get that job done? If we are going, we ought to get moving."

"Yes, as soon as I can get my jacket and boots on," Elise said.

The voice broke into his thoughts again.

You're a wimp! You may as well tell the truth now. You keep blowing it anyway.

Tony shivered.

"Leave me alone, "he blurted.

"I beg your pardon?" Elise said, "I don't know what you're talking about."

"Oh, nothing, I was just thinking of something else."

Watch it.

"All this stuff has to be carried out to the car, Tony," Elise said, "Would you do that for me?" She pointed to a pile of neatly folded rags, two aluminum pails, and a bottle of Pine Sol. Tony snorted, demonstrating his distaste for the job at hand.

"I have never cleaned a toilet in my life," he declared, sticking his chin out stubbornly, "and I'm not going to do it now."

"Then you had better find another place to go," Elise replied with a smile. Tony didn't answer.

He carried the cleaning supplies to the car, stacked the pails and picked up the box of soap flakes and put everything in the trunk with a grunt.

"Why are we taking Oxydol?" he asked.

"In case I have to put a load in the washer," she said, "I don't expect to, but you never know."

"Okay, but I'm not cleaning toilets," Tony repeated.

Elise opened her mouth to voice a retort, but closed it again without speaking. Tony got in the driver's seat, glared straight ahead with the air of a man on a dangerous mission. She laughed at him.

"What?" he asked.

"I was just imagining you going behind a bush in the winter-time, "she said sweetly.

The motor roared into life, and the car lurched forward. Tony jammed the brake on inches short of the garage wall. "Of all the nerve, "he complained, "expecting us to clean toilets."

"Focus, Tony. I think you need to reverse," Elise said. Tony didn't answer. He gripped the steering wheel and reversed the Buick suddenly, throwing Elise forward. She clutched the seat belt she had not had time to buckle up before Tony started the car moving again. Once out of the garage, he gunned the motor without looking where he was going and backed too quickly down the driveway. After narrowly missing a passing car where the private road met the street, they sat for a moment in silence, before turning onto Maple Street.

"I may have to fly in on my broomstick unless you get it together," she said with a charming smile.

"No comment," Tony said, eyes straight ahead.

***

"It smells of salad dressing and onions in here." Elise sniffed the air when she unlocked the door of the Community Centre.

"And egg salad sandwiches," added Tony. "Who supplied the refreshments last night?"

"The ladies were responsible for everything. One of them makes the pinwheel sandwiches and other fancy dishes. Nice group of people, and they clean up after themselves, so we don't have to do any of that."

Hot water and aluminum buckets filled with the clean scent of Pine Sol worked overtime to cancel out the food odours left over from the reception the night before.

Elise dipped a large string mop into the soapy liquid, and wrung it out by pushing a pedal with her foot.

She slopped it onto the floor.

"Reminds me of my mother," Tony commented. "On cleaning day, she would put down a puddle of soapy water and then wring the mop out until it was almost dry and pick it all up again. I used to wonder what good it did, but now I see. I have never mopped a floor, either."

"A good experience for you then, "said his wife, chuckling. "Just wait until you get to the toilets. A real thrill waiting for you to enjoy."

"Don't push it," he warned, testily, although he was beginning to relax. "I suppose you expect me to tell you what happened last night, too. Brad said I owe you an explanation. I wasn't really acting. I have conducted an orchestra before," he blurted.

"I guessed that," Elise said, "by the way you made eye contact with the musicians, especially the English horn player. You may be a novice floor-mopper and toilet-brusher, but you are not a novice orchestra leader. Who are you, Tony?"

"A big goof," he said, forfeiting yet another opportunity to tell the truth. "I should talk to Brad first. I intended to come clean this morning when I met him, but we had to cut short the meeting," he said somewhat truthfully." If you can wait until I have spoken to him tomorrow morning, I will try to tell you everything," he added, stalling for time.

"I'm dying to hear the rest of the story, and I don't want to wait. You do owe me an explanation," Elise said, "and you should do it as soon as you can, you need to tell me the truth. I wasn't born yesterday, you know."

"I will soon, I promise you."

"What's preventing you from telling me now? I heard some remarks at the reception, and I think you are lying to me. Why don't you come clean?"

"Please wait," Tony pleaded. "I need to tell you in my own time. Have a heart, eh?"

After a moment of deep thought, Elise asked, "if you have directed an orchestra before," she said, "then you must know about the three wrong notes I played in *New World?*" She put her hand over her mouth and laughed nervously.

"And also, the two bars you missed in *Waltz of the Flowers,*" he said, "but don't worry about those. By the time you rushed to *The Mirlitons,* you'd won the race by a nose. I think you earned the trophy."

"You heard that?" Elise asked, with downcast eyes. "Do you think the audience heard it?" She looked up and met his gaze. A slow smile began to relax Tony's face. First his eyes twinkled, then his mouth twitched until he suddenly broke into a great smile. They both laughed out loud.

"Not everyone noticed, "he said, with a broad grin.

"But you did, "she whispered.

"Of course, I did," Tony said.

The voice cackled again, *Careful Tony.*

"I hear you, Frank," murmured Tony.

"Who?"

"Oh, nobody you know," Tony said, his eyes beginning to blur.

Too much for one day, he thought. Now she knows just enough to be nosy, I don't know what to do. I cannot run away again, and I cannot stay here.

"Come on, Tony," Elise said briskly. "Let's get this job out of the way so we can go home and have dinner."

"Okay," he said, glad to allow Elise to set the mood.

"I still want to know the truth about everything," she said, "but right now is not the time. We have work to do."

"Thank-you," Tony murmured.

TWENTY

Elise put disinfectant into the toilet bowl and brushed energetically. He grimaced when he saw her get down on her knees to wipe the floor clean. He moved away so he would be out of her range of vision, but still be able to see what she was doing. He went into the hallway and industriously polished the doorknob until it shone. He muttered, "Ewwww," when he heard the water running in the bathroom.

To his horror, she called out, "Come here, dear, and give me a hand, please. "With a great deal of trepidation, he stuck his head around the corner, and murmured a weak, "Yes?"

"I have four more to do. I like these bathrooms because they are not the usual stalls, but they do take more time to clean, "she said. "If you would carry the pail and change the water and Lysol, we could get the job done much faster."

"Okay. Uh, that is, um, I mean, uh, would it help if I, ah, sort of, I mean, wash two of them for you?" Tony stammered.

"Oh, would you? It would really help. Thank-you. It is tiresome job, and I would appreciate it so much. Be sure to put on clean rubber gloves for each bathroom."

And so, Tony, uttering, "OH, "and then, "Eww," followed closely by "Yuck," actually got down on his knees, and for the first time in his life, cleaned a toilet, all the while thinking that he would hate to go behind a tree during the winter. In spite of himself, he was amused. Not only that, but his fertile mind was beginning to visualize the possibility it really could happen.

After cleaning the first bathroom, he went on to the next one, same procedure. When he was done, he pulled the gloves off and put them in the garbage, and scrubbed not only his hands, but his arms and up past his elbows with strong disinfectant soap, rinsed them thoroughly and dried on a generous measure of paper towel. He looked in the mirror before he left, and saluted the man reflected there. The man saluted him in return.

"Yuck!" he said. Tony was sure the man in the mirror said, "Yuck," before he walked away.

It was already twilight when the cleaning supplies were finally piled in the Buick for the trip home. Tony snickered when Elise hid the number panel from him while she punched in the security code. She turned out all the lights, except the outside motion- sensitive bulb.

"Do you think I will break in and steal the paper towels?" he asked.

"We have plenty of towels at home, but we *are* almost out of toilet paper. It's just routine," she said with a giggle.

When they stepped outside, the motion sensitive light shone on the pathway. Tony opened the car door for her. Before he started the motor, Elise laid her head on his shoulder, and whispered something in his ear.

"Shh, it's our dirty little secret." He squeezed her hand. "And I hate the idea of going behind a bush, so I am glad I passed the test."

TWENTY-ONE

Monday morning dawned with another snowstorm, the flakes huge, soft and wet.

"It's so pretty coming down, isn't it?" Elise said, as she parted the drapes on the big picture window overlooking the gardens, their summer splendour hidden under five inches of newly fallen snow.

"I have never thought snow was pretty," Tony growled. "It just means I have to shovel the driveway when it stops."

"So does everyone else."

"That does not make me any happier."

"It's a fact of life. In the winter snow falls and we shovel. I'll help you if you like. Before you came into my life, I shoveled plenty of snow drifts away," Elise said.

"You should not have to do that kind of work, "he objected. "It's bad enough you were expected to do toilets yesterday. You won't be shoveling snow today. It is a man's job." Tony pursed his lips and looked defiant. "I'll have time to do some of it before Brad picks me up. I hope this is our last meeting."

"Why? He is just trying to help you."

"I have snow to shovel," Tony said.

"Snow clearance is everyone's job," Elise said. "Julie helps Brad when their eldest son is not available. There's no reason why I shouldn't help too. Sometimes she works with him even if Tommy is there. They often end up having a friendly snowball fight."

"I do not want a snowball fight," Tony said, with an abrasive edge to his voice. "I will work until Brad comes around the corner. And don't you try to finish the job before I return," he ordered. "The snow will wait. It's a man's job," he ordered.

"What if no man is available?"

"You have me."

"We can worry about the snow later. It's still falling so there's no need for anyone to clear it until it stops. Come and eat breakfast now."

Elise made a special effort to please Tony with the Blue Willow dishes, snowy white napkins and the crocheted place mats made by her own hands, knowing how he loved pomp and circumstance.

He usually lingered over his breakfast, but this morning was different. He barely noticed the place mats and he seemed stressed about the meeting with Brad.

"What does he want this time," she asked.

"Who knows?" Tony said irritably. "I hate having to rush. If I don't get out there and shovel that driveway now, he'll be here before I even get started. I hate making him wait."

Tony had just finished the snow removal when a horn blasted, and Brad's car turned onto Maple Street.

Brad tried to look relaxed. Hoping to avoid upsetting Tony again, but at the same time, get the information he needed, he tried a different tactic. He called out, "C'mon, boy, let's get this show on the road, eh? I haven't got all day, y'know."

"Boy? I'm old enough to be your papa, young man," Tony replied, as he threw two more shovelfuls of snow to the side of the driveway. "I'm ready for you." He looked at his watch. "Don't panic, "he said, "You are earlier than you said." He stood the shovel up just inside the garage, put his work gloves on a shelf above it, changed into his dark blue windbreaker which was hanging on a peg, and pulled on his best black leather gloves.

"Brr! This coat is cold."

Brad sat in the driver's seat and waited while Tony stomped the snow off his boots and got into the front seat beside him. "Did you recover from helping Elise with the cleanup yesterday?" he asked. "We guys left the lighter jobs for Elise and Lorraine. Cynthia even came in to help out yesterday."

"Uh," began Tony, "I wouldn't call cleaning the bathrooms a light job," he complained. "I helped her with them though. Did two and she cleaned the other three. Dirty job for a woman. How come you didn't do it?"

"She and Lorraine couldn't lift the stage extensions, is why. Those babies are a couple hunnert pounds each. We treat our ladies well, "Brad explained." That's why we get to keep them."

"Keep what? The ladies?"

Brad nodded his head wisely. "We don't want the girls to do any heavy lifting. Our compensation benefits won't cover us if a female worker is injured lifting more than thirty pounds. Cleaning up after a concert involves a lot of lifting and the girls don't have the strength like we men do for lifting jobs."

"Oh," said Tony, "I have never worked with a stage crew before."

"I know," Brad said, "I guess you just took it all for granted. If you were on the other side, you likely wouldn't know about those things. "

"I was never required to do that kind of work," Tony said. "When a concert was over, my work was finished."

Brad nodded sagely, choosing to pass over Tony's second faux pas. "It's quiet at Headquarters this morning," he said, maintaining a friendly tone. "Sunday's are the busiest time, after the usual Saturday night parties. By Monday mornings there are only a few muggings to deal with, maybe some mischief in the school grounds. John Billyboy has a weekend reservation in the drunk tank. I'll get Sam to sign him out so I can have the rest of the day off. I reported to work at four this morning."

"Do you go to work that early?" asked Tony, in surprise.

"Yeah, I have always been an early riser, "he said with a shrug. "A robbery once a week keeps things interesting. Robberies and fights are always between four and six a.m."

"I can think of more entertaining things to do than deal with robberies," Tony said, grimacing. Brad threw back his head and laughed. The car shimmied on the icy highway.

"Watch your driving," warned Tony. "Can you imagine the headlines if we had a collision?"

"I might have to give myself a ticket," Brad said, chuckling.

Tony smiled smugly. *Serve him right,* he thought. *He thinks he knows everything.*

They pulled into the parking lot at the police station and went inside. Cpl. Louis Richelieu sat at the desk.

"The snow hasn't been cleared from the parking lot yet," Brad said casually. "If we had an emergency call, and got stuck in a snowbank, the shit would fly."

"I'll deal with it right away. How come you're back here on your day off?" asked the receptionist.

"I like this place," Brad shouted over his shoulder, as he and Tony went into his office and closed the door.

"Run out there, will you, Tony, and grab a couple cups of coffee from the machine, eh? Two creams, no sugar," Brad said. He dug in his pocket and found two quarters and rolled them across the desk at Tony with a broad grin. "My treat." He sat down at the desk and opened his notebook while Tony went for the coffee.

TWENTY-TWO

"Not bad java for the paper cup variety, eh?" Brad said, as he took a gulp of the rich, brown liquid. He screwed up his face and frowned, "Bitter as hell, but at least it's hot."

"I hear a company called Starbucks is opening in the States," Tony said. "Supposed to be best coffee in the world. It will be more than twenty-five cents, you think?"

"Yeah," said Brad, "I heard about that. In Seattle. Cost an arm and a leg, but they say it's worth every dime, y' know. Of course, it won't catch on in Canada. It'll be something like a dollar a mug when they start selling it by the cup."

"Oh *fook*!" Tony said, rhyming the four-letter word with *hook*, as he tried out North American slang in his thick Yorkshire accent. "What do you mean, when they start selling it by the cup? Are they too cheap to give you a cup to drink it from?"

Brad snickered in spite of the seriousness of the discussion. Somehow the word lost its nastiness in the pronunciation. "They're just selling beans right now, not cups of coffee. And Starbuck is the name of some character in a story. A dog or something," he said, stifling a grin.

"I don't know it," Tony said. "So, we get a handful of beans and have to make our own coffee?"

148

"Have you ever been to the States? Things are different there," Brad said. Tony started, gulped and fidgeted with the zipper on his sweater.

Stop fidgeting. Doesn't go with all the lies you tell.

He straightened his shoulders, pulled the zipper up to the top and patted it firmly in place. He felt hot and sticky.

"Changed planes in New York once, "he said.

"Oh, really?" Brad said, "How long were you there?"

"Uh, just long enough to make connections."

"Where were you when they put the first man on the moon?"

"I don't remember."

"I was there, "Brad boasted, with a swagger, "I saw the rocket ship take off. My throat was sore from yelling. I was about sixteen at the time."

"That's nice, "Tony said, "I should go now. "He stood up and looked at the door.

He knows you're lying. I think he knows who you are. You keep giving him clues.

"Tony," Brad said firmly, "we just got here, and we need to finish this conversation today. I think there are some things we have to clear up before we can go any further."

"But I want to go home now," Tony complained.

"Sit down, please. I'm sure you don't have to rush away this quickly."

"What do you want to know?" he said, sitting gingerly on the edge of his chair.

"How did you manage to conduct the Symphony Saturday night?" Brad asked. "*New World* is difficult, but you directed it like a pro. Had you directed it before? It seemed like it wasn't the first time you conducted it."

"Oh, I did a little acting when I was younger," Tony lied. "Just happened to be that piece I directed in a play. A lucky break, eh?'

"Very lucky," agreed Brad, "and so convenient that I have a problem accepting it."

Tony pushed his chair further away from Brad, and stared at the closed door.

"Do you smoke?" Brad asked, abruptly changing the subject.

"I used to. Why do you want to know?" Tony said. He leaned his elbows on the desk.

"Somebody left a pack of Pal Mal in the bathroom last week. We may as well smoke them. Nobody's coming back to get them now."

"Uh," said Tony, "I quit four years ago. Elise won't like it if I come home smelling of smoke."

"She'll never know," Brad insisted. He reached his hand into the drawer and pulled out the familiar black and red package.

"Not my favorite brand, but it is hard to turn them down, "Tony said, moistening his lips.

"I hid them at the back of my drawer for just such an occasion. Only three left," he said. "We'll get one each out of it anyway. Toss ya for the third one when we get to it," Brad said in an offhand manner.

"I haven't flipped for anything since I lived on the riverbank in Vancouver," Tony said. He clamped his mouth shut and looked nervously around the room. Brad ignored the slip and busied himself with dumping two tailor-mades out of the pack, measuring them against one another, and then made a pretense of handing the short cigarette to Tony with an exaggerated flair. Tony rolled his eyes, but watched him closely. He thought, *Oh, that game, eh?*

"Want a light?" Brad asked as he held out the flaming match.

"Thanks."

He watched Tony light up and inhale deeply before he puffed his own cigarette into life and exhaled a haze of blue smoke with a loud sigh of pleasure.

"How long did you live in Vancouver?" Brad asked.

"Three years," Tony replied, "I met Yvette there."

"Oh, I didn't realize she was living in the same place. How come you took up with her? Did you just need a woman?" Brad flicked the ash off the end of his cigarette into a Coca Cola bottle he found on the floor beside the garbage bin, ignoring the ash tray on the desk. Tony looked away.

"No, nothing like that. She parked her bike against my tent late one night after being evicted from her apartment. She was two days late with her rent. I thought it was one of the guys being funny and I came out in my underwear. She averted her eyes." He half smiled at the memory.

"Plenty of rowdies waiting for a chance to take advantage of a pretty young girl. They teased her constantly because she appeared so young and innocent. I was afraid one day they would gang up on her. It probably looked like I was saving her, but I began to get my own act together after I met her. I guess you already know that."

"You mean they seemed to be threatening her?" Brad asked, putting his cigarette on the rim of the ashtray.

"Their talk made me edgy. I hate that kind of thing."

"I don't blame you. So, you married her soon after you met her then?" Tony nodded his head and Brad continued. "How did you get from a homeless camp into a mansion? Your house must be the largest one in Rocky Creek."

"It is a beautiful house," Tony agreed, not noticing Brad's reference to the homeless camp. "At first we lived in a little house that Captain Jim McCormack found for us. He performed our marriage ceremony."

"Did you get a job?"

"Yes, I knew a fellow involved in the stock market

and he hired me part time. Things just went ahead from there. I bought this old house and began fixing it up about a year after we were married. I liked having money because I was able to give back to the Sally Ann when things picked up. They were very good to me."

"How did you raise money for a down payment?"

"It was a tax sale. Money-wise it was a steal, but barely livable."

"I take it you musta had some training in finances. You couldn't have just jumped into stocks and bonds without any knowledge of the business," Brad persisted, "and then you had to be bonded so you could do the legal work so no doubt you changed your name legally. Did you have money saved?"

"Yes, I had some money when I came to Canada. Not much, but enough to cover my expenses. I had other jobs before I got involved with music in Leeds. Real estate, and that sort of thing, you know. Of course, everything had to be legal once I started working in the stock market. However, I do not remember what I did about the name."

"Leeds, England?" asked Brad, raising his eyebrows. "Is that where you worked under Richard Lawrence?"

"I beg your pardon?" said Tony, looking bewildered, "What do you mean by that? I don't follow you."

"You said yesterday that you had worked under Richard Lawrence. Did you forget?" asked Brad.

"Oh, you must have been mistaken. I told you he's dead."

"No, you said that you knew he was still alive, and you used the rumour of his death in a plane crash to cover your own disappearance," Brad said, nodding his head.

"I did not, "lied Tony.

"Yes, you did," Brad replied, "If you like I'll dig up the tape and let you hear it. It's your voice, and make no mistake, Tony, you told me yourself that you used that as an alibi. I have it on tape, and can prove it."

152

"Tape? You taped our conversations without my knowledge? Isn't that illegal?" Tony asked indignantly.

"You saw me turn it on, "Brad said, "I didn't do it behind your back. I'd have remembered what you said anyway. Why bother to lie about something that silly? Richard Lawrence is a common name, and there must be a dozen guys named Richard Lawrence. I know three right here in Canada."

"Really?" Tony said. "I've never known anyone by that name. You must be mistaken. "

TWENTY THREE

"Let's break and have another smoke. I'll toss you for the third cigarette. "Brad fished a quarter from his pocket and flipped it nonchalantly. "Heads or tails?" he asked.

"Tails," said Tony, "two out of three."

"Naw! Straight across the board. Heads, I win, tails you lose," Brad said. He grabbed the cigarette without looking at the coin, lit it and snickered. "Surprised you fell for that one."

Tony felt his hackles rise at the unfair way Brad had taken advantage of him, but he guffawed loudly to cover up his molten anger. "Got me that time!" he said amiably, while the fury boiled up inside him.

Bastard! What a snake.

"I hear ya," Tony mumbled.

"What did you say?" asked Brad.

"Nothing. What are you talking about?" Tony said.

"Forget it," advised Brad.

"I will," answered Tony.

"You need to tell the truth, so we can get this finished. Is your real name Richard Anthony Lawrence, and are you the former director of the Leeds Classic Orchestra? Did you walk out on them? "

"Why do you want to know?" Tony asked defiantly.

154

"You should wonder what the law will do to you if you keep lying. You know I have a good reason for asking you questions. Don't you want to clear your name?"

"I wish you would not treat me like a criminal," Tony complained. "Why do I have to clear my name? What are you trying to pin on me?"

"If you answer my questions truthfully, we can both get out of here a lot faster. May I remind you this is my day off? It's worth your while to be serious." He folded his arms. "I'm here as a friend, Tony. I want to help you to come clean. You do like sleeping at home, don't you?"

"Of course, I do. I am glad this weekend is over because I went to a concert I did not want to attend, then took part in it against my will." He put his hand up to stop Brad from commenting. "You knew all along I was a musician. You tricked me."

"Not intentionally, Tony," Brad said. "You came to my rescue because you understood my dilemma and I am grateful to you for doing it."

"But you're sure playing it up now."

"That's not my game," Brad said sharply, "I guessed months ago that you knew a lot about music, and then yesterday when you revealed your identity to me – by mistake maybe – I realized I had to get to the bottom of the mystery. If we can't prove your identity, you could be deported."

"Deported? Why?"

"You told me yourself that Richard Lawrence was reported missing in a plane crash, and then you contradicted yourself and said you are Richard Lawrence."

"Yeah? What do you mean? I told you nothing of the kind," Tony snapped.

"Tony, I am trying to be patient. You can't be dead in England, yet be alive in Canada. In order to trace you, I need to know what name you used when you married

Yvette. Lorenzo or Lawrence? You've been fooling around for the last six years, using aliases and pretending to be what you aren't. It's time you told the truth."

"Am I under arrest?" asked Tony, holding out his hands for the handcuffs he expected Brad to produce.

"Please answer my question."

"I married Yvette as Lorenzo. Same as I married Elise. Are you going to haul me in for that?" He pulled his hands back and stared at Brad.

"No," said Brad, "I already know who you are. It's not against the law to use an alias unless it's for a criminal purpose. You've left yourself wide open to a lot of questions by your lies and acting "

"What do you mean by acting?" Tony asked, "I am not an actor. And I'm not a killer, either."

"I know that, "agreed Brad. "I'm not sure what your game is, but I wish you would come clean. Who are you? I can't help you sort things out unless you tell the truth."

Tony sighed loudly before he replied. "I really am Richard Anthony Lawrence. Please don't blow my cover."

"I'm a police officer, not a gossip!" Brad said shortly. "Just tell me why you came to Canada. You did get a passport so you entered Canada legally. Your rationale is confusing. If Richard Lawrence is listed as a missing person this creates an odd situation. Can't you see that?"

"Obviously you've been investigating me," Tony said, with a deep sigh. "I am unable to explain it any better. I guess that's what I'm saying. The man is not dead, but his name no longer exists. It looks like you already know some things, anyway, so why do you keep interrogating me?"

"I did some discreet checking around. It didn't make sense until I came across a poster of you in Leeds. What I don't get is how Lawrence could have successfully hidden his identity long enough to get out of England, then to turn up here without somebody recognizing him. There has to be a reason for this kind of behaviour."

Tony stared into space for about ten seconds before he answered. "Street life is different. There is respect for what you don't want to tell others," he said. "My past was my business. I slept under hedges in the park and in ditches by the side of the road. When it rained or snowed, I holed up in the airport lounge and pretended I was waiting for a plane. I resembled a tourist with my suitcase, and my clothes were fairly decent."

"So," said Brad, "is that how you dropped out of sight?"

"No-one cared what got me there nor did they connect me to Lawrence. Homeless people spend their money on survival, not concerts in Queen Elizabeth Theatre. I never had to explain myself."

"Did you beg on the street? You had to eat, "said Brad.

"Odd jobs, yard maintenance, busking. I played bad guitar and my singing was even worse, just for dimes and quarters."

"You've got to be kidding!" Brad exclaimed. "You busked in downtown Vancouver? I can't imagine you with a beat-up guitar case accepting pennies. But that does explain why I thought I'd seen you before."

"I knew that. I recognized you, too." He looked down. "I can keep a tune, but I have a terrible voice. They probably paid me to stop singing," he said ruefully. "When you drop out of society there are hard choices to make. You give up a heated home, a wife and kids, a dog and a cat." He stared down at his shoes in deep thought before he looked up again.

"You never stopped wanting a relationship with a woman, though," Brad said, looking squarely into Tony's face.

"Everybody needs someone. Yvette needed me as much as I needed her.

June Carter Powell

TWENTY FOUR

"How long did Yvette live on the street?" Brad asked.

"A short time – it was too dangerous for her. I told you how I met her," Tony said, irritably. "I am sick of answering questions. My thoughts are foggy. Can we meet again tomorrow? I promise I will give it all to you then,"

"She was so young," Brad said, ignoring him. "What did she die of?"

"She was twenty-eight. Must we drag that poor kid's name through the mire? You keep asking me the same questions." Tony wiped his brow again and coughed. "I am sick of this whole thing," he complained, "it's like you think I'm making it all up."

"Was there something odd about her death?" Brad insisted.

"No," Tony said. "I know it does seem odd that she neglected to tell anyone she was ill, and then she collapsed on the street. I was shocked when the doctors discovered she was having a series of mild strokes at night. I remember she always had an odd habit of putting her hand up to her forehead. I guessed she might be having headaches. Nothing was different but I made an appointment for her to have an eye examination, just in case there was something we had missed," he explained.

159

Tony covered his eyes for a moment and drew in his breath with a whistle. "I am not happy talking about this," he said.

"You were married to her, "Brad said, "How could you miss that she was sick? I don't get it," he said, ignoring Tony's discomfort, made more evident by his odd habit of seldom using contractions.

"True, but it was a simple relationship. I was proud of her for the things she had achieved, like learning to read and write. She was eager to learn although it was difficult for her. I was fond of her, but she wasn't that kind of wife."

"What was she then? An unpaid housekeeper?"

"Oh, no!" Tony exclaimed, with a sigh, "I married Yvette because I felt a deep admiration for her. She was a beautiful girl. I knew she had some challenges, and I wanted to protect her from the harsh side of life on the streets. It was an environment she had been thrown into through no fault of her own."

"Did she ever talk about her life before that?" Brad asked. "Did she attend school?"

"Yes, her home life was abusive but she even fell through the cracks in the school system."

"How far did she go in school?" Brad said.

"I think it was in the middle of grade six," Tony answered.

"So, she really didn't have much of an education."

"No, "Tony answered. "Sometimes support workers are provided to help with day to day living, after leaving school, but Yvette was overlooked. Perhaps because she appeared normal and well groomed. Even in the camps she always looked nice."

"Did she buy new clothing?" Brad asked.

"She had no money for clothes," Tony said. "It was all free clothing from church bins. It was amazing how she knew what matched and what looked well on her. Yvette

appeared normal, but when she tried to converse it
became evident that she was challenged. She was also
unable to read the social cues."

"Lots of people are like that."

"Invisible handicaps are very subtle. She was teased a
lot. Often there is an element of caring for each other in
the homeless situation too, but in her case, if I had not
been there, one or more of the men would have taken
advantage of her. I could not stand by and watch that
happening," Tony said.

"I understand."

"When we moved here, with my help, Yvette ran the
household very well," Tony said. "She could cook a basic
meal and follow directions, and she was exceptionally
clean."

"Could she read?'

"She could read and write at what was probably a
grade three level. I base my assumptions on the fact she
read pre-teen age girl's books, like *The Bobbsey Twins*.
Even so, she loved being Mrs. Lorenzo and she was an
excellent companion." He smiled with pleasure at the
memories. "We were very happy together."

"I noticed her in church the few times I went," Brad
said, "because she was a truly lovely girl. My wife
guessed Yvette had some challenges, but I'd never have
known it by her appearance. I remember that she loved to
sing the hymns in church." He looked at Tony with a
mischievous grin.

"Oh, yeah, she did that alright. She was a sweetheart,
but she was tone-deaf. Yvette had a tinny singing voice
that was quite unpleasant," Tony said. "I thought my
voice was awful, but hers even topped that." He smiled
broadly.

"That must have been hard for you, with your keen
ear," Brad said, becoming serious again.

"No, it fit in with my new image. She never sang

much around the house, so I did not get the full assault of her enthusiasm." He laughed with a humorous, but kindly manner. "The girls at the church said she sang the hymns as if she meant every word. I stayed home most of the time, but I met with the pastor once after she passed away. He said nobody ever suggested that she keep the volume down. In spite of her everyday challenges, Yvette's enthusiasm for life made everyone love her."

"She was quite a character, in other words. Was she sick a long time before she died?" Brad asked.

"She did not appear ill, but I guess she was having headaches. The day she collapsed on the street I took her to the hospital by ambulance. Even now I blame myself for not realizing she was seriously ill. I cared for her twenty-four hours a day after she was discharged. She died two weeks later, and I have always been puzzled why they let her come home if she was really so sick." Tony sat with downcast eyes.

"If a patient is unable to vocalize her problems, I guess they could go unchecked. You shouldn't feel guilty, though. You nursed her through those dark days, and surely you did all you could," Brad said.

"I tried to tell myself that, but it was hard to understand how she could have died so quickly. She needed medications to control the stroke symptoms but the only time she saw a doctor was after she collapsed. I thought it had to be my fault even after the doctor explained that people with challenges are often quite stoic about feeling pain and will put up with discomfort. Some just accept it as normal and tell nobody."

"Did she ever complain?" Brad asked. "That is unusual if it was that severe."

With his index finger Tony traced her initials on the wooden surface of Brad's desk. He looked up and said, "No, unless Yvette was asked a direct question, she would not have volunteered how she felt. After she died, I went

162

to a psychiatrist in Vancouver and he told me that is sometimes a trait of people with Asperger's Syndrome although she was never diagnosed as having it. I would rather not see him again because a man outside the door told me it was my fault."

"What man?" asked Brad, frowning. "Not the psychiatrist. He would never tell a patient that."

"I don't know," Tony said, "but this guy keeps on telling me I am guilty. He says I deserve to die, too. A few weeks ago, he egged me on to climb over the guard rail where the lookout is," Tony said. "I stumbled and rolled toward the river and he said I was worthless, and I should die. He said it was easy and nobody would care."

"Did you recognize his voice?"

"His voice seems familiar, but I am not sure where I heard it before."

"Do you remember how you got back up the hill?"

"I think I grabbed a small tree. It took a few minutes to stop shaking but I managed to crawl up the bank on my hands and knees. I tore my pants and cut my knee, but I don't remember anything else about it — except being awfully sore and bruised for a few days."

"What did Elise say?"

"Of course, I got the third degree, while she bandaged up my knee and bitched about the blood stains on my clothes. She said my pants were too torn up to be mended."

"My wife would have said the same thing, "Brad said. "It's a female thing, you know. Didn't you think it was stupid to climb over the guard rail in the first place? It was a dumb thing to do, Tony."

"I did not think it was that dangerous," Tony stated. He looked down at the floor.

"I think," Brad said, "we guys have to understand that women are natural care-givers, and that tendency kicks in when something happens to their man. They don't mean to molly-coddle us."

"I know," Tony said.

"Were you nervous about driving home after that experience?" asked Brad.

"Yes and no," answered Tony. "I don't recall much about the trip home other than knowing I had to get there. I must be mentally ill. I can't remember things. What is wrong with me? Do I have Alzheimer's Disease? Dementia? Am I insane?"

"Hold it!" Brad said, raising up his hand for silence. "You aren't any of those things. You are feeling stress, though, so I'm taking you home now. I want you to rest for a couple of days before we talk again. I can help you get your life straightened out if you will trust me. Can you remember if you changed your name legally from Richard Lawrence to Antonio Lorenzo? That's very important. Come on, Tony, think."

"I started the process. There was an announcement in the Vancouver paper of my intention to legally change my name, but I don't know what year it was," he said at last, "I do not remember."

Tony became defensive again, but Brad gently coached him, "Relax, Tony. It has been a tough few days. We have dug into things in your past that you may have preferred to forget. We'll wait until next week to talk again."

"Thanks," Tony said. "I want to go home."

"I won't soon forget how you came to my rescue the night of the concert, so it's my turn to help you now. It's a fair exchange," Brad promised.

"Yes," Tony murmured.

"Who is the psychiatrist you are seeing?"

"Dr. Rodney Brown, on Broadway."

"Supposed to be a good doctor, "Brad said, "I have heard of him, but I haven't met him."

"I thought he was okay until he let that fellow in the

building. Now I wonder. I would prefer not to see him again."

"Hmmm," Brad said, "Was he another patient?"

"I do not know who he was. His voice reminded me of a man named Frank. I did not like him being there. If he is there, I don't want to see Dr. Brown."

Brad frowned and looked puzzled. "Oh, so you do remember someone who spoke like him. Was he in the room with you when you were talking to the doctor?"

"I think so." He repeated that he didn't want to be there if that man would be there too.

"Who is this guy called Frank?"

"I have no idea because I have known a few men called Frank and he does not sound like any of them. There was a slimy guy in the camp, but I never knew his name. The women were scared of him. Always trying to get into Yvette's tent. He would have forced her."

"Hmmm. It makes sense that you don't like him. Was his name Frank or something that sounded like Frank?" Brad asked.

"I wish I could remember," Tony said after a moment of deep thought. "What if I don't want to see Dr. Brown again?"

"It would make it difficult for me to help you. Maybe one more time? Do I have your permission to handle the change of name information? I have ways of getting the facts quickly. If you'll let me look after this, we can probably have our answers within a week." Brad checked the time, and said, "It's getting late. Let's get out of here."

Tony nodded his head and pulled on his jacket quickly as if wanting to put an end to the discussion, but Brad lingered, an anxious expression in his blue eyes.

After what seemed to be an interminable pause, he said, "Tony, I've been thinking. When the Christmas holidays are over, would you like to take over the orchestra? I am just a stand-in until we can hire a real director. I believe we have found that person already."

"Oh, no, I'm not ready for that. It's your baby. I could give you some conducting lessons though. You look like you are rowing a boat when you conduct, and you hold the baton like a hockey stick."

Brad threw back his head and laughed heartily. "This ship's about to leave port in five minutes so let's go," he said. "All aboard! You owe me a beer for that shot."

"I'll buy you a whole case."

"I'll be up there fastening the jib, "said Brad, smiling broadly.

"It's a rowboat. You have oars, no sail and no jib," Tony informed him, making rowing motions with his arms.

TWENTY FIVE

Brad waited until Tony entered the house before he left. He waved at two men shoveling snow a couple of houses down from Tony's place. They both stopped working and watched as he drove away.

I'll bet they wondered why I took him home in the police car. And in uniform. These small communities are all ears and eyes. Sometimes mouth, too. He better get this solved or the property values up here will drop. It doesn't take much in this kind of neighbourhood to get people talking. *How do I go about getting to the bottom of Tony's problems? Maybe I could talk to Dr. Brown, but then, again, he might not co-operate because of patient privacy.*

***

Tony took the basement steps two at a time, and flung open the hall closet, hung up his jacket and took off his boots.

"Elise, I'm home," he shouted. "Where are you?"

"I'm right here, Tony," she answered, from the living room. "Why are you yelling?"

"Oh, sorry," he said, "I didn't realize I was talking so loud. I am glad you are here because Brad upsets me sometimes. He's so--so like a policeman. Never satisfied with me just answering questions simply. However, by the time he dropped me off, he was in a good mood and was laughing." He crossed the kitchen in three long strides and reached out to enfold her in a hug.

"You've been smoking!" Elise exclaimed, pulling away. "I can smell it on your clothes."

"Brad was smoking so I did, too," Tony said. "Somebody left a pack of cigarettes on the window sill.so we smoked them."

"Did you want to smoke? You quit a long time ago."

"No, but I thought I may as well."

"How many did you smoke?" Elise asked, holding her nose.

"Only one but Brad smoked two. Why are you giving me the third degree? I'm not a child," Tony said, suddenly feeling angry, "It's not like I smoked a whole package. You always ask a lot of questions. Can't you...."

"Forget it—I'm just glad you're home," Elise said, "I'd like to relax with you is all."

"I know, and I didn't mean it." He sniffed the air. "Got any coffee brewing? I could do with one that doesn't taste like Styrofoam."

"Okay, and I can have lunch ready in a jiffy. Maybe we could talk a bit? It's lonely in this big house sometimes," she said, with a wistful look in her blue eyes

"I forget about that sometimes. Brad asked me if I would like to take over directing the orchestra in January." he said. "It felt good to be asked even though I knew it would be hard for him to give it up."

"I think you could, "Elise said. "Will you do it?"

"I'm not ready to do that yet. But you do know I used to direct an orchestra? I know you guessed that," Tony said. He put his hands on her shoulders and turned her around to face him.

Elise looked up into his eyes, and smiled slowly. "I don't know anything for sure," she said, "but I think you've been holding out on us. You must have had experience conducting an orchestra before you came here.

168

I bet you were famous and had girls running after you and crying like Elvis."

"Not quite that dramatic," he said, with a chuckle, "and Praise the Lord for that. Elvis can have it! I couldn't handle being chased or making women cry. I did have a following in my country though. Do you know where I am from?"

"I think you lived in England, and you are really Richard Lawrence, director the Leeds Classic Orchestra." she said. "At the reception I heard that fellow from England say it was uncanny how you resembled him. He said even your arm movements when you conducted the orchestra were like Richard Lawrence," she said, her voice becoming accusatory.

"I was sure you were on the right track," he said, not noticing her mood change. "I thought you would guess the truth long ago."

"I knew darn well you were lying to me, but I still can't understand why you would go to such lengths to fool me. I don't even know who I'm married to."

"I wanted to tell you, but I couldn't bring myself to do it. I knew it would be difficult to answer your questions at that point. The truth is I walked out on my orchestra. I was nervous to face the crowds anymore."

"*Your* orchestra? What's that supposed to mean? Wasn't there more to it than that?" Elise said, her cheeks flushing.

"Yes, but I don't want to go there today." He tried to draw her into an intimate embrace. When she pulled away from him, Tony looked surprised and hurt.

"Oh, bully for you, Big Shot!" she retorted. "You should have told me a lot sooner," Elise said with a frown. "I'm not impressed. Now I don't even know if we're really married. If you aren't who you said you are, maybe we're just shacking up. What else have you lied about?" She pushed him away and stared at him, a frightened look in her eyes. "For all I know, you could have a bunker under the garage where you lure young girl hitch hikers for your…"

"Elise!" he cried, "That's not fair. I've just had a rotten few days with Brad and now you're giving me the gears, too." He made a grab for her.

"Me not fair? Too bad!" she snapped, avoiding his clutch. "What about me?" She broke free and ran out of the room. "You took advantage of me," she shouted. Her voice faded away as she rushed around the corner, ran into the hallway and part way up the stairs. She turned back and blurted out, "How could you do this to me?" Angry tears ran down her cheeks.

Tony caught up with her, and put his arms around her waist to prevent her from going any further. "Elise! You don't understand." He held her firmly so she couldn't move away.

"Neither do you!" Elise retorted. She tried to push his hands away, but he held her tightly. "I don't want to just shack up with some guy. You weren't being honest with me. For all I know you're a criminal." She pounded his chest with her fists and turned her face from him. "I want to get away from you. You're nothing but a pain in the ass," she cried. Breathing heavily, he let his arms drop.

"I'm not just some guy, he said, "I am your husband, the man you married."

"Oh, yeah! Do you have to remind me?" she said, turning blazing eyes on him.

"Don't be like that. You know I get depressed easily. I got upset because I had to wait so long for the change of name process to go ahead. Brad said he will help me to make sure I did everything right. And I'm not a criminal."

"Oh, come on! Milk it for all it's worth, why don't you?" she said, sarcasm dripping from her voice. "Just because you get depressed doesn't give you permission to lie and cheat. How do I know that you aren't some

170

horrible fugitive hiding from the law?"

"Because I'm telling you so. And I am not milking it for all it's worth, as you so sweetly put it." He lifted her chin with his cupped palms, and looked into her eyes. "No more lies," he promised, "I'm tired of lying."

"And I'm sick to death of listening to them." She elbowed him in the ribs.

"Ow!" he yelped. He jumped out of the way and massaged his side.

"You've lied so much you don't even know the truth anymore. I'm going over to Lorraine's place, and don't you try to stop me."

"Oh, please don't involve Hank and Lorraine in our business again." Tony pleaded. "The last time you did that, I could feel them looking at me oddly. They'll think I threatened you or became abusive."

"You'd better not try it," Elise warned. "Now get out of my way so I can get some stuff together. Lorraine is my best friend"

"When are you coming back?" Tony asked, his cheeks flushing.

"When I'm damned good and ready," she said. She stuck her chin out in a stubborn square. Tony thought she resembled a bulldog, but he kept it to himself. He hadn't expected her answer to be quite so abrasive, but he rationalized that the old cliché is true. There are times when caution really is the better part of valor.

"You really think I'll allow you back?" he said, his voice rising with mounting anger.

That's right, tell it like it is, Tony.

"This was supposed to be a nice day just for you and me, and now look what you've done. You ruined everything!'

"Me? I ruined it? Why, you lying creep, how dare you talk to me like that? You'll be lucky if you ever see me again. Let me past you. I don't even want to talk to you anymore. I may never trust you again." She removed his hands from her waist, and ran up the stairs to the bedroom. She slammed the door so hard it bounced open again. She slammed it a second time. A Wedgewood plate fell off the wall in the hallway with a resounding crash. Fragments of porcelain scattered over the marble floor. Tony flinched at the depth of her anger.

He walked cautiously around the porcelain shards and downstairs into the kitchen. He thought about sweeping up the pieces of her favourite plate, but couldn't be bothered. Instead he ignored them and sat at the table. He rested his head in his hands and listened to Elise banging things upstairs.

It was the first real fight since they had met. Well, there had been times when the air was blue with unresolved issues. If he could only go back in time!

Why didn't I tell her ages ago? I had plenty of chances and I blew them all. What a fool!

You've got that right, Tony.

The last thing he wanted right then was to be chastised by someone he couldn't even see. He looked in vain for the person speaking the words. It was the same voice that had hounded him for ages, familiar, grating. Maybe it really was Frank. If only he could remember what Frank looked like.

Brad had suggested the voice was coming from his own tortured thoughts and that Dr. Brown could help him get rid of it. He gritted his teeth. One part of him wanted to believe Brad was wrong while the other half wanted to believe he was not hearing a phantom voice at all and it was a real person taunting him.

He stood up and looked despondently out the front room window, trying to gather his thoughts together. What should he do? Wait a while before going in to talk to Elise and hope by then she has calmed down? Maybe a good idea.

He walked slowly up the stairs again, stalling for time. He stopped twice to reconsider his options.

"I should have done this four years ago," he whispered to himself. He held his aching head with the tips of his cold fingers. With a heavy lump in the pit of his stomach, he worried whether he was doing the right thing. Certain he was correct in trying to talk to her, he pounded on the bedroom door. No answer.

He could still hear Elise stomping around in the room. He tapped lightly this time. When she still didn't respond, he opened the door a crack and called, "Elise, I would like to talk to you." Still no answer. He opened the door wider, and took a step inside the doorway, but changed his mind abruptly as he dodged a flying missile in the form of a silver hairbrush.

Elise held her hair drier over her head, but when she saw him standing there, she let it fall to the floor. She sat heavily on the bed and glared at him, her frustration boiling over again.

"Get the hell out of here and leave me alone," she yelled, her voice breaking, "I've had all I can take of you and your fairy tales. Why don't you go back to where you came from?" She leaped to her feet, picked up a book from the bedside stand, and aimed it at his head. The weight of it flung her forward and made a loud *plop* as it connected with the door jamb.

Tony made a quick getaway just as the heavy volume fell to the floor. He noted it was the *Complete Works of William Shakespeare* and probably weighed at least sixteen pounds.

Angrily he flung the door wide open and roared, "Let me get my bloody suitcase and I'll leave. I don't have to put up with this. Who the hell do you think you are? Queen ****?"

"No, that was your last girl-friend, "she yelled. She put her hand over her mouth. "Oh, no, that was Yvette," she said very softly, her voice almost inaudible. "I shouldn't have said that!"

"Queen **** was a hellava lot better than getting stuck with her wicked stepsister, Princess @&*^%?" he snarled, as if he hadn't heard her last comment.

"Well," she snapped, "Your Majesty Prince Lardarse, you deserve to be hooked up with Princess @&^%?"

There was dead silence for about ten seconds while they both tried to digest this turn of events.

Elise dashed her angry tears away with the back of her hand, cleared her throat loudly and looked at the ceiling. She covered her mouth, then flicked an unruly curl off her forehead. Finally, she sat down on the edge of the bed and focused on his nose. He needed to wipe it. How could he stand the drip suspended like a glistening pendant dangling from one nostril?

Tony nervously pulled his left ear, grabbed a tissue from his side of the bed, and blew his nose with an uncouth honk. After the fact, he remembered that Elise recoiled at such bad manners. He looked into space, avoiding her stare. Finally, he turned to face his furious wife.

"I'm glad you blew your nose," Elise said, quietly, her anger beginning to dissolve, "because the drip was driving me crazy."

"Thank-you," Tony said, "I'm really grateful that you are glad."

"Uh," she said, looking into his eyes, "and I am glad that you are grateful."

"Well, I'm glad that is settled," he remarked.

"Me, too," she said.

Gradually a faint smile softened the grim hardness of her face, while the shadow of a grin replaced the glum straight line of his mouth.

"Uh, do you think Our Majesties could talk for a wee bit without any more verbal diarrhea? I'm not leaving, by the way," he said, with an apologetic smile. He walked over to where she was sitting by the bedside table and knelt down before her.

"Me neither," she announced, as she smoothed her disheveled hair.

"I feel guilty. It's my fault for not being honest with you. I should have trusted you more." He stood up for a minute, and looked nervously around before he sat down beside her. He reached out and slipped his arm around her. "Come, let's talk."

"I wish you had treated me as an equal," she said, allowing herself to be pulled into a loose embrace, but indicating by the space between them that she was not quite ready to surrender completely.

"I am sorry, "he said. It wasn't very much to say but he couldn't think of anything else he wanted to tell her. Just three tiny words from the heart.

"I'm sorry, too."

He gathered her into his arms and held her without speaking. His own eyes were moist. He wiped them on his shirt collar.

After what seemed an eternity, she dried her eyes on the sleeve of her white blouse, leaving a faint mascara mark on the cuff.

"I don't know why it was such a shock when you finally told me the truth. I had already guessed at the concert that you really were Richard Lawrence. It was at the reception after the concert actually, "she said. "I wanted you to tell me yourself because it wasn't enough for me to guess at it. I felt betrayed when you kept me waiting."

"I know. I understand that. I was in the wrong. Let's go downstairs," he said, "and be careful of the broken glass on the floor by the top stair, because I haven't cleaned it up yet."

"Okay," she said in a wee small voice. "I'm

completely worn out. That took a lot of energy."

"I bet it did," Tony said, "I feel horrible right now; just the thought of losing you makes me ill. My whole body aches. I feel so guilty."

"I thought I was going to be sick. My head is still pounding. I shouldn't have lost my temper," Elise said.

"It was my fault. I shouldn't have lied to you. Prince Lardarse, eh? That was imaginative." Tony smiled.

"I've never been called the wicked stepsister before. Princess @&*^% is quite a mouthful," Elise said.

"A good match for the prince," Tony remarked. "It's what he deserves."

"I'll have to think about that. We were both angry."

"Nothing a person says can be unsaid, no matter how many times we apologize. It means that we allowed the tension of the past week to get to us," Tony agreed.

"Let's try to put it behind us," Elise suggested. "Anger is such an awful thing. Please don't lie to me anymore. I don't understand the need to tell untruths."

"I know and I have another thing to tell you, too, and I hope you will be okay with it."

"What is it, Tony?" Elise asked warily.

"I have been seeing a psychiatrist in Vancouver for several months," Tony said. "When I went there for meetings with my stockbroker I also had appointments with Dr. Brown. I will see him again after Christmas."

"I wish you had told me that before, too."

"No more secrets. And now I'd like a drink. How about you? Red or white wine?"

"Rosé," she said, a weak little giggle escaping from her lips.

TWENTY-SIX

A fire burned in the fireplace, the flames casting dancing shadows on the cool, beige walls of the front room.

"Only three days to Christmas," Tony said needlessly "It's on a Saturday this year," he informed her. Conversation between him and Elise was still somewhat stilted after the nasty exchange they had had that afternoon.

"I have all my shopping done," Elise said. "Let's do some kid stuff this year. We could fill each other's stockings? What do you think?"

"I haven't even started my shopping," Tony admitted. "I have been busy talking to Brad. I think the stockings might be fun. I have not had a stocking since I was about eleven years old, but if we put the tree up we might feel more festive. I wanted to put it up today, but I'm still bushed from dodging various unidentified flying objects." He moved to sit cross-legged on the floor in front of her.

"Yeah?" Elise asked, with a crooked smile. "Me too. Tomorrow would be a better day. My mother loved Christmas. We always put our tree up the weekend before the twenty-fifth, so she could display her handmade decorations. We did stockings for each other when we

177

grew up, too. It was fun."

"Was it a big tree?"

"No, we had one of the first artificial trees made. Mother couldn't bear to kill a living tree for a week and then throw it out in the snowbank to die alone in the cold."

"Oh, one of those funny looking silver trees," he said, ignoring her compassion for a real tree.

"Yes, but with our handmade decorations it was quite pretty. Mother's sister decorated eggshells to make delicate Faberge-style hanging balls."

"Was that Valerie?" he asked, "Did she make the ones you have, then? I keep forgetting to ask who had made those."

"Yes, Auntie Val was very artistic. Did you have a real tree at home?"

"An imported one from Canada," he said with a chuckle. "That seems so funny now. We seldom ever got snow for Christmas where I lived. Most kids thought it was special when we did get a little bit, which melted away after an hour or so anyway, leaving a wet, muddy mess."

"Well, we're sure getting our share of the white stuff this year," Elise said, "You may never want to see snow again after this winter."

"I disliked it because it was usually wet and nasty because the temperature never dropped low enough to make the snow stay frozen like it does here. I could make a mean snowball when I was a kid, but I hated getting snow down my neck. More like having a pail of muddy ice water poured over you."

"I loved everything about winter, even the snowball fights," Elise said with enthusiasm. "It was a time to let go of all the polite behaviour and burn off energy by throwing snowballs at your friends. We would make them earlier in the day and stash our supply inside a fort until the fight started."

"You?" Tony asked in surprise. "You had a fort?"

"Of course. Sometimes the girls would be against the boys, but mostly we chose two captains who would select his fighters. When the fight got really serious, we'd hide behind our fort and pelt snowballs."

"Wow, you really did that?"

"I was a tomboy, you know. In winter it would get dark by four o'clock. We couldn't wait to get outdoors right after dinner to have a snowball fight under the stars. We'd hide until everyone arrived. Then the fight would begin. Sometimes the battle got downright serious and we'd pelt snowballs at anyone who dared to come down the street. Usually the victim would make a few snowballs to throw back at us. I got one of my male schoolteachers in the back of the head once." She giggled delightedly.

"Was he angry?" asked Tony.

"He certainly wasn't pleased," she said, "but he never did know who the culprit was, and of course nobody would snitch on me. He didn't even suspect I could throw anything that fast."

"How come? If he was one of your teachers, he must have known you were no angel," Tony said.

"Oh, I imagine he did, but he didn't realize I had such powerful throwing arm. I was the smallest kid in my class," she said, "and quite well behaved normally. All that changes when involved in a snowball fight."

"There's nothing wrong with your throwing arm now."

"What do you mean by that?"

"By what?" Tony asked, feigning innocence.

"I'll make some hot chocolate and we can have it by the fire before we go to bed," Elise suggested, changing the subject. "Do you want whipped cream or a marshmallow on the top?" She pushed herself out of the deep sofa and stood up.

"How about both?"

"You'll get fat."

"It's too late to worry. Look at my girth. And you did call me Prince... He pulled up his shirt to reveal his bare, hairy chest. "Come back here and hug me first." He grabbed her sweater and pulled her onto the sofa again.

"Promises, promises!" Tony said after an embrace.

"Mmmm," Elise whispered in his ear. "You must think I'm a bad girl. Last night I slept with Tony Lorenzo and tonight I will sleep with Richard Lawrence."

"I like bad girls." He stood up and pulled her to her feet. "I have to wash my hands for that hot chocolate," he said.

As he walked toward the bathroom, he gave her a mock salute. When he reached the door, he turned, and with a cheeky grin, stepped inside and closed it. A hot drink by a flaming fire and a warm woman — what could be better?

TWENTY SEVEN

Tony slept in the next morning. A brisk wind was blowing around the old house, getting into every crack and moaning like a banshee. His bed felt so warm and comfortable that he didn't want to leave it even for the delicious aroma of freshly brewed coffee and whatever Elise was baking. He hoped it was for his breakfast. He sniffed the air and reconsidered. The bed was nice, even if he was alone in it now, but a hot breakfast might be nicer, he thought. He hadn't been alone in it last night, he remembered, a lecherous smirk on his face. He was glad Brad didn't want to continue the interviews until the following day, because he had other things in mind.

Tony stretched and got out of bed, put on his bathrobe and wandered down into the kitchen.

"Hi, honey!" he said, a happy smile on his face.

"Did you have a good sleep? When I crept out of bed this morning you were snoring softly," Elise said.

"Really? I never snore," he declared.

"No, of course not," Elise said, "It must have been my imagination. It inspired me to parody a song with apologies to Stephen Foster."

"What song?" asked Tony, warily.

She sang the parodied words to the tune of folk song

Beautiful Dreamer.

> *"'Beautiful dreamer, how sweetly you snore,*
> *I'd like to stay with you, but you sound like Eeyore.*
> *What musical bass notes you make with your nose,*
> *You're rhythm and harm'ny from your head to your toes.*
> *Beautiful dreamer, how sweetly you snore.*
> *I'm leaving this bed; I can't take it no more.' "*

"I didn't think I ever snored that loud," he said, "if I really snore at all, that is." He laughed.

"There's more verses to the song. Do you want to hear them?" she asked

"Okay if I pass?" Tony said, changing the subject, with a twinkle in his eye, "What are you baking? It smells like the coffee cake my mother used to bake for Sunday morning breakfasts when I was a kid?"

"Just like a man," she said, "you prefer food to poetry."

"Especially poetry with me as the subject," he said, raising his eyebrows in mock horror.

"I felt so good when I got up this morning that I wanted to make something special to tempt you. I do care about you, even if I haven't known who I've been sleeping with for the last four years," Elise said.

"Well, you do now, and Brad will help me get some things straightened out. I'm grateful to him for that. It's in exchange for me helping him at the concert. I like Brad, a nice guy."

He's a cop, don't trust him. He could turn on you any time.

"Who said that?" asked Tony.

"What are you talking about?" said Elise.

"I don't know. Maybe somebody left the radio on in the laundry room."

Elise stood still and listened. "It was not on when I walked past the door five minutes ago. Just tell me how come you like Brad now when you didn't like him at all before the concert?" Elise asked.

"Okay," he said, "if you are unable to hear it, probably the radio isn't on."

Am I really just hearing voices? He shuddered involuntarily. *What a horrible feeling it gives me!*

"You didn't answer my question. Why didn't you like Brad yesterday and now you call him a nice guy?"

'Well, things change, I guess. He's really an okay fellow. Yesterday when I told him he held the baton like a hockey stick he got a real charge out of it."

"Wasn't he angry?" asked Elise.

"No, he was good natured about it," Tony answered. "He even laughed when I offered to teach him how to conduct."

"Because he didn't get angry, you changed your mind about him, then. However, he is awkward, and he forgets to give the orchestra a downbeat, so we never really know when to start playing."

"He is serious about wanting to learn, and I am willing to teach him." Tony said.

"I like Brad and I would be happy to see him really learn how to direct an orchestra," Elise said. "When will you be finished talking with him?"

"I have an appointment with Brad tomorrow, then nothing until after the holidays. Today belongs to you and I."

"What shall we do with it?"

"Go back to bed, perhaps," he said with a chuckle, his eyes sparkling with merriment.

"Hmm," she murmured, as she buttered a generous wedge of coffee cake and put it on his plate. "Let's eat first. At your age. . .?"

TWENTY EIGHT

The next morning Tony waited by the front room window for Brad to pick him up for what he hoped was the last interview.

Tony relaxed, knowing the worst was probably over. *Brad has done his homework well, and obviously knows all the details now, so there is no need to hide anything from him. All I have to do now is to confirm what he already knows.*

At nine o'clock Brad arrived in his own car to pick him up, Tony was glad to see he wasn't in the police cruiser again.

He was right on time as usual, wearing his Russian hat, the flaps down over his ears, chin straps swinging back and forth as he walked out to the car, yanked open the door and hopped in.

"How are ya?" Brad asked.

Tony said, "I'm okay. Do we have time to go back in the house and have a quick cup of coffee before we go? I'd sure like one. I wasn't quite finished breakfast when you arrived." Tony smiled weakly.

"Sure," he said. "Did you wear that funny looking hat while you had your toast?"

"No," Tony said. "I jammed it on my head when I saw you come up the drive. How come you are not driving the cop car this morning? I'm sure my neighbours

184

have enjoyed imagining I am about to be incarcerated."

"Do you really care what your neighbours think? I'm in for a cup," Brad, said consulting his watch, "We have a few minutes to spare."

"I worry about Elise having to answer questions."

"Elise is tougher than you think," Brad said. "Living with you hasn't been easy the last while."

"The coffee just finished perking so it will be hot," Tony said, choosing not to acknowledge Brad's remark. Some things were better left unchallenged.

The two men walked back into the house together. Brad kicked his boots off and bounded up the basement stairs behind Tony. "Smells good in here," he commented. "I got you really upset yesterday, didn't I?" he asked, turning to Tony at the top of the stairs.

"I am fine this morning though. It's not easy talking about some things, but I know it has to be done. We could just hang our jackets over the back of our chairs," Tony said, taking off his winter coat. He draped it over the armchair at the head of the table. "I'm sure you will want to get going as soon as we finish our coffee. Here, I'll pour yours first." He laughed self-consciously, "My wife is out this morning, or she'd have the cups we used a few minutes ago in the dishwasher already. This is your cup, isn't it? And I had this one." Tony held out the green mug with gold and bronze maple leaves on it.

"Yes," agreed Brad, "I had that one earlier. I don't need a clean cup yet." Tony poured a cup for Brad before pouring coffee for himself.

After killing thirty minutes drinking the aromatic brew, Brad was anxious to go. He got out of his chair and pulled his socks up, an important part of getting a move on.

"This is good stuff, and I could stay all day and drink coffee. I like this better than what we get from the coffee machines. Come on, get your jacket on, Let's go."

Tony snugged his collar around his neck as he stepped out into the cold.

"I hate winter," he complained. "I don't see it serves any purpose at all. What difference would it make if winter was skipped?"

"Quitcherbitchin'" Brad said, pretending to be impatient, "we can't do a thing about it, so get into the car and I'll turn the heat up after the engine has been going for a while."

"Is quitcherbitchin' a word?" asked Tony.

"It is now," said Brad. "I like it, and it fits the way I feel at the moment. My office will have heat, so you'll live until we get there."

"Probably," Tony agreed solemnly.

It wasn't far to the Police Station if one took the main road, but Brad enjoyed cruising through the outskirts of Rocky Creek. He liked the idea of doing a little neighbourhood sleuthing while he was on the road. He had no hunches today, but it was a good habit to stay alert.

When he had driven past acres of apple orchards in the sparsely populated rural district, with a few homes in the distance, and a farmhouse on the right, Tony suddenly said, "Stop!" Brad slammed on the brakes and came to a full stop.

"What's wrong?" Brad asked. "Why did you want me to stop? I thought you were anxious to get to where it's warm."

Tony had already jumped out of the car and was digging in the snow at the side of the road. At first, he thought Tony was probably obeying an urgent call from Nature and looked the other way. When he got out of the car to check the reason Tony was taking so long, to his amazement he saw that Tony was holding a very young black kitten. He had rescued it from a mound of snow so high that every part of it, except its ears were dusted with snow.

Tony held the wiggling animal against his chest. The little fellow nuzzled in the warm jacket and finally stopped struggling.

"What the hell? We're supposed to go to the shop so we can talk, and here you are. . . "

"Sorry," Tony said. "Look, he's only a baby. I can't leave him here to die. It's too cold out here for a tiny kitten." He hugged the kitten close to him and stroked his furry head. The kitten purred loudly and began to make sucking sounds on Tony's wool coat. Even Brad, who much preferred dogs, had to smile. Tony looked up at him with an entreating expression.

Brad sighed. "It's somebody's cat, for God's sake. Put him down and get back in the car now. This is nonsense," he said sternly.

"No," Tony said, thrusting out his chin. "He's only a few weeks old. He must have been dumped here to die. Just his head was sticking out, so someone tried to bury him. I have to take him home. I can walk back if you don't want to help. This is more important. We could meet another day."

"No, we have to get this over with today," Brad insisted, "Look, he's a stray cat. I'm not having some damn cat in this car, that's final. If it was a dog, I could see it, but a cat. . ."

"There's no difference between an abandoned puppy and a discarded kitten," Tony said, standing his ground.

"Okay, okay, let's go," Brad said, relenting somewhat. "I haven't got all day to fool around. If that animal pees in my car or in my office you are going to be sorry," he warned. "Do you understand? Keep the damn thing under your coat and don't let anybody see it. Do you get it?"

"Don't get your shit in a knot!" Tony said, becoming dangerously mouthy. However, he obeyed and got quickly back into the car. He undid the buttons on his windbreaker and held the kitten against the warmth of his body. He pulled the jacket around him like a blanket and disregarded the snow that melted onto his coat.

"Mind your tongue," Brad said, his exasperation in danger of boiling over. "I'm taping every word you say," he threatened. "This is the dumbest thing I've ever seen. Just don't let it stick its head out of your coat again until I take you home. I don't want my staff to think I'm off my head. If it pees, it had better be on your coat, not on anything of mine."

"You have a tape recorder in your own personal car?" asked Tony, innocently looking around for it on the dashboard.

Brad frowned in righteous indignation and glared straight ahead. "You're just lucky I don't," he said.

Tony didn't answer. *Hmmm! He isn't really so tough after all. He's human, too.*

Oh yeah?

The road to the police station seemed much longer than usual, and the scenery Brad loved, not quite as picturesque. *Tony will never cease to amaze me*, he thought.

Brad was silent for the rest of the journey to his office, studying Tony thoughtfully along the way. *How could I have allowed this joker to pick up a stray animal and transport it in my car, of all things? Thank God, it's not the cop car or I'd be in hot water.*

After a moment or two of observation, Brad smiled to himself. "So you have a soft spot in your heart for animals, eh? Tony?" he muttered. "Or an underdog, like Yvette. Like me, when I couldn't go back onstage at the concert. Tony came to the rescue.

"Do you like animals, Tony?" he asked. *He acts like a jerk most of the time, but if a kitten can get to him, maybe he really does have a nicer side to him.*

"We always had pets when I was a child," Tony said.

"So did we," answered Brad. "Did you have dogs or cats?"

"Both," said Tony, "but cats are most often abandoned, and my mother couldn't bear the thought of a homeless kitten."

Don't tell him too much. He's trying to trip you up.

"No, he isn't," Tony said.

"I beg your pardon?" Brad said, glancing at him curiously.

"What?" Tony said.

"I heard you say, 'he isn't,' whatever that means. Unless you were talking to yourself."

Shut your big mouth, Tony. You will let the cat out of the bag.

"No," Tony said. "The cat is fine, and it isn't in a bag. It's in my jacket."

"What?" said Brad.

As the two men entered Brad's office a few minutes later, Tony said, "Well, we don't need to guzzle away on more coffee anyway. I feel as if my kidneys are floating."

"I've never heard that comparison before." Brad said.

They were greeted by the staff like old friends, and even Tony was addressed by his first name.

"Nope," said Brad, "after that wonderful brew of your wife's, the paper cup variety would be like poison. Does Elise do all the cooking at home, or do you have hired help for that?"

"No, "Tony said, his eyes shining with pride. "We only hire help for house cleaning and serving when we have a large dinner party. Elise does all the cooking and meal planning. She is very domestic, and loves to experiment with new dishes, and new flavours." He had removed his jacket and was cradling the kitten in his warm hands, totally ignoring Brad's warnings about what would happen if the little animal had an accident on the rug. "He has stopped shivering now," Tony said, referring to the kitten.

"You lucky dog," Brad said, paying no attention to the cat. "You have it all, Tony."

"I do," he answered, with a superior air. "I think I have some problems, though. That old man says I am unhinged, and now I wonder if he's right." He looked up at Brad and gave him a questioning smile.

"Different, yes, but that's beside the point," Brad said, looking at the animal poking an inquisitive paw toward Tony's keys. "I think we're both a little daft at the moment but let's get back to business here, so I can get you and this feline out of my office without anybody seeing it." Against his better judgement, he reached out and rubbed the little guy's ear. "Have you told your doctor that this man talks to you sometimes?" he asked.

"No, I have not discussed it with Dr. Brown. Wouldn't he know that already? We were right outside in the hall by his door when it happened."

"Probably not, unless you told him," Brad said, "Did you say it was a man's voice who accused you of causing Yvette's death?" he asked.

"Yes," Tony said, "he says some awful things to me. I hate him."

"Does he have a name, Tony?"

"Now we're getting somewhere," Brad said under his breath. The poor guy must really be hearing things. *I'll get in touch with Dr. Brown right away.* It would be quicker to phone but he may not think it's the right thing for me to do. I'll draft a letter tonight and fax it to him.

"I don't know," Tony said. "I have never asked him, but he sounds like someone I once knew. His name was Frank." He looked bewildered. "I don't understand," he said.

Brad raised his eyebrows and asked, "Do you drink much? I remember you said you hit the bottle after your fiancée jilted you. What was her name again?"

"Jane Morrow, the opera singer," Tony answered. "It's not drinking. I do that behind closed doors. Why do you want to know?"

"I was just wondering if you're writing a book? Are you sure you don't go to the wine cellar and take a bottle or two up there when you're working?"

Tony stopped short and stared out the window. "No," he said, "I am not writing a book and I am not drinking. I've been practising conducting an orchestra. I have tapes of my orchestra in Leeds and I like to conduct the music. Insane, eh?"

Brad said, "No, not insane. Maybe not even eccentric. Most directors practice with a recording, so when they come to rehearse the orchestra, they know the music. That's what I do. Does the man ever speak to you when you are conducting?"

"No. That's funny, isn't it?"

"Maybe not. What does Elise think about it?"

"She doesn't know," Tony answered, "I always close the door and lock it and she never comes up to check on me. She respects my privacy."

"I see," said Brad, "so maybe you can tell me what Elise does to get you annoyed."

"Well," answered Tony, "she's so cheerful all the time, and she giggles like a teenaged girl. She enjoys people."

"Wouldn't you rather have a cheerful wife than one who criticizes you? I would," Brad said, "Is there anything specific she says or is it just the tone of her voice that reminds you of something?"

Tony hesitated before he answered. "I guess she reminds me of Jane. She waves her arms when she talks on the phone, and she is self-sufficient," he explained.

"Who is Jane? Could you tell me again who she is?" Brad repeated the question.

"She was my fiancée, "Tony said, "but she left me at

the altar at our wedding. It was called off."

"Oh, yes, you did tell me that. It must have been hard on you," Brad said.

"It was awful. My best man said she was crying. She didn't know how to tell me."

"That would be insulting. No wonder you went out and got drunk with him," Brad said. "However, you are married to Elise now, and you must have put Jane out of your mind a long time ago."

"Oh, yes, I am happy with Elise," Tony said with a contented smile.

"You just said that sometimes Elise makes you think of Jane," Brad reminded him. "How do you feel about her now?" he asked. "Does the singer still bring up happy memories for you or are they all unpleasant, hurtful thoughts?"

Tony tilted his chair backwards, teetering precariously on the two back legs. The kitten blinked his eyes and peered over the side of his bed inside Tony's coat pocket. "We worked together for a long time and we did have a lot of happy times, but I guess I would not take Jane back now even if I had a chance," he said. "It's funny, but I don't think of her that way anymore. She has never married, you know." He leaned forward, and with a bang, the chair landed on the two front legs again. He grabbed the desk for support.

"Then what is it about Elise that makes you compare her to Jane?" Brad prompted.

"I think it's because Elise has strong opinions the same as Jane did." Tony said, "I believed a woman was supposed to be a helpmate to her husband."

"There are times a wife is a helpmate. However, often it's the husband who is the helpmate. In a good marriage, we help one another and that's how it should be. It is not a bad thing when a woman knows what she wants for herself," Brad assured him.

"I like to look after my wife," Tony said, "I wish Elise would consult me before she decides to do things. The least she could do is find out if I approve before she makes plans."

"So if Elise was more like Yvette and needed you to take care of her, it would make you happier. Didn't you feel tied down when Yvette needed so much from you?"

"I used to long for someone to talk to on my own level. Yes, Yvette was a little taxing sometimes. I did like the fact she needed me, though," he explained.

"Don't you think Elise needs you?"

"No, whatever she wants she is able to do without asking me for help," Tony said. He scratched the kitten's head with the point of his finger and refused to make eye contact with Brad. He focused on the furry beast.

"That just means that Elise is an intelligent woman, not that she doesn't need a husband," Brad said. "She is capable of making her own decisions. Isn't that the kind of woman you want for a wife?"

"Well, I like to be consulted on some things. Like with the music. She didn't listen to me when I told her it wouldn't work here in Rocky Creek. She went ahead and got a ride with someone else after I told her I didn't want to take her all the time and needed the car often myself. She didn't even tell me that the plans were to clean up the hall, so we got reduced rent. She doesn't share things with me."

"You were wrong when you said the music would never work," Brad said. "Just because she wanted to join the group and do her own thing, doesn't mean that she can get along without you. You have no faith in her ability to decide for herself. She still wants a husband. There are some things that every wife needs that only a caring husband can give to her. Love, security, friendship, not to mention companionship."

"She should have asked my permission before she

made plans to run off and join an orchestra!" Tony
snapped. "Yvette would never have done anything
without asking if I minded."

"No, because Yvette's decisions were dependent
upon you entirely. What I get out of this is that Yvette
looked upon you as a parent while Elise is your equal."

"I suppose so," Tony said rather grudgingly, "I
thought of Yvette as my wife even though her needs were
more those of a child. She needed my approval, and Elise
doesn't appear to care if I approve or not."

"That doesn't make sense, and you need to realize
that Elise is not like Yvette. What you object to is that she
knows what she wants out of life and doesn't need your
permission to follow her heart. It's a good sign that she is
mature. I don't expect my wife to ask for my approval all
the time, just because we're married. I make some
decisions, of course, but I don't feel slighted if she wants
to take charge of her own life. I guard her safety and do
all the big jobs at home, and I don't allow her to lift things
too heavy for her to manage. I would fight for her if I had
to." Brad banged his fist on the desktop with such force
that Tony jumped, and the kitten ran for cover as fast as
his short little kitten legs could carry him. He peeked from
behind the trash can, one unfocused blue eye looking
warily from the shadows.

"Okay," Tony said, his voice muffled because he was
on his knees under Brad's desk coaxing the kitten to come
out from his hiding place. "I recognize that I can't solve
my problems without help. That's why I chose to see Dr.
Brown in the first place."

Brad rolled his eyes as he watched Tony carefully lift
the little ball of fluff and place him inside his Russian hat
and tuck him in like a father comforting a frightened
child. *Amazing*, he thought.

"I respect you for feeling that way," Brad said,
concentrating on anything but the kitten, "because it

shows that you understand your position. So let's discuss the old man. Do you know what he looks like?"

Tony didn't answer right away. He sat down again by the desk, deep in thought, stroking the kitten, who had already fallen asleep inside the fleece- lined hat.

After a long pause, he said, "It does seem odd that I have never seen him. What is going on?" He rubbed his forehead.

"Do you think the old man is just a voice?" Brad said, scratching his ear thoughtfully. "How do you know it is an old man? It would be difficult to say he is old if you don't know what he looks like."

"His voice sounds old. Like Frank's voice. I don't understand. I don't know what he looks like. Are you saying that I am imagining things?"

Tony jumped to his feet and glared at Brad. "What makes you think I'm losing it? I work in real estate, I own stocks and bonds, I own my home. I am successful. You're looking at me like I am a fool."

"Tony, you are definitely not a fool!" Brad protested. "I am trying to help you find out what is happening. You have been very anxious and tense, and filled with worry. You have someone who talks to you often. You can hear him even if you can't see him. Unless you have the power to go into another dimension, there has to be an explanation for it." He smiled wryly. "If he is just a voice, then Dr. Brown is the person to help you sort it all out."

Tony sat down again, took a handkerchief from his pocket and blew his nose. He shook his head repeatedly and muttered under his breath. "I don't have to take this B.S. from you!" he said, finally. "You aren't really trying to help me. You just want to prove I'm nuts. I know your type."

Brad waited for Tony to calm himself, without speaking.

"Just crazy people go around hearing things that

aren't there." Tony said. He fiddled with his belt buckle. Finally, he looked up and stared into Brad's eyes, as if waiting for an answer.

"I wish I knew, but I really don't. I think it is stress related, but I don't know for sure," Brad said apologetically. "I do know that if one is overwhelmed by anxiety, he can believe his thoughts are being spoken by another person. I have only my first year of psychology so I can't answer your questions accurately."

"I have certainly been anxious," Tony agreed, "I was worried about someone finding out my real name, especially Elise. Now both you and Elise know, it is not so bad. I mean, the world didn't come to an end." He smiled guiltily.

"That's a good sign," Brad said, with a wry grin. "However, you still need to talk it over with Dr. Brown, because you don't want the anxiety to continue. He really is the one to help you. But you are on the right track. Identifying the problem is the first step and following through is the next one. I know you can do it."

"Thanks," Tony said. He stood up and reached for his jacket. "I'd like to go home now. I need to do some serious thinking. I'm glad he didn't pee in my hat." He stroked the soft black fur before he gently lifted the sleeping kitten from his hat and placed it in his coat pocket.

The police officer sighed and looked the other way. "I'm glad too," he said, with a snort, but a smile curved his lips. "Let's go now. I'll warm up the car for a few minutes, so the kitten won't get cold, and you won't complain," he said, "I don't imagine the little guy is a big fan of winter, either. He must have been nearly frozen in that snowdrift." He slid his feet into his boots, and retrieved his official winter hat from a top shelf. "Your winter bonnet is almost the same as mine," he said jovially. "Good choice. These hats are worn by the Mounties everywhere in winter."

"Yeah," Tony said, "Elise calls this my funny hat, but it is comfortable and I like it. Little Rocky warmed it up for me," he said.

"You're lucky that's not all she did in it," Brad said, "and what makes you think Little Rocky is a boy cat? It looks like a girl to me."

"No way," Tony insisted, "a girl cat would be whimpering. He's a guy cat. Look at his broad nose, and the way his ears are low down on the sides of his face."

"That's because she is only a few days old, not weeks as you thought; even puppies are like that. Her eyes are just open but she is unable to really focus yet. It's a girl cat and she's cold. She hates winter, but she's brave and won't complain like you do," Brad teased.

"I wasn't complaining," Tony said, "Snow is fine as long it is on the mountains." He set the dark grey Russian hat evenly on his head and grinned.

"And in another province preferably," added Brad with a hearty laugh. "How do you get that thing so even on your head? It's like you used a level on it," Brad said, pointing at the hat.

"I'm a straight shooter is why," Tony said with a smirk.

"Come on, Maestro, let's get the hell out of here. I want some lunch."

"Maestro?" asked Tony, raising his eyebrows. "I wonder if I will ever be called that again?" He looked thoughtful.

"I think you will," assured Brad. "It's in the stars. And hide that black cat when you walk past the front desk, willya?"

TWENTY-NINE

Tony buttoned up the flap on his coat pocket to hide the kitten from the staff at Brad's headquarters. He smiled at Brad who was trying to be nonchalant while the two men walked past the receptionist's desk.

"C'mon, let's get you home," Brad said, trying to hurry Tony along. He appeared to want to stand around and chat.

"Yes," Tony agreed, "Elise will wonder what is taking me so long," he said, but he continued to loiter, making conversation with the receptionist.

Brad swung the door open and put his hand on Tony's shoulder, ushering him outside and toward the car.

"I'm sorry that I have to use the cruiser to take you home. I'm working a few hours after lunch today and then I want to have dinner with my wife tonight. The kids are both going skating this evening, so we'll have a rare night alone."

"That will be romantic," Tony said. He settled back in the seat and checked to see that the kitten was comfortable before pulling his coat collar snugly around his neck. The little body on his lap was warm and had quit wiggling.

Brad couldn't help grinning. "Actually," he said, "the

quiet is more what we are looking for. Romance happens; quiet must be stolen."

"We have no children, so our evenings are almost always quiet, "Tony said. "It must be difficult when you have to steal time for yourselves. I wouldn't like that. If I had married Jane, we would have had children, but Elise and I are too old to start a family now."

"You now have a cat," Brad said, "a baby cat that you will probably have to feed in the middle of the night. She is only about ten or twelve days old."

"How do you know?" asked Tony, "I thought you disliked cats."

"I don't dislike cats, except in my car when I am working. I am not supposed to take animals to work. Not even a dog. I was just worried about that. I know she's young because her eyes are not focusing very well yet. It's like she opened them only a few hours ago. They are still blue, and she can't really see yet."

"Do you think so?" Tony said. He undid his coat buttons and checked on the kitten again. "He sure sleeps a lot, but I thought he was almost three or four weeks old. If he is that young, he won't be eating solid food yet. His owners must have thrown him out to die in the cold. Who could do that?"

"People do things to unwanted animals, but maybe the door was left open for a minute and she slipped outside without anyone noticing," Brad explained. "It may not have been a case of just tossing her out to die."

Brad thought to himself, *The wee kitten is probably too young to have managed to travel so far away from his home but Tony will just stress if I tell him what I think really happened. Maybe she is one of a larger litter? Where are the others? The little one is safe now and that is the only important thing.*

"Well, he will have a good home with us. Elise will take care of him."

"What if she doesn't want a cat?" Brad asked.

"Elise would never treat an animal badly," Tony said, "I know she will want it."

"I would like to see her reaction," Brad said, with a nod of his head, "It will be like bringing a new baby home. You can call her from here. She might appreciate getting a phone call from you to let her know you are bringing a kitten home."

"She'll be fine with it," insisted Tony.

"Okay, it's your call," Brad said, letting the subject drop. "We will have to meet one more time."

"How come?" asked Tony, his annoyance threatening to overflow again. "I thought our interviews were all finished. I am sick of having all these appointments. Will there be an end to it soon? I don't feel as if I am in charge of my own life anymore. Are you still trying to prove I am either a criminal or insane?" He uttered several maledictions that caused Brad to come to his own defense.

"The interviews about who you are, and were, are finished. We have to find out if you took all the legal steps when you married Elise. Those things could cause you problems in the future. Things like getting your old age pension and stuff like that. I have an easier way of finding out things than you probably do, so let me help you."

Tony calmed down somewhat, "You know," he said, "I am worried about the change-of-name being legal." He stroked his chin thoughtfully and sounded more subdued than usual. "I did put in the application, but I was moving around a lot in those days so I'm not one hundred percent sure if it went through. I was very impatient, too. Drinking too much, maybe."

"That's what I want to find out. It will help a lot when you know for sure everything is legal. And if some steps were missed, we can easily fill in the blanks. It's easy when you know all the moves. We can do that after Christmas."

Tony noticed the kitten seemed very restless. "What's wrong with Little Rocky," he said. "Do you think he wants out of my hat?"

Brad leaned toward him and peered into the hat Tony was now using as a cradle, instead of his pocket. "Come on, Papa, let's get his child home," he advised. "She needs her dinner. I hope Elise knows what to feed her. I think maybe she has to go to the bathroom. She seems restless."

Tony stroked the furry little creature, but it seemed unable to get comfortable. "Do you think he is afraid of the car?" he asked Brad.

"I doubt it," Brad said. "She is too young to notice much, and when we drove here it didn't appear to pay much attention to the movement of the car. Perhaps nature is going to make a call. "

Tony lifted the kitten and looked curiously underneath him.

"Oops!" exclaimed Brad. "Tony, grab some paper towels from the box under your seat. Put them under the little creature," he said with a chuckle. "I have to concentrate on my driving, or we'll slip off the road into the ditch."

"Okay," muttered Tony, leaning over to pull the box out and extract a couple of sheets from it.

"I think we got it before the widdle got the lining of your hat too wet," Brad said, "but let's get her to your place right away. It was bound to happen sooner or later."

"Where's Elise when I need her?" Tony lamented.

"You'd better wonder if she knows how to wash your Russian hat without the colour running!"

Tony was sure that Elise was looking out the window overlooking the driveway when Brad drove in. She probably heard the unmistakable sound of the cruiser coming to a full stop.

Yes, there she was at the window

I'll bet she is trying to see what I'm carrying in my Russian hat instead of wearing it on my head. She'll wonder why it's filled with paper towels, too.

Tony unlocked the door and came up the stairs very quietly, rather than rushing up two steps at a time as he usually did.

Tony crept into the kitchen holding his hat close to his body, not even complaining bitterly that Canada was the coldest place on earth. He even forgot to tell her how much better the climate was in England. Instead he gave her a shy smile.

"What have you got in there under all those paper towels?" Elise asked, giving him a peck on the cheek.

"Something special," he whispered, "and you'll never guess. Somebody tried to freeze this little guy to death in the snowbank by the orchards on Ollie's Ranch Road," he said. He came closer to her and held the hat so she could see inside it.

"What is it?" she asked, "A kitten?"

"Yes, isn't he cute? He was shivering when I picked him up. Brad said he has just opened his eyes. Someone must have thrown him out, or he escaped some way," Tony explained.

"How awful," Elise murmured. She reached inside the hat and lifted the little ball of fluff up and examined it. "He is frightened," she said. "Let's take him into the kitchen and see if he will take a bit of diluted milk. I'll call the vet for a check-up before Christmas and he'll tell us what to do. We mustn't let him die. He's so cute. I love him already."

Tony smiled a satisfied smile behind her back as he followed her into the kitchen, took a clean towel out of the drawer and spread it on the counter to put the baby on. *Elise is a pushover, too,* he thought. *I knew she would be okay with it.*

"Is he old enough to know he should use a litter

box?" she commented.

"He christened my hat in the car and we just mopped it up with paper towels. I hope you know how to wash it."

"Do you mean that you found him before you even got to Brad's office?" Elise asked. "That was hours ago. I'm surprised he held it that long." She stroked the long, unruly fur, ignoring Tony's hat completely. "Is it a boy or a girl? Looks like a girl cat to me. She's having a bad hair day." She smoothed the kitten's head gently and rubbed the tiny ears.

"A boy, I think, although Brad thought it was a girl. No wonder his hair looks messy. He was in the deep snow and so scared when I picked him up. Brad was sure worried he was going to pee on the floor in his office. Tell you what—you put some newspapers down for him and I'll nip to the general store and get some litter. We might have to teach him how to use it."

"He is too young to use a litter box yet," Elise said.

"Oh, what's he going to do? Pee on the floor?"

"He's a tiny baby. He knows nothing about litter boxes."

"Well, I will go now, and ask what we can offer him to eat and then tomorrow take him in to the veterinarian. Brad thought he was too young to be away from his mother."

"I think so, too. The reason she looks like she's having a bad hair day is because she is probably part Persian," Elise explained. "When she gets older the fur will be long and thick. Our Persian kittens looked like that until they got older and their fur thickened up. She is so cute, and I'd hate to lose her just because we don't know what to do." She looked at the clock. "The vet's office is still open so if you wait a few minutes I'll give them a call and you can pick up a bottle and some food. They have milk formula especially for kittens. Sometimes a mother cat may have five or six hungry babies, and be too weak to feed them all."

When Elise called, she was able to speak to the technician on duty. "Tony will pick up the necessary articles," she explained.

"You may not be able to look after her, Mrs. Lorenzo," the woman said. "If she's that young she shouldn't be away from her mother. But bring her in at 10:00 a.m. tomorrow," she said. "Dr. Lewis will see her. I'll send two little kitten bottles for you to try out, and an eye dropper in case she isn't strong enough to nurse. And how about a soft fabric cat carrier? The kitten could sleep in it at night and it would be warmer than the metal cage type, and better than a cardboard box. It has a solid bottom in it," the technician suggested.

Before Tony left the house, Elise said to him, "I think this little cat is dehydrated from lack of milk." She pressed the tip of her index finger against his head, noting that the skin remained depressed when she moved her finger away.

"Oh, no!" Tony said, "Does that mean he will die?"

"No, but it does mean *she* may have been away from her mother for longer than you think. "

"How come you keep saying 'she' and "her'? It is a boy cat."

"I don't know what gender she is because it is hard to tell this young. However, dehydration is an important issue, and we need to get some liquid into this little body right away, so off you go," Elise said, pushing him to action.

"What shall we do?" Tony asked, looking worried. His face drooped as he reached out and touched the tiny face.

"I have a couple of eye droppers so I'm going to get started while you are away. I'll feed the baby some warm water just to keep it from getting really dehydrated," Elise said. "Hurry, Tony and get there before the vet closes the office for the night."

Tony grabbed his jacket at the bottom of the stairs as he ran through the garage and out to the car parked in the driveway. Elise smiled when she heard the door slam, and Tony start the motor.

As soon as Tony left the house, Elise quickly found everything she needed and prepared a glass of clean, lukewarm water for the kitten.

"Come on, little kitten," she said, picking the baby up and stroking the fur. "This won't have too many calories in it, but it will be good for you until Tony comes back with the milk. Oh, no, don't cry! I know, your little tummy is hurting. There, now — it will soon be all better." She wrapped the little one in a small hand towel, and cuddled her.

She held the kitten in her left hand and with her right hand put the eye dropper so it was just touching the kitten's tiny lips. Tears came to Elise's eyes and ran down her cheeks as she gently eased the warm water into the kitten's mouth. Tiny sharp claws dug into her hand as the kitten tried to knead her skin to encourage the milk to flow.

The poor little thing would have starved or frozen to death out there in the cold if Tony hadn't rescued her. This baby will live, she decided. Against all the odds of its survival, this little miracle would live.

More than two inches of snow had fallen since Tony left home that morning, but the temperature had risen somewhat since then, which meant the snow would melt in the daytime and freeze again at night, making driving treacherous.

He drove carefully back to the town centre and went into the clinic where they were waiting for him with a package of kitten food, eyedroppers and two kitten-size bottles.

The veterinary technician, next in line to the veterinarian himself, had said not to be disappointed if the kitten did not survive. It was risky to even try to save a kitten that young. She even suggested that it might be more humane to put him to sleep right away. Tony was horrified. He paid for the bottles and formula and dashed out to the car to get home as quickly as possible.

It was already icy and treacherous. Tony was glad he had rescued Little Rocky before the weather turned really cold. He rushed home as quickly as the bad winter road conditions permitted, wondering what he would find when he arrived home.

The first thing the little kitten did after having a full stomach of kitten formula was to wet on Tony's lap.

"Look what your cat did to me." Tony shrieked as he leaped up. "Now I'll have to send these pants to be dry-cleaned and they smell of cat pee." He looked pathetic as he held the kitten at arm's length with its feet and head dangling. Elise couldn't stop chuckling while she rescued both Tony and the little fur ball from each other.

"Stop that! It isn't funny!'

"It is, too," Elise said, laughing even harder. "Little Rocky just became Roxy. She is a girl."

"How do you know that?" asked Tony indignantly.

"Because I looked when I was cleaning her up while waiting for you to come back. She couldn't help wetting on you. Her little tummy isn't big enough to hold all that liquid and she is just a baby. She is too young to have any control, and you will have to get used to it."

"Ugh!" Tony said, "How long is this going to go on?" he asked, holding the wet patch away from his body. He pursed his lips and frowned.

"Until she learns how to use the cat litter box, she will wet her bed like any other baby. She has no mother to take care of her and we can't put diapers on her so when

you pick her up make sure to put a towel on your lap.
Now run and get changed and I'll take care of her."

"A girl, eh? It figures," he said as he made a quick
exit.

Elise didn't answer but she glared at his retreating
back. "What a sexist creep. Sometimes I wonder what I
ever saw in him." She mouthed the words to his
departing back.

He dashed up the stairs to change his clothes. When
he returned a few minutes later he had fully recovered
from the experience and wanted to see if Roxy was okay.

"I hope I didn't scare her when I jumped up," he said,
"I didn't expect her to wet on me."

"With her tummy full, she is too groggy to worry too
much. After she finished eating, I burped her like a
human baby and got up a bubble. It was the cutest little
burp you ever heard," Elise said. "She is adorable."

"And so helpless," Tony added, looking into the new
cat carrier that would be her bed for the next few weeks.

"The poor little soul has a lot to learn," Elise
explained, "and she is tired now and has already fallen
asleep. Roxy got over it and I hope you did, too. We may
have to feed her with an eyedropper for a couple of days
because she is not strong enough yet to suck from the
bottle."

"Isn't it just like being fed from her mother?" asked
Tony.

"Not quite," Elise told him, "The hole in the nipple
may need to be made larger with a hot needle."

"You know how to do that?" he asked.

"Sure, I do."

"Roxy is a good name," Tony said, "I like it. A
feminine version of Rocky."

"While she is asleep, we could decorate the tree,"
Elise suggested. "She probably won't bother it this year
because she will sleep until it's time to feed her again. She

will be like this for the next three weeks at least. When she gets stronger we will have to keep an eye on her all the time."

"When will she be able to drink from the bottle?" Tony asked.

"A couple of days," Elise explained. "It depends upon how many feedings she missed from the time she was outside until you brought her home. It doesn't take long for a kitten so young to become weak and unable to nurse. The rubber nipple is harder than the real one, too, but we can soften it up."

"Is that why the vet thought we couldn't look after her?"

"Yes, it takes lots of patience. I hope she doesn't remember the bad experience she had, being separated from her cat mother, being cold and hungry," Elise said. "We are her new parents now and we have to make her kitten memories good ones,"

"Oh," Tony said, wistfully. "We can do it, can't we? She won't die, will she?"

"No, dear, she won't die if I have anything to say about it," Elise said.

"I'll get the decorations from the storage room and meet you in the den," he said, looking relieved.

It was a tiny tree standing on an end table that Elise had bought at a second hand shop several years ago. She had sanded it down and applied several coats of fresh varnish. It always made her happy to turn an old piece of furniture into something new.

"Why do you bother?" Tony had asked when she proudly showed him the beautiful table. "You can have any new piece of furniture you desire," he said. "There's no reason to put all that work into some old thing. Just say the word and we can have a new table made to your specifications."

"I want this one," she said stubbornly.

"After all that sanding and varnishing you only have an old table with fresh varnish on it," he said.

"No," she said, "I have a beautiful stand for a beautiful Christmas tree. Not only is the tree special but now the stand is special, too. New isn't always better."

"I suppose you will tell me we are decorating the house just for Roxy this year?" he asked.

"She's too little to care. You said so yourself. We are decorating it for ourselves," Elise said.

"I don't really see what you are talking about. Isn't Christmas about children? Just because our child is a cat..."

"Before the Christmas season is over Roxy will be strong enough to have an interest in the tree and the dangling ornaments. She will eat anything she can get into her mouth. Tinfoil is lethal to animals," Elise explained patiently, "This table is too high for her to pull the decorations down. We could keep the door shut all the time, but then we wouldn't be able to enjoy the decorations ourselves."

"Oh," Tony said, unconvinced. When Elise left the room to prepare the two mugs of eggnog, he lifted Roxy onto the table so she could see the tree at close range, ignoring the fact that her eyes were still not focusing.

She sniffed it somewhat lethargically and with physical encouragement from Tony, poked one of Elise's hand-crafted decorations onto the floor.

Yes, she's a girl cat alright, he thought as he placed her back into her bed and went about cleaning up the pieces of the shattered ornament, hoping to hide the evidence from Elise. *A boy cat would know better.* He finished picking up the last few shards just as Elise came back with the steaming eggnog, laced with rum.

They sat together on the love seat in the den sipping from the invigorating Christmas drink.

"At approximately ten days old," Elise said, "she's not strong enough to do more than sleep, eat and wet the bed. It will be a lot of work to look after her."

"She certainly does that with a great deal of enthusiasm," Tony agreed, with a half smile. "At twelve dollars a can for the powdered stuff it will sure add up. What are the directions?"

"Add warm water and stir. I will make up enough formula for one day and warm it up for her for each feeding," Elise explained. "It will probably last for a week right now, but by the time she's six weeks old, it might only last a couple of days. Likely then it will be time to wean her and change her diet to canned meat for kittens."

Tony leaned over and looked at Roxy sleeping peacefully. "I don't think she even cares about Christmas as long as the kitten bottles are filled and we are willing to love her," he said

"She probably won't have any recollection of the cold day she spent in a foot of snow, and she might not even remember her little mother, you know," Elise explained.

"That's sad, but ignorance is bliss, I guess," Tony said. "She must operate solely on instinct. Cry when hungry, wet or uncomfortable. Do you think the experience will influence how she develops as a full-grown cat even if she doesn't actually remember it?"

"It's possible," said Elise.

Tony learned all about parenthood firsthand. He willingly got up in the middle of the night and while Elise changed the blanket in the carrier, and heated up a bottle of milk for the wee baby, Tony filled a quart jar with warm water, wrapped it in a towel and placed it in Roxy's bed to keep her warm until she cried to be fed again before daylight.

Tony also took a turn feeding her. It was awkward at first. Her sharp claws were out when she kneaded on his arm like she had probably done to encourage her mother's

210

milk to flow.

Getting simple in your old age, eh, Tony? When are you going to start dusting the furniture and sewing fancy aprons?

The voice taunted him by yelling in his ear, telling him off, and chiding him for being weak and stupid, but Tony managed to turn it off for the very first time since it started. He was busy taking care of Roxy.

"I think," Elise said to him, "you could look after her now while I go to the store. Would you mind doing that?"

"Sure," Tony agreed, "You haven't been away from Roxy for almost a week, so you should get out of the house. I'll be fine," he assured her. Under his breath, he said, "She hasn't noticed the broken decoration and I don't intend on telling her. She'll be so excited over the diamond and pearl necklace I bought for her. My taste is impeccable. She'll be blown away."

THIRTY

Elise enjoyed shopping at the General Store in Rocky Creek. Horace and John Caruthers made a special effort to provide extras for customers such as Elise Lorenzo.

John stood up when she entered the store now. "I didn't know you played the stand-up bass so good," he commented, "and that husband of yours shore surprised everyone at the concert. How long did it take him to learn to wave that stick to the music? He shore was a good actor."

"Oh, ages," Elise told him, "but Brad knows how to teach even the most difficult student."

"Well, I hope Sgt. Thomas ain't gonna give up his day job," said John, snickering, "We need him here in Rocky Crick."

"I don't think we need to worry too much about that," Elise said, "although experienced directors are not exactly a dime a dozen in Rocky Creek. He'll be around to do both jobs for a long time, I am sure. He cares about the people here," Elise said as she paid for her purchases,

"I'll carry this big box of groceries out to the car fer ya, Misses Lorenzo," John said, as he hoisted the box up in his strong arms.

"Did you enjoy the concert?" Elise asked.

"Oh, yes. Me and Horace sure enjoyed it. We don't

get much real good music here, y'know."

As they piled the groceries in the back seat, Elise thought about the concert. If only John knew the truth! "Why, thanks, John, that's very kind of you."

After he put the big box in, John began to walk away, but he stopped suddenly and said, "Wait! I gotta ask you a question. You ain't in a rush, are ya? Horace has just gone in the back door, and he can mind the store for a bit by hisself."

"What would you like to know, John?" she asked, feeling that it must be something important for him to leave his younger brother alone in the store for that long.

"What is a core-ang-glace?" John asked, pronouncing the words phonetically.

"Did you read that in the program?" she asked.

"Yep, but I dunno what it is," he said.

She thought over the question before she answered it. "Cor anglais is just a funny name for the English horn. The words are French, but the instrument is English. It's not really a horn at all. It's sort of a cross between the oboe and a bassoon. It's a double reed instrument like the bassoon, only much smaller. "

"Really?" said, John, looking somewhat vague. "Thanks," he said, "that clears things up real good. I never seen one of them played before, ya know."

"Do you play an instrument, John?"

"Not exactly," he replied, speaking slowly and carefully. "Least not good enough to play with you professionals. Sometimes I rattle a couple of spoons and people say I'm darn good, though."

"We are not professionals, John."

"You sure sounded like it to me and Horace," drawled John. "Guess I better get back to the store or my brother will be wondering if I'm tryin' to get away without working. He is only sixteen, you know."

"Brothers can be like that, but a little responsibility

might be good for him," Elise assured him. "You have a happy day, and any time you want to know something, you be sure to ask me, eh? I'll be glad to help you." John went back to the store, stopping to wave a cheery good-bye before he opened the door and went inside.

Twenty minutes later Elise hopped out of the car and hauled some of the smaller bags of groceries into the house. Tony hurried down the steps to the garage and carried the last large box up to the kitchen for her.

"You must have bought the whole darn store," he complained.

"Not even half of it, but John and Horace have a good selection of stuff in that store and it's quite fascinating to look it over. I saw some lovely old-style serving dishes, with lids on them, made of crockery so they can be used in the oven. John is going to put them away for me for next week"

"Are they like the ones you said your mother had?"

"Yes, I have always loved that style, I bet your mother had some just like them, too. They had lids on them, and you could use them for either cooking or serving. They are so convenient."

"I seem to remember she did," he said. "Was there anything else interesting in the store today? John has a big selection of merchandise."

"Yes, he has almost everything there. I like John and Horace. Very genuine people."

"I like them, too," Tony said. "They were at the concert."

"He said he and his brother enjoyed it. John said he played the spoons, but we were too good for him to come and play with us. He called us professionals," Elise said. "He was surprised you played the stick so well. He thought maybe you were waving it in time to the music, not that we were playing the music in time with the stick."

"Interesting," Tony said. "Did he seem as though he might like to learn how to really play any percussion instruments, like the drum or cymbals? If he likes rhythm maybe he would like to try."

"I enjoy watching the percussionists play," Elise said, "but I doubt if John even thought of learning to play any instrument properly," she said. "He may not realize one has to practice constantly to become really good player."

"Hmm," said Tony. "It takes a percussionist ages to achieve split second timing and accuracy. I wonder if the two of them could be taught drums so they could join the orchestra? If they are really interested, I am sure it can be arranged for them to have some lessons. I could set up a fund for that. It would help both students wanting to join the orchestra and teachers alike."

"That would be a wonderful project for the New Year."

Elise and Tony had agreed earlier to do *the kid thing* Christmas Eve and fill one another's stockings.

"How do we do this?" Tony asked.

"We can make our own rules," Elise explained, "but when my sister and I grew too old for Santa Claus we still wanted the stockings, so we chose names and only filled that one stocking. It was fun and we got some useful things in it.

"Where do we put them?"

"Oh, we hung our stockings at the head of the bed, but in our case, we don't have anything to hang it onto so we will just lay the stocking on the bedside table or even on the floor for the overflow items."

Tony was up bright and early Christmas morning to turn on the tree lights, and present Elise with a beautifully designed red felt stocking. He had put two Japanese oranges in the toe of the sock, some chocolate and several small gifts. At the top, near the loop to hang it up by, was a plastic and felt Santa Claus figure with a red bag on his back filled with mints. He had also included a whisk broom because he liked the red handle.

Roxy slept through Christmas morning, except to cry for her breakfast, wet her bed, eat, and go back to sleep. She didn't show any appreciation for the red bow tied to the handle of her new portable bedroom, in the soft green cat carrier. She didn't even look at the purple litter pan, and the two cans of kitten food. When Tony showed her the white double bowl cat feeder, she turned her head the other way, but she did sneeze a soft, "chuff-chuff," when presented with the felt catnip mouse. She reached out a soft black velvet paw to touch it, and Elise murmured "Aww!"

Tony grinned and nodded. "She likes it," he said. Elise rewarded him with a motherly smile.

The stocking Elise filled for him had a Japanese orange in the toe, too, a chocolate bar, a bag of Licorice All Sorts and miscellaneous items for his office, such as pens, pencils and paper clips.

Under the tree were the bigger Christmas gifts. Tony was pleased with the black bow tie, and the navy blue hand knit sweater, and he was very impressed with the gold cufflinks from Elise but when he opened his gift from Santa, Tony was puzzled.

"What on earth is this thing?" Tony asked. He held it up and frowned.

Elise chuckled. "It's a ratchet," she said. "It's part of a socket set. I thought it would be useful to you."

"Oh, thanks," he said, in a monotone. "Santa Claus must think I would know how to use it. Do you even know what it's for or did you pick it up because you thought it was cute?" He snickered.

"Of course, I know what it's for. My father always had at least one in his toolbox. The angled teeth hold another tool like a wrench or a driver, so what you are

216

trying to turn won't move in the opposite direction. It allows motion in one direction only, but it's not from me; it's from the guy in the red suit."

"Oh," said Tony, raising his eyebrows. "You are a smart cookie!"

"No," she said, "I just did as my father told me, but I still learned a lot that way."

The birdseed and the wire container of bird suet with a tag that read *from Roxy*, caused Tony to smile indulgently.

"Roxy is too young to enjoy bird watching yet," he said.

"She will soon be old enough to enjoy it. A bird feeder is kitty television," Elise said, chuckling. "It's more a gift for her than it is for you, but you get to fill the feeder."

"I wonder who gave me that?" Tony said, when he saw the bag of cat litter. "I hope I get to try it out very soon. I like the little shovel that goes with it and the natty royal blue strainer."

Elise loved the gifts Tony gave her, while he was impressed with the gold cufflinks. He noted that they were of a number of karats to be impressive.

THIRTY-ONE

When Tony received Brad's request for help in preparing for the spring concert, he was pleased, yet nervous at the same time.

"I am honored that you would call me," he said. "Under the circumstances I would not have been insulted if you had overlooked me. Is there anything specific on your mind?"

"Well, yes," Brad said. "Have you given any thought of taking over directing the orchestra? You are so much more capable of doing it well than I am."

"Heavens no!" Tony said, "It's your baby. Without you, this orchestra never would have happened. I am not ready to even think of that. Have you chosen a date for the Spring Concert yet?" he asked.

"I thought you might be interested. We could be ready for a concert on March 11th. It's the second Saturday in the month," Brad said. "I haven't even thought of a program yet, but we had better hurry up because we have to plan a rehearsal schedule."

"I could give you some conducting lessons, and then we can make some decisions together," Tony offered. "I will not be ready to take over directing for a long time. I can help, and offer suggestions, but you are doing fine so let's not make any changes just yet."

"Okay," Brad said, "I'll continue but you know I have absolutely no idea how to direct anything that is really important. The easy stuff I can do, but I am lost when it comes to the bigger works."

"You are much better than you think," said Tony. "You have some very good ideas, and with help you will develop directing skills. It will be a challenge for us both."

"I would enjoy that. You are very generous. I guess *New World* was not really a practical choice for our first concert," Brad said. "I didn't have the courage before today to talk about what happened at the concert in December. I am still embarrassed."

"*New World* was not only a challenge for you to direct but it was too difficult for a new orchestra to play, although they did well, thanks to Cynthia's experience," Tony told him. "With more time it will not be beyond the musicians and with training you'll be surprised how easy it will be to direct. I am willing to give you some conducting lessons. The next time you conduct it, you will feel secure." He filled his coffee cup for the third time. "I can give you some advice on pieces suitable to play, too. Do some popsy pieces that everyone knows, and add in some classics as time goes on, to get them accustomed to hearing more serious music. Sometimes you can mix and match and come up with a better concert." He studied Brad's face as he drank his last cup of coffee of the evening.

"That's a great idea!" Brad exclaimed, "I feel better about it already and I accept your offer of lessons. I am one lucky sod," he said, chuckling. "You are right, music I know would be easier for me to learn on. I've been like a kid. I wanted to have everything at once."

"Programming is an art," Tony said. "If I am really serious about going back into the music scene, I need someone to practice on. You can be my guinea pig."

"How lucky can this guinea pig be?" Brad said, "If

the newspaper picks it up the headline will read *Former director of the Leeds Classic Orchestra chooses Sgt. Bradley Thomas as his piggy.*"

The two men had become fast friends in the weeks following the Christmas concert. Now they sat together at Brad's old farmhouse talking about the spring concert coming up. Sitting at the spacious, but unpretentious dining room table, they had chatted well into the night.

"I had better go home," said Tony, "I did not warn Elise I might be this late."

"She'll forgive you."

With a lot of back slapping, guffaws and various piggish snorts, the two men parted company. Tony jumped into his car and drove straight home. He knew Elise probably wouldn't have waited up for him. Tony said a belated prayer just in case.

THIRTY-TWO

The week went by quickly and it felt as though Spring was just around the corner even though there was fresh snow on the ground. Daytime temperatures had warmed up considerably and seed packages were displayed in the grocery stores already. The local nursery had a window filled with baby tomato plants, and Tony was certain he'd heard a robin's admonition to cheer up that very morning.

He wasn't sure why he felt so elated after dinner, but as he tripped down the basement stairs on happy toes, he felt an excitement he hadn't experienced for years. Nothing had really changed in his life, but he felt a sense of relief that cancelled out most of the stress he had endured for so long.

He still slept on the couch in the den, his feet still hung over the end, and Elise still refused to accept him until she had proof he was really Antonio Lorenzo, the man named in their marriage contract. He tried to convince her that she was married to the man, not necessarily his name and it was legal, but she was not in the mood to listen.

"Do you not think," he asked her, "that you are carrying this thing way too far and making it more complicated than it really is?"

Elise replied a stubborn, "No."

221

"Then," he said, "there is not much I can do about it. We just have to wait." He turned his face from her and grimaced toward his feet so she couldn't see the frown.

It was true; until Brad received the letter from Statistics Canada saying they had already acted upon his change of name application, Tony had no way of knowing whether he was legally Tony Lorenzo or still Richard Lawrence. Ten years ago, he had been too busy trying to survive on the street to check out his status or to pick up his mail. It was his own fault that he had moved often and used a string of aliases so nobody could trace him.

He had been told that the marriage was legal but if Elise had any doubts, he realized she was not the kind of woman to hide them. He felt sure she had no desire to burn her brassieres to prove she was liberated, like a group of women in Vancouver had done recently, but she was a straight shooter. The good news was that she had only moved him out of the bedroom, not out of the house.

***

As soon as dinner was finished, he put on his warm work gloves and his Russian hat and went outside to clean up the driveway for what he hoped was the last time this winter. The wind tugged at the chin straps, flapping them back and forth until he tied the laces firmly under his chin.

The new-fallen snow was dry and sparkling, just right for making snowballs. He leaned on his shovel to watch a group of kids playing in the vacant lot next door. They had built a sturdy snow fort and were busily stockpiling snowballs. That meant a good fight was scheduled shortly. The pile was getting higher and higher with each added layer. A good twenty feet away another fort was being built. By the opponents, he guessed. There was little activity in the second fort but a lot in the one next door to his driveway.

He wondered if Elise would enjoy playing in the

222

snow, now she was grown up. He knew he wouldn't like it one bit. So juvenile. But then again. . .

Even if he felt he shouldn't have to shovel snow, the only way it was going to be cleared was if he grabbed the shovel and went at it.

If he played his cards right, in another year he might be famous again. Then he would hire somebody to shovel the snow for him. Perhaps he wouldn't be able to handle fame any better now that he did ten years ago, though.

However, none of this was going to change the fact that his wife refused to sleep with him until she knew she was married to him. He was mighty sick of sleeping in the den.

Once upon a time. . . women wanted to sleep with him, but that was another time. He shouldn't even be thinking of those days.

He began to think of snowballs. When he was younger, he had loved playing in the snow. The kids were having so much fun that he almost imagined himself right in there throwing a few too. But no, he was not going to lower himself to that level.

Oh, I suppose you think you're too good for snowballs, Mr. Fancy-pants.

Tony looked over his shoulder. Who said that? It was the same voice that had taunted him for years. It had been silent for a couple of weeks. In fact, he realized the voice didn't taunt him as often now as it had done a long time ago.

It was still an unpleasant voice but less accusatory than it used to be. He looked around, half hoping someone was there, but afraid that Brad and Dr. Brown were right, and it really was his own tortured thoughts after all. He gripped the shovel with both hands and breathed deeply in an effort to calm himself.

"I am no longer worried, and you can go to hell," he said aloud to the voice. Only the North wind wailed in reply. He shuddered and a nerve in his right cheek fluttered. He shook his fist angrily and said, "I know what I want out of life and I intend to get it. So get lost."

Tony imagined he heard a whisper as the wind blew one more gust before it departed.

The air was quiet. Even the shouting from next door had stopped shattering the evening air. He wondered if the kids had abandoned their new fort. How odd that they would have worked so hard during the last hour to build such a sturdy fort just to leave it unused. It was a good fort. He liked its construction. The walls were thick and strong, built to withstand an evening of youthful tumbling and mock fighting. What a waste to abandon a strong fort like this! Somebody should pay attention to it.

Ten minutes passed. It was so quiet that the clink of his metal-handled shovel startled him as he leaned it against the side of the house. He walked over to the fort and looked inside it.

"Oh, oh!" he exclaimed as three boys jumped out of the shadows and yelled in unison, "Hi, Mr. Lorenzo!"

"Just wondered where you were," he said, trying to cover up his embarrassment. "Well, you guys have fun. Must be nice to be a kid." A big smile spread over his face. *Caught red-handed.*

"It is," the middle-sized boy said. Tony thought he recognized him as the one who had delivered the flyer advertising the formation of the orchestra. It was so long ago, a year at least.

Tony thought, *I wonder if he remembers how rude I was to him when I told him to go away.*

He held his ears as the yelling and shouting started up again and got louder and louder as the snowball fight got into full swing.

He headed back to his own driveway and began shoveling fast to get the job done so he could escape from the screaming group of kids. Soon it turned into an urgent desire to run away and hide.

Such a racket! Do they have to scream? Why do kids think they have to shout when they are having fun?

Snowballs flew through the air with reckless abandon. The kids yelled with excitement and their laughter was even louder than before. The guffaws of the boys and the giggles of the girls were filled with youthful exuberance. Tony almost envied them.

He went back to work and forced himself to ignore the kids, but he had a difficult time ignoring the snowballs that came closer and closer to him. When a wet one hit him in the back of the neck he was startled, yet not suprised it had happened. Feeling the cold, icy fingers of winter running under his collar made him angry for about ten seconds. He opened his mouth to shout a threat—but then he hesitated. The kids were not being vindictive; they were just having fun. It may even have been an accident. He decided to give them the benefit of the doubt.

The group retreated. He chuckled to himself when he saw them peering around the entrance to the fort. Their actions reminded him of Roxy.

He mused, *They think I'm angry. Well, I bet I can still throw a good snowball.* He relished the thought.

"Come out here and fight like men!" he roared, even though he detected some girlish voices mingled with the male fighters.

The Voice butted into his thoughts, momentarily holding him hostage.

You miserable old man! Still wallowing in self-pity. Why didn't you jump over that cliff last summer? You'd be free of that money-grabbing Elise.

"No!" he hollered, his voice lost in the shouts coming from the fort.

You miss Yvette. Admit it. I can take you to her any time you want. See that car coming down the hill? Go jump in front of it. Yvette waits for you.

"Yvette was a wonderful wife," he said aloud, "but she is in heaven now. She would want me to stay here and enjoy my life. Yvette does not want me to join her in death."

He was sure he heard a wail as the wind changed direction. He stood still and listened. It was quiet. Where were the kids?

He threw down his shovel and trudged through the snow again and presented himself at the fort entrance. "What's wrong with you guys?" he roared into the cavern. He waited and listened. *They're plotting*, he thought. As he walked away, he called out, "Don't tell me this good fort is going to be wasted on a bunch of sissies?"

A snowball hit the side of the garage above his head and exploded in a rainbow of opal and emerald crystals.

"About time I got some action from you guys!" he yelled, as he brushed the snow away from his eyes and nose. He scooped up a large handful of snow and expertly rolled it into a perfect snowball, round, hard and shining. He pelted it at the largest boy, followed by another and another until he was right in the middle of the best darn snowball fight of his life. He felt the tension of the past two weeks drop from his shoulders. He laughed, and he guffawed, and he chuckled like a kid. He even shouted. It felt good to shout.

Tony caught a shaft of light coming from a window overlooking the driveway. Elise must have heard the shouting all the way from inside the house and had opened the drapes to get a better view.

There was no time to wonder because a snowball zinged through the air, and smashed to smithereens by his feet. He noticed that two boys and a girl had joined him on his side of the drive, so he concluded that he had his own warriors. Magically a supply of ready-made snowballs ended up on his side too. He was impressed —

the kids were going to play fair after all. They were not only sharing their warriors but their ammunition as well. He knew all along they were good kids.

He thought briefly about being his old pompous self, but the moment passed as quickly as it came. Pompous behaviour wasn't working for him anymore. Instead he made a huge soft snowball and threw it with force at the biggest boy, the one he felt sure had thrown the first one at him. It exploded in a mass of glistening diamonds as light from the rising moon splashed across it.

When the streetlights came on, the kids seemed to know it was the signal to go home for dinner. One by one they looked for their belongings in preparation to leave the fight.

Someone declared that he had lost a glove. A scurry as several boys and a couple of girls were down on their hands and knees searching for the lost article. Tony enthusiastically dug and scraped the snow away as he joined in the hunt. It became a challenge to be the first one to find the glove.

"I found it!" he shouted, waving it over his head.

He never did know how it happened but with lightening quickness he was at the bottom of a dogpile, laughing and jostling for position. Snow flew in every direction. When he got a mouthful of it, he just spat it out and wiped his face on his scarf. When his hat disappeared, he didn't even get upset when someone shoved a girl's toque on his head.

"Hey, who belongs to this?" he called out, as he yanked it off and waved it over his head, the blue pompoms swinging back and forth as if beckoning their owner.

"I think it's Joanne's," somebody yelled. "She wears pompoms."

"Good, they don't suit me!"

"Doesn't go with your beard," remarked a male

227

voice, chuckling loudly.

A shrill whistle pierced the winter air as a father somewhere called for his children to come home.

"That's my dad," said a voice, "I have to go home right now. See ya tomorrow, guys." One by one the warriors gathered up their things and headed for home. until Tony thought he was alone.

He sat in the snow and savoured the moment. Getting up on all fours, he looked around curiously before standing up.

He found his shovel right where he had tossed it. He threw it over his shoulder, carried it into the garage and hung it on a peg by the door.

When a small boy covered with snow stuck his head around the doorway, Tony was startled.

"Mr. Lorenzo," he said shyly, "I came back to ask you if you'll be able to come out and play again tomorrow?"

"You're darn tootin' I will," Tony answered with a grin. "Why don't you just call me Tony? It's much easier to say than Mr. Lorenzo. What's your name, young feller?"

"Jimmy," the boy said.

"Would you like me to drive you home, Jimmy?"

"Nope, I just live over there," Jimmy said. He pointed to a house with a Christmas tree still on the balcony. "Bye, Mr. Tony. We had fun, didn't we?"

"Yep," said Tony. He had never said *yep* before. It had a nice ring to it.

He walked to the end of the driveway with Jimmy and watched the boy trudge through the snow and cross the road to his house. As he approached his door, Jimmy turned and waved goodbye.

Tony walked slowly back up the drive toward the house with twenty-four windows. He felt certain he had passed the hardest test of all.

It was an honour to be accepted as a friend by a small

boy.

THIRTY-THREE

It was February when Tony received a call from Brad that a letter from Statistics Canada addressed to Tony, had arrived in his mail bag at the Police Station. Tony hung up the phone and sat down at the table to finish breakfast.

"Who was that?" Elise asked as she refilled her coffee mug.

"Brad," he said, holding his mug out to her for a refill, too. "He's finally received the letter from Victoria regarding my change of name paperwork. He wants me to come to his office and pick it up."

They sat together without speaking while Tony squared up his place mat and cutlery. He chewed in silence until he had eaten two pieces of toast. He got up and paced the floor, still ruminating thoughtfully.

"I hope it's good news. It's lonely sleeping by myself on that damn couch in the den." he complained. "My long legs hang over the end and I can't get comfortable." He looked straight at Elise and focused on her forehead.

"I agree," she said, without wavering. She leaned in and planted a kiss on his ear. "My feet get cold in our big bed, too. What if it isn't good news and we still have no proof we are married to each other?"

"He has all the connections," Tony answered. "It's been nearly three months since I told you about it. It has to be good news."

"Can you imagine how long it would have taken if you'd tried to do it on your own?" she asked.

"Probably another ten years. Even with Brad helping me, I still had to pay for two searches to be done. It was a real mess." He glugged the coffee down in one big gulp, took his dishes to the kitchen and set them on the counter. "Brad is very thorough so I see no reason why the news would be anything but good," he called over his shoulder as he walked away.

"Well, don't be too long. The tension is killing me."

"Tonight's the night," he promised. "Brad says It is in an official brown envelope and the stamp is on straight, so it looks authentic." He shrugged into his coat, picked up his briefcase and walked out the door.

"A good sign," she said throwing him a kiss.

***

When Tony arrived at Brad's office, he was carrying an odd shaped box. He plunked himself down on a chair and parked the box in the corner.

Brad studied the parcel carefully. "You must be excited," he said.

"I am," Tony said. He stood up and stretched before he walked over to Brad's desk, shifting from one foot to the other, barely curbing his desire to snatch the letter off the desk and rip it open. He hadn't realized how anxious he was until it he saw it within his reach.

Brad picked up the letter, swishing it like a fan, punctuating each word with a wave of his hand, "This...could...change...your...life," he said. Slowly, teasingly, he held out the long official envelope to Tony.

Brad studied Tony's expression as he read the letter. He glanced at the parcel standing upright against the wall. "Good news, Tony?" he asked.

"It's over, and I am officially Antonio Johhann

Lorenzo. I'm relieved," Tony said.

When Tony dropped into the chair, an explosive laugh escaping from his usually reserved demeanor, Brad leaped up and pumped Tony's hand. "Congratulations," he said.

"I can't tell you how pleased I am," Tony said. "Besides which, that bloody couch I've been sleeping on the past three months seems to get smaller every night. Last night I damn near ended up on the floor."

"It must have been difficult for you," Brad said, covering his grin with the back of his hand. "It's a load off my mind too. You do realize you could have been in a bucket-load of trouble if we'd neglected to look into that?"

"It came as a surprise to me when you told me I could have been a suspect in my own alleged murder by leaving a trail of aliases and addresses," Tony said.

"There could have been a lengthy investigation with media coverage. Not every day does a guy get convicted of his own murder." Brad shook his head in amazement. "How did you come up with the new names?" he asked. "My imagination wouldn't be nearly as good as yours.

"Antonio was my second name, and the other names I used are just ancestral family names."

"Are you of Spanish origin?" Brad asked. "I only browsed through the information you gave me before I sent it in, but I remember you were born on Foulness Island, off the south coast of England." Brad said. He leaned back in his chair, and tapped his fingers on the desk.

"Granny lived on Foulness," Tony explained. "Papa was born in England of Italian heritage, and Mama was from a tiny village called Castel Grande in Italy. Very close to Mt. Vesuvius. Lorenzo was Papa's family name before it was anglicized to Lawrence. My first language was Italian. Both countries are where music was first developed."

"So you just went back to the original name," Brad said. "Congratulations. I can contact the authorities in Britain to let them know Richard Lawrence is alive, living under a different name."

"It had not entered my mind the way I did this made me a suspect in his disappearance," he said.

"Your name is cleared. Now you can go on with your life the way you want to."

"Thanks, Brad. I appreciate all you have done for me and I think I might even forgive Jane Morrow for jilting me. She probably does not give a damn, and has not thought of me for years, of course." He laughed ruefully.

"Are you going to tell her?"

"Heavens, no. It's just for my own satisfaction. She may not even remember who I am now," he said.

"She probably credits you with helping to launch her career. That must be a satisfaction to you."

"It is," Tony agreed.

Brad was still looking at the box Tony had carried in. "Hey," he said, "aren't you going to show me what's in the funny box? Where did it come from?"

"I picked it up at the Bus Depot on my way here."

"Oh, it came by Greyhound," Brad said. "Tell me what it is before I open it myself. It looks like a machine gun, but even you wouldn't be so brash as to bring one here," he said, the familiarity of a special friendship affording him the luxury of borderline rudeness.

"Just paying you back for the suspense you put me through before you gave me the letter," Tony said. He picked up the long box. "Do you have a pair of scissors? They put enough packing tape on this thing to send it all the way to Europe and back."

"Where did it come from?" Brad handed him a long letter opener. He leaned over and peered at the return address on the parcel. "Vancouver?" he asked.

"Yes," Tony answered, as he cut off the tape, and

with a flare, whipped off the lid to reveal a black leather case with silver clasps.

"The case is handsome," said Brad, coming closer to look. "Why, you clever old dog! I do believe you bought yourself a musical instrument. What is it?"

"A viola! I wanted you to know about it first. I am planning a surprise for Elise tonight. We have a dinner date." He opened the case and took off the blue satin bag covering the instrument. "It's very old, made in Germany in 1814. I had it appraised, and then I had a Luthier set it up with new strings and clean it up. Isn't it a beauty?"

"How come you got an old one?" asked Brad, frowning. "Surely you would have rated a nice new shiny instrument?" He watched as Tony held it in his arms as if it were a baby. "What's a Luthier?" he asked.

Tony laughed. "A violin maker. Old is better, when it comes to hand crafted musical instruments."

"Oh," said Brad, backing up a step. "How much is this worth?"

"I paid twelve thousand dollars for it, U.S. funds," said Tony. "It was a steal."

"At that price it should play itself," Brad said.

"It takes a lot of skill to play a viola."

"Are ya gonna play it for me?" asked Brad. The tension had leaked away from the room after reading the letter. The two men stood comfortably in one another's presence.

"I'm not sure I remember how to play it," Tony said.

"Oh, come on, just a little tune, eh?"

"I haven't touched a viola for, well over ten years. I sold my beautiful instrument before I left England, and I can't tell you how that hurt me," Tony said. "I couldn't bear to touch another viola all those years. I do not yet have a shoulder pad to soften the hardness of the wood against my shoulder, but I am glad it came with a chin rest."

234

"Do you want to borrow my scarf?" asked Brad, coming closer to have a better look.

"Yes, please," Tony said, stalling for time. He watched as Brad got his wool scarf from the coat closet.

After deliberating as long as he could to delay the demonstration, he folded the scarf into a cushion and laid it over the bony part of his shoulder before bringing the viola up under his chin.

The magical moment when he drew the bow across the strings was ambushed when Brad shuddered and exclaimed, "That's awful! Can't you do better than that?"

Tony laughed. "I hope so eventually," he said. "I did warn you. I have to tune it up before I try to play anything."

Brad watched with interest. "Will that make a difference?" he asked.

"Probably not," Tony said, with a crooked grin. "Ten years is a long time."

He took his time turning the pegs, and plucking the strings one after another. He cocked his head to one side as he listened to the sound before the tuning was accomplished to his satisfaction. "I should be able to turn the tuning pegs and bow the strings at the same time, but I will not be able to do that just yet. I haven't the strength in my neck muscles to hold this heavy instrument. It takes lots of practice to develop that kind of strength."

"Play us a tune," Brad insisted. "I want to hear what it sounds like."

"I will be rusty," Tony said, still trying to delay the inevitable, "You may not want to hear me play anything just yet. You expect miracles."

"Stop making excuses. If you can tune it, why can't you play it?" inquired Brad.

"That's the easy part," Tony explained. "With practice I will be able to play something. I can't even depend upon muscle memory anymore. It's too soon."

"What's muscle memory?" Brad scrunched his brow at the unusual phrase.

"It is when the fingers appear to remember certain moves after some years of study. They call the groups of notes *riffs* because the patterns appear in many pieces of music. Musicians memorize the note patterns because they occur so often. You must have heard the term *riffs* when you conducted the jazz band."

"Yeah, but I thought it just applied to saxophone and clarinet music in jazz."

"No, to all kinds of music. Even Beethoven used the technique." He opened the case as if he planned to replace the viola in it.

Brad put his hand on Tony's arm. "You were gonna play something for me," he reminded Tony.

"Are you sure?"

"You can do it," insisted Brad.

He watched as Tony carefully rubbed a bronze-coloured stone on the bow hairs.

"What's that stuff?" Brad asked, leaning over to get a better look.

"What stuff? Oh, you mean the rosin? You must have seen Elise rosin her bass bow at rehearsals. Haven't you noticed all the violin players rosining their bows before rehearsals commence? Rosin makes the bow cling to the strings. Otherwise it would just glide over them without making any sound at all."

"Oh, yeah, I do remember seeing that. I guess I just didn't pay much attention."

Finally, Tony lifted the instrument to his chin and haltingly scratched out something that vaguely resembled the old folk tune, *Twinkle Twinkle Little Star.*

"Oh, I recognize that one!" Brad said. "How come it sounds like you're scratching on a chalk board? Is that how the viola is supposed to sound? It looks like a big violin, but it sounds dreadful." He winced as if in pain.

"No," Tony said, "I just need to practice. Aren't you going to applaud my efforts?"

Brad did a couple of dutiful claps. "That's all you're getting," he said.

"Thank-you, thank-you!" Tony bowed low with an exaggerated flourish, much to Brad's amusement.

"That tune is said to have been composed by Mozart," Tony said.

"You do the curtain call well," Brad said, "Can you curtsey, too?"

"No, girls curtsey. Guys just do a slight bend from the waist. It is part of the Suzuki method of teaching. Students copy what they see and hear. They learn by example."

"There is a Suzuki piano method, too, so I have heard of it. I would think the kids get bored."

"No. We teach little ones to listen to sounds and try to make similar sounds at the first lesson. Children taught by this method are comfortable playing in public because stage presence is practiced right from the beginning. Bowing to the audience is very important. Funny, but that word *bowing* means to accept the audience's praise is spelled the same as *bowing* which means to use the bow to make a sound on a violin, but the two words are not pronounced the same."

"Isn't that confusing?"

"No, it doesn't seem to be," Tony said. "Dr. Suzuki was very specific about teaching manners to his little musicians."

"Who is Dr. Suzuki?"

"A music teacher in Japan who used a totally different approach to music, and even taught little kids who couldn't read music at all."

"Really? How did he do that?"

"He taught music exactly the same way we teach little ones to talk. It is the language of love. The child would be encouraged to listen to a song and to mimic

237

each note on a tiny violin. The child listens to the sound and the rhythm rather than trying to read and transfer symbols to an instrument. It's much easier than the traditional method. Of course, at some time the child learns to read music," Tony explained.

Just then, the office door flew open and Brad's secretary peeked in. She looked worried.

"What are you two doing in here?" she demanded, her eyes on the viola. "Were you trying to play that thing?" she asked, pointing her finger at it. "Sounded like you were torturing something." She turned to Brad and asked, "What should I tell the rest of the staff out there? They want an explanation for the terrible squealing that was going on in here."

"Don't worry about it, Laura," Brad explained, laughing. "He was just showing me what Dr. Suzuki taught him. He says he needs to practice. What do you think?"

"I'd say so. Are you finished?" she asked, "Maurice was going to call 911. We all thought you were getting killed in here."

"Don't worry, Tony's leaving soon," Brad said. "I'll make sure he goes quietly. You can go back to work now. And please explain why Maurice was going to call 911 when you are already in the police station."

"It just seemed the thing to do," she said, backing hastily out of the office. She closed the door behind her. Brad rolled his eyes and Tony chuckled.

Brad locked the door after her and secured the windows. "Just in case the paparazzi try to come in," he said. "Can I try it now?"

"Sure," he said, "You can't do much worse than I did."

Brad lifted the viola to his chin and clutched the bow in his right hand as if he was wielding a pool cue. He scraped it across the strings kitty-cornered, catching the bow hairs on the curved ribs of the instrument.

"Stop!" Tony said, as he hastily rescued his viola. He clipped away the damaged hairs of his bow, using the small pair of scissors attached to his key ring.

"You better stick to waving a baton and tickling the ivories on your piano. Man, was that awful."

"What does Elise think of you buying a viola?" asked Brad, when he had recovered from the embarrassing experience.

"She does not know. I wanted to tell you first because you encouraged me to go back to music again and I appreciate it."

"I am honoured," Brad said. "What's your game plan? When will you tell her? She deserves your respect. She stuck with you even when she knew you weren't telling her the truth. Women instinctively know when we guys tell untruths."

Tony nodded in response. "After dinner tonight I will tell her."

"It would be very good to see Elise happy again. The last few months have shown on her face. I'm sure she will be happy to know you will join us for the next concert." Brad felt for them both.

"It may be Autumn before I am good enough for that," Tony confessed.

"That long?"

"Maybe. What will Hank and Lorraine and some of the other musicians think about me playing the viola? I think Elise will be pleased but maybe not everyone. I might take some lessons from Cynthia. I will need all the help I can get."

"Quit worrying," Brad said. "They will all be happy to welcome you and I know Elise will be overjoyed. Unless you demonstrate your current musical prowess, that is."

"Heavens no, I will not play it in public for a while

yet. Except to make Elise laugh."

"She will be relieved your change of name is complete. Make your evening into a romantic date, and celebrate together," Brad advised. "These last few weeks have been rough so take advantage of the good news."

"They have been even harder than I imagined," Tony said. "We will celebrate tonight, and I intend to make every minute count."

"Do you have plans, then?" asked Brad.

"Sort of," Tony said, "but I think what we'll do is just let it happen. You know, play it by ear?"

"If you are serious," Brad told him solemnly, "I think you need to start playing it by music."

"Who asked you?" murmured Tony.

"It's free advice as a bonus," Brad informed him.

THIRTY-FOUR

Tony left his boots on the shoe tray inside the garage door and slipped on his house shoes. He walked noiselessly into the adjoining laundry room and looked around for a safe place to hide the viola in the meticulous room until after dinner. The excitement was almost more than he could bear.

The case was too long for him to hide it under the towels, or in the laundry basket. "Ah," he said, "the gardening shelves!" He carefully placed it on one of the wide shelves at the end of the room. It was nearly invisible between a tabletop garden fountain and a bird bath. He stood back to admire the way the smooth stone sculptures with gold antiquing complimented the rich, black leather case.

"Perfect!" he said before he sprinted up the stairs two at a time.

Elise was standing by the stove in the kitchen stirring a large pot of spaghetti sauce while she listened to the news on the kitchen radio. Tony was unable to contain his good news any longer. Incoherently, he babbled about the result of the name change while he grabbed her and swung her unceremoniously around the kitchen.

"Slow down!" Elise exclaimed, placing a silencing finger on his lips. The spoon had flown out of her hand when Tony swept her off her feet, splattering spaghetti sauce all over the stove and the spotless floor. After she had managed to catch her breath, she washed the spoon under the faucet and cleaned the stove while Tony got down on his hands and knees to wipe the rich red sauce off the floor.

"You had better have good news, Mister, after making a mess of my kitchen," she warned. "Come and sit down and start all over again." She took his hand and led him to a chair before sitting down at the table across from him. "Okay, now tell me," she said.

"Yes, good news," he crowed. "The name-change is complete, and I am legally Antonio Lorenzo and have been for the past seven years, so I was worrying for nothing. I moved around so much I guess I- ah, I mean the -ah- the lawyer, couldn't catch up with me," he blurted. A nervous laugh followed his stuttered words. He waved the letter back and forth. "It's all right in here," he said.

"Oh, my God! Let me see it," she demanded. She grabbed the envelope from his hand and slid the letter out.

Tony straightened the placemats while she read the letter. He focused on her face as her expression went from surprise to satisfaction.

"This is the best news I have ever heard," she said, "and I am so proud of you." She pushed her chair back from the table and stood behind Tony, her arms around his shoulders. Leaning down slightly she rested her chin against the back of his neck.

"You sure are short," he said with a laugh.

"I am not–you are tall." She gave him a squeeze.

"I'm overwhelmed," Tony said. "My hands are shaking." He held them out over the table. "I keep wondering if I will suddenly wake up and find it's all a dream."

"Well, this letter should bring you back to reality,"

Elise said, as she urged him to stand up so she could hug him.

As if on cue, the radio played *The Blue Skirt Waltz*, the song that Tony and Elise had made their own five years before when they first started dating.

He asked, "Will you have this dance with me, beautiful lady?" She nodded and he led her to the centre of the floor where they enjoyed an intimate waltz. When the song ended, Elise did a pirouette on her pointed toes. He bent her backward over his arm and planted a genuine Hollywood kiss on her lips.

"You've been practicing," she said. He gave her a cheeky wink.

Roxy fled to the stairway and peeked between the turned spindles to watch the proceedings.

"She probably thinks we have lost it entirely, "Elise said through her laughter.

"Roxy might be right," Tony said. "I was worried that I was going to be charged with my own murder."

"What? How could they do that?"

"It's a long story," he said, "and if Brad had not followed my journey from then to now, it could very well have happened. My name is cleared. We should celebrate. Do you want to go out for dinner? It is too late to get a reservation, but perhaps the Hilltop Diner in Chilliwack would do a special for us."

"I could put all the food away in the freezer for another night," she said, "but I made your favourite meal and it's almost ready to eat." She stepped closer to him. "We could have candlelight and wine right here."

When he nodded, she said, "Let's eat in the dining room, just we two. This is too important to share with anyone else. I want to be alone with you." She stood on tiptoe and kissed him.

"I feel that way, too," Tony said. And he did. He realized more than ever that she was the special someone he needed in his life.

Happy tears rolled down her cheeks. He kissed them away. He drew her closer. "Thank-you for standing by me these last months. I know it hasn't been easy."

"It was worth it."

"I have another surprise for you after dinner tonight. I hope you will like it."

"What is it?" she asked. A mischievous twinkle had crept into her blue eyes.

"You'll find out after we have done all the cleanup. I hope it will make you very happy. It has been hard to keep it a secret, so I do not want to give it away yet."

"I can hardly wait," Elise said. She was smiling as she went back to the stove.

"I hope I can," he said, unable to believe how his life had changed since he'd opened up to her.

Tony looked forward to his dinner date with Elise of candle-light and wine, and wonderful food. He was excited that she wanted to celebrate alone with him, but he wondered, with some trepidation, what she would say when he played the viola for her later that evening. Well, scratched a tune on it anyway.

That will certainly add to the surprise. *I have not played for ten years.* As the old saying goes, *If you do not use it, you lose it* is definitely true when it comes to music. This evening should be interesting.

THIRTY FIVE

The round oak table was beautifully laid with two Royal Albert table settings, Pinwheel crystal champagne flutes and wine goblets. A single yellow rose in a tiny crystal vase stood to the right of each place mat. A golden candelabrum was in the center, three tall white candles flickered seductively.

Tony escorted Elise to the table on his arm and pulled out her chair. He waited for her to be seated before he slid her chair in and then took his place across from her.

"I'm glad we took the leaves out of the table. It is so cozy and intimate this way. You have truly set out a feast for us. I was raised on pasta. I'll bet we are the only couple in Rocky Creek who think pasta is a festive meal." He breathed in the tantalizing aroma of the rich spaghetti sauce and succulent meat balls with pleasure.

"Oh no, there are many Italian families here."

"You are a better Italian cook than most Italians," Tony said.

"Only because of my dear little stepmother's influence. She would have been so proud to sit at our table tonight. I can picture her happy smiling face. I think she'd like you."

"I had forgotten you had a stepmother. What made

her so special?"

"My sister and I were too young to remember our birth mother. When we lost Papa too, she was there for us. We always felt loved and I believe we were."

He reached out and placed his hand over hers. "How is it that we have been together for years and yet we are just beginning to get to know one another?" he asked.

Elise answered, "Did I never tell you that Mama Anna was from Northern Italy? I thought I did long ago. She was only seventeen when she came to look after us and two years later, she married Papa."

"I guess I was so consumed by my own problems," he said, "that I closed my mind to everything else. I am sorry I was so thoughtless."

"I understand," she said, touching his arm.

As they talked, Tony played the perfect gentleman. A large bowl was piled high with the pasta course, and garnished with a sprig of fresh oregano. He filled both plates and sprinkled a generous amount of freshly grated Parmesan cheese over each plate. Elise served the green salad in matching salad bowls and passed him the silver tray holding a choice of salad dressings.

"These dishes are so elegant," Elise said. "The last time we used them was when we had the dinner party meeting to discuss the orchestra."

Between mouthfuls, they reminisced about that evening.

"Brad was watching me like a hawk that night."

"I didn't notice."

"I felt like a felon as he studied my every move."

"I thought he was just interested in what you had to say."

"No, he obviously had other things on his mind that night and I felt his eyes on me all evening. Anyway, let us forget Brad tonight."

Tony filled his glass and touched the edge of Elise's

glass with his. "May I propose a toast to my wife," he said and sipped the bubbling liquid. "Mmmm, I like this champagne."

"Thank-you, dear," she said.

"I thought I would have to jump-start Hank's truck that night, so he could go home," Tony cackled, unable to disregard the memories of that evening. "When I looked out the window, I couldn't believe my eyes. He had parked that rusty old crate close to my brand new Buick."

Elise chuckled. "Yeah," she said, "Hank is an interesting man, very genuine, I think."

"Long live Hank," Tony said, lifting his glass. He downed it with one gulp and wiped his lips on a white linen napkin.

"Then Brad. . ." he said, "drat the man, he actually got down on his hands and knees and mopped up muddy water. I was shocked to see our notorious sheriff on his knees in my foyer."

When he offered a toast to the chef Elise accepted it gracefully.

"Hey, that's me," she said. An excited giggle escaped her lips.

"I do owe a toast to Brad," he said. He refilled the glasses with champagne losing no time in drinking most of the bubbly immediately. He sputtered as he tried to laugh when the bubbles went up his nose

"I thought you were an experienced champagne drinker," commented Elise, handing him his napkin.

When he had recovered, he added, "Thanks to Brad who knew exactly how to obtain all my papers and was willing to help."

She clinked glasses with him again, and offered two toasts, one to Richard Lawrence's memory and the other to Tony's Lorenzo's good fortune.

He accepted both toasts on his own behalf.

"Is that legal?" asked Elise.

"I hope so," Tony said. He tossed it down. "It's fine with us," he said, slurring his words. He toasted Roxy, who was playing with a small object she had found on the floor.

Elise picked up a tiny porcelain angel with gilt wings and turned it over in her fingers. "I wonder where she found this?" she said. "It looks like a piece of one of my handcrafted ornaments."

"I forgot to tell you," Tony said, choosing to skirt the issue rather than tell the truth. He remembered exactly what had happened. "Roxy. . ." he said.

Tony! the voice admonished.

He put his hand to his lips and paused, a sick feeling at the pit of his stomach.

"It was my fault," he said. "I knocked it down, and then I hid it so you would not find it. I was wrong. I encouraged Roxy to touch it with her little paw. She would not have even noticed it if I had not lifted her up so she could see it."

"I loved that ornament because my sister made it. It was my favourite one," she said, "but I suppose things happen. I am glad you told me, because I was going to have a word with the cleaning lady."

"I'm sorry, "he said. "I was ashamed to tell you."

"Perhaps Valerie will make another one for me. The little angel isn't broken, just the eggshell, so she can make another one using the same figurine. Not everything in life is so easy to fix."

"Right, "he said. He shifted his chair, and squared up his place mat again. Elise frowned as she watched him fidgeting.

"I acted like a stuffed shirt that evening, "he said, glad to change the subject.

"A little bit," she agreed, her laughter tinkling like sleigh bells on a winter's night.

"When George wanted his sushi well done. I thought

his manners uncouth. Fred wasn't sure which knife to use."

As they reveled in each other's company, they laughed at things that were funny and things that weren't funny at all. Being together was almost as intoxicating as the champagne.

"I can't eat any more pasta," Elise said. "I think all this champagne is getting to me."

"Oh, I can eat and drink any time," Tony declared dramatically, "especially if it is an authentic Italian dinner, the sauce simmered for hours until all the flavours have blended."

"Just like Mama used to make," they chanted in unison.

"I hope you didn't forget about my surprise."

"I did not forget it. It has to be presented at just the right moment," he said. He leaped unsteadily to his feet and bowed to her with a great show of theatrical pomp. Elise grabbed him around the waist to prevent him from landing in her lap. She gave him a push as he grabbed the table for support.

"Wow," she said with a slightly off-key snicker. "I can't wait. It sounds grand."

"Oh, it is!" Tony sat down again, breathing heavily from the exertion.

"We should have piped the pasta in like the Scots do with their haggis on Robbie Burns Day," Elise suggested.

"We can still honour the pasta," Tony said. "I propose a toast to Mama!" he said.

"We did that already."

Tony gave Roxy a meatball from his plate when Elise wasn't looking. The little cat ate it under the table, leaving the onions in a neat pile on the floor. She emerged to carefully wash up, laundering both ears, and her tail, with special attention to cleaning the spaghetti sauce off her whiskers.

"I can't remember when I had such a good time. Were you shocked to see me playing in the snow the other night? I enjoyed myself that night, too."

"I was surprised" she said.

"I shouted too, just like the other kids," he said.

"I heard you."

"I learned a new word, too. 'Yep.' Do you know it?"

"Yep," she said.

"My mind is foggy. I need coffee," Tony said. "I hope I can walk a straight line. Let's take dessert into the den and eat by the fire. Do you think I'm tipsy?" He stumbled and she took his hand.

"Maybe."

"Must be the night air."

THIRTY-SIX

The candles burnt out one by one. Elise looked at the three short stubs of solidified candle wax. "It was a good party," she said.

"If we look anything like those three candles it must have been a rollicking success," Tony agreed.

"Roxy wasn't drinking, but she was partying. She even climbed the curtains."

They cleared the table and then took their coffee and dessert into the den. Tony pulled the heavy drapes closed to shut out the rest of the world.

They settled on the large turquoise davenport for an intimate evening by the fireplace. He was glad Elise wanted to share tonight alone with him. He put his arm around her shoulder and held her close without speaking.

Shadows danced on the walls, while the warmth of the flickering flames cast a cozy ambiance into the handsomely appointed room.

Roxy jumped lightly onto Tony's lap and made her way up to his chest, her fur glistening in the light of the crystal chandelier, her tail perpendicular.

He smoothed the long dark fur. She purred happily and nuzzled his chin.

251

"Did you have a good day guarding the house from all those nasty stray cats around here? I bet you helped Mom get dinner, too." Roxy purred even louder and flicked the end of her tail as if it were an ostrich plume.

"Mow!" she uttered a one syllable reply.

Tony got to his feet. "Now, sit still and close your eyes. This is the moment. Don't move a muscle," he warned and left the room.

He returned with the viola case under his arm. "Keep your eyes closed. You, too, Roxy," he said. He set the treasure carefully and as quietly as possible on the coffee table.

He opened the case and took out the instrument, folded a white tea towel and placed it on his shoulder before he raised the viola to his chin and scraped out a halting rendition of *Charlie Brown and Snoopy*, an exercise from his first music book.

Elise opened her eyes wide and uttered, "Yeek!" as she leaped to her feet. Roxy scaled the drapes and stared down at Tony from her new vantage point perched on the antique curtain rod, her golden eyes as big as saucers.

"I don't think Roxy likes music," he said. "And I thought 'Yeek' was a little over the top, too."

"Well, we were both shocked," Elise said, laughing. "Is that a viola? It seems bigger than Cynthia's violin."

"Yes, I bought it a week ago and had it outfitted with new strings. I want to join the orchestra next year, so I plan to get a refresher course," he said, sticking out his chest.

"Wow," said Elise. "Will you take lessons from Cynthia?"

"Do you think I need them?" he said and they both laughed.

She pulled a footstool over to the window to stand on. He steadied her while she guided Roxy to rappel halfway down so she could reach her before she destroyed the designer drapes.

Elise fired questions at him. "What made you decide to buy a viola? Did you play it before? I thought you were a conductor. Can you still play it?"

He tried valiantly to answer each question but was stymied when she said, "Maybe you can play *Harold in Italy* for a concert next year."

"Not likely." He chuckled amiably. "Rocky Creek isn't ready for *Harold in Italy.*"

"More likely *Harold in Italy* isn't ready for you, dear," she teased. Tony grinned self-consciously, but declined to answer.

"Play it again, dear. I'm sure you can do better than that."

"Not much, but okay, I will try again. Ten years is a long time."

Tony lifted his viola to his chin once more and after scratching out a few harsh notes, managed to play an old Italian aria from memory.

"O Sole Mio is one of my favourites."

"You recognized it?"

"Of course. It's like riding a bike. You never really forget how to play. I can tell you once played beautifully. It will come back. I know it will." Elise touched his arm affectionately. "May I look at it?"

She took the instrument from him gently and turned it over to examine the back.

"Oh, what a beautiful bloom." She traced the exquisite pattern with her index finger. "The mark of a true craftsman," she said.

"I was sixteen when I changed from the violin to the viola," he said, "ages before I became a director of music. I played solo performances in Europe between directing concerts with the Leeds Classic Orchestra. Before I came to Canada, I sold my beautiful viola. I thought music caused all my troubles. I missed it, though."

"Wow!" Elise said. "Were you a child when you started music?"

"Almost three," he explained. "I had a child-size violin the length of a salt box. It seemed really big to me then."

"I'd like to try it but the champagne is making me dizzy," Elise said. "How do you ever make your big fingers play this little thing?"

"Let me help you," he said, taking the instrument from her while she settled herself on the davenport. He allowed Roxy to sniff it before giving it back to Elise.

"You spoil that cat," Elise complained, good-naturedly.

"We both do," he said.

He sat back to listen, a smile spreading over his face. "I wonder what she smells. Maybe old varnish, and oils used a couple of centuries ago when artistic hands shaped this instrument in an ancient workshop oceans away."

Elise applied herself to the task carefully. "I'm used to playing a huge instrument taller than a man, so this feels tiny to me."

"It's actually big for a viola," Tony explained.

"How big is it? It seems small to me."

"About twenty-two inches. I tried some smaller ones but I liked this one best."

"My bass is nearly seven feet!" she exclaimed, "This is backwards to me," she said, pursing her lips. "I started on a tiny violin years ago, but I've been playing the bass so long I have no clue what to do."

Tony picked up a gold brocade throw cushion and laid it on her lap. "Just stand it upright on your lap like a miniature bass and you might be able to figure it out."

She struggled to co-ordinate fingers and bow while holding the viola upright, the bottom of the instrument resting on the cushion as if it were a string bass. She dragged the bow over the strings and honked out a few shaky unmusical notes, off key. Tony stuck his fingers in his ears and closed his eyes as if in pain. "Yeek!" he exclaimed.

She exploded into giggles. "Thanks," she said.

After she made several ear-splitting attempts to draw the bow across the strings it began to sound less like a hack saw and more like a viola bow. Tony eventually realized she was playing the opening notes to Haydn's *Surprise Symphony*. "It's a surprise, that's for sure," he said.

He sang, *"Papa Haydn played a joke, On the staid and sleepy folk, Struck a chord and they aw-o-o-oke, Papa Haydn's joke,"* while Elise scratched out the melody.

"Where did those lyrics come from?" she asked.

"My Grade One piano book. When my teacher, Mrs. Gable sang the words with me, I would laugh with delight," he explained.

"My bass teacher wasn't nearly so accommodating. He chanted 'one, two, three, four,' at the top of his lungs while I struggled under the weight of my instrument. Sometimes he would bang his heel on the floor in time to punctuate each beat."

"Were you scared of him?"

"No, Petro was a young prodigy in those days. I was inspired by him. He was also very handsome with curly black hair."

"I'm jealous." Tony pursed his lips in a pout.

"I wonder where he is now?"

"I propose a toast to Petro, wherever he is," Tony said. He offered her another glass of champagne. "We really should christen it."

"Oh, no, it's not a ship," she said, as she pulled it out of his reach.

"I didn't mean we were to break a champagne bottle over it!"

They drank to Petro and to Mrs. Gable, who had long

ago passed from this world.

"I can imagine her giving harp lessons to young angels on Cloud Nine," Tony said. "She was a wonderful woman." He offered blessings to her soul, while Elise suggested impishly that he may have to recall the lessons she taught him as a child.

The toasting threatened to carry on well into the night, until the bottle was empty. When Roxy was caught licking the rim of the bottle, it put a definite end to the toasting. It had been a fun evening of love, promises and contentment.

"I hope you are going to let me move back to our bedroom tonight," Tony said, "because I think my back is developing a permanent hump. The davenport in here is too short and narrow for me." He stood up and massaged his lower back.

"I had plenty of room, but my feet were cold."

"They won't be cold tonight!" he promised with a bawdy wink.

"What if there's a mistake and we are not really married?" Elise said, looking nervous again.

"No chance of that. Brad is very thorough. He does not leave anything to chance."

"I know but I want to make sure."

"You saw the letter. What more proof do you need?"

Elise sighed and looked down at the floor. "I don't like getting nasty surprises. Let me see the letter again, please."

"Alright, Elise, I will get it for you," he said, rolling his eyes. "It's not necessary but…"

Tony obligingly ran up the stairs to his office, and brought the letter down to her. He opened it and placed it in her hands. "Read this," he instructed. "It says that I have been legally Antonio Johann Lorenzo for seven years. That includes the year of our marriage. It is legal and you are my wife."

"Was your marriage to Yvette legal?" She read the letter twice before replacing it in the envelope.

"Yes. Through the court process her name was legally changed from Lawrence to Lorenzo."

"I thought you were married as Lorenzo. I am confused."

"Yes, we were, but her name had to be changed at the same time mine was. I came to Canada as Lawrence and assumed Lorenzo after arriving here," he explained. "*Lorenzo* has both Spanish and Italian roots. *Lawrence* was an anglicized version of my old Italian family name."

"Do you have papers to prove that? I need to see that in writing."

"You really are determined to be a party pooper, aren't you?" he said, struggling for patience. "Brad obtained all the papers, so I *can* prove it."

"Okay, I believe you. When can I see them?"

"Brad will bring them all over next week, but I can phone him now and have him look it up if you want," he said.

"Yes, that would make me feel better. Have you figured out how you will re-enter the music scene?"

"More important is how I will re-enter my bedroom," he said. He looked pointedly at Elise and gritted his teeth. She laughed self-consciously and nodded her head.

"Is that a 'yes'?"

"After I have proof," she said.

It was only ten o'clock, but Brad was in the shower when Tony called so Julie gave him the message. Tony waited on the line while Brad dried himself and put on a bathrobe. Finally, with a great deal of shuffling of papers and grumbling, Brad agreed to read out the crucial paragraphs over the phone to Elise.

When she hung up the phone, she was smiling. "Yes, he says it's all legal now," she said.

"Well, about time you believed me," Tony said, as he gave her a big bear hug. "You are a nut case when it comes to being proper. We've already lived together for over four years, so what would it matter?"

"It matters to me," she said. "Now before we head upstairs, tell me how you will deal with the music."

Tony sighed, giving in to her request. "It will be a long journey. I am not as good a musician as I once was, so I will have to go to the beginning and review the lessons Mrs. Gable taught me.

"After I have repeated those exercises, I will play a variation on the theme to develop the music. I will also play some musical filigree and even some double stops and harmonics until I get to the Second Ending."

"The Second Ending? Isn't that the pattern one must understand to play *New World Symphony*?"

"Not just the *New World Symphony*, but it's the stepping-stone toward playing many other pieces of music."

"Ten years is a long time. Will it be difficult for you to come back?"

"Yes, it is but I know I can do it," he said determinedly. "I have my wife back and music in my life again. What more can I ask for?" He leaped to his feet, shimmying his shoulders forward and sideways as he danced an Irish jig. Puckering up his lips, he accompanied the jig with a piercing whistle solo.

Roxy peered suspiciously from behind a table leg. She swiped her paw over her ears, one by one, as if to clear away the unpleasant sounds.

"I didn't know you could dance and whistle like that," exclaimed Elise.

"One of my hidden talents, and I'm not even Irish," he said.

He coaxed Roxy from her hiding place by rattling the cat treat can until she finally came out. She waved her tail in rapture as she crunched each flavoured bit.

"Our own new world is just dawning. We will take a curtain call together. The three of us," he said, drunk with happiness.

"Mow," commented Roxy. She bunted his knee with her head.

"You, too, sweetheart!" Tony stroked the shiny black fur.

"I am very proud of you, Tony." Elise planted a kiss on the tip of his nose. "If Dr. Suzuki had heard you play *O Sole Mio* tonight, he would be proud of you, too. He'd know for sure you have indeed come to that Second Ending."

About the Author

June Carter Powell lives in Kamloops with one husband, Michael, and two cats, Francie and Smoker. Although an octogenarian, she plays the viola in *Kamloops Brandenburg Orchestra* and in *The Thompson Valley Orchestra* as well as *Ordinary People*.

Her mother always said she embellished most stories to make them more interesting, so June thought she should use this talent somewhere. Creative writing!
Published works include *Under the Blue Wig*, *The Second Ending* and short stories in *Grandmothers' Necklace*, and several IAG publications, *Kamloops Tapestry, Away From Home, Blue River, Dark Waters* and *Kaleidoscope*, and *Collected Works*